Einstein's Fiddle

RICHARD ADAMSON

Black Rose Writing | Texas

ISBN: 978-1-68513-606-2
PUBLISHED BY BLACK ROSE WRITING
www.blackrosewriting.com

Printed in the United States of America
Suggested Retail Price (SRP) $20.95

Einstein's Fiddle is printed in Minion Pro

PRAISE FOR
EINSTEIN'S FIDDLE

"Thank God Rick Adamson is here. Inarguably deft and hilarious."
–Bill Scheft, former Thurber Prize finalist, Emmy-nominated writer for David Letterman

"A hilarious small town murder mystery that Janet Evanovich fans should flock to."
–Sublime Book Reviews

BLUES OF AUTUMN, Richard Adamson's previous Tanager mystery, has well over 1,000 five-star reviews.

To Helene

Einstein's Fiddle

CHAPTER ONE

If I'd answered the phone the way I was supposed to, none of this would have happened. Not to me, at least. Sure, I would have heard about it on the news. Watched it on TV. Followed all the rumors and lies on social media. But I would never have been a part of it. But hey, when you're new to a gig you make these little mistakes.

"Hello?"

"I'm calling with reference to your mother."

The morning sun smiled bright and warm through the front window of my store, yet the caller's icy words froze my heart solid. "My… mother?" I asked.

"You can relax, she's all right."

"What are you… I don't… Has there been an accident?"

"Not yet."

"Pardon me?"

"Don't worry." The tone of his voice warmed up a degree or two bringing it barely above absolute zero. "I assure you that Amy is alive and relatively comfortable. May I presume you wish her to remain in said condition?"

"What the… Who is this?"

"Don't play the fool. You know who it is." The caller sounded male. But just barely. "Your mother is doing well," he said. "And if you wish her to remain in good health I think it's time we came to a final arrangement."

Final arrangement? I didn't understand. But that's not unusual for me at this hour of the day. Things often don't make a lot of sense to me before noon.

The caller went on, "If the fifty thousand didn't mean enough to you, maybe Amy's life does."

"Amy? Who's Amy?"

He ignored my question. He clearly had an agenda all his own. "I'll give you twenty-four hours. And don't forget, one word to the authorities and all negotiations, both past and present, shall be considered null and void. And so, I'm afraid, shall be your mother." He paused, either for dramatic effect or to think up something even crazier to say. He decided to go with the latter. "And you'll have nothing left but your precious alpacas."

Alpacas? Now I really didn't get it. I don't sell alpacas. Never did. My shop – the pet store in which I was now standing with a sweaty telephone clamped to my bewildered ear – sells no live animals. Just feed and supplies. And none of them related to alpacas. I would have reminded the caller of this seemingly irrelevant fact, but it was too late. The line had already clicked dead.

I checked the display of the landline phone I was using. No luck – it just flashed, *Private Caller.* I started to dial my mother's number so I could check on her, but I was interrupted by Stanley. He was barking at something outside.

Stanley is a dog, although, I guess the word *barking* may have given that away. He is a pooch of few words, so when Stanley says something, it deserves immediate attention. At this moment, he was trying to draw my notice to a man standing outside who was tapping an impatient knuckle on the front window. The man didn't look happy. Neither did the bull mastiff on the end of the leash he was holding.

The gentleman pointed to his wristwatch and gave me the international sign for, *Unlock your door, idiot. Sign says you're open.*

I waved and gave him the international sign for, *Be right with you, kind sir, right after I check up to see if my mother has been kidnapped.*

I finished dialing. And as I waited for an answer, I counted each ring – I always do when I phone Mom. Her hearing is fine, but her legs have slowed up considerably.

Four rings.

Mom lives alone. Since Dad died, she has remained in the family house in Buffalo. Her daughter, and coincidentally my sister, lives close by, in Lockport. I'm just a few hours east, here in beautiful downtown Lake Placid.

Eight rings.

If Mom doesn't answer, I'll have to try her cell phone. Trouble is, mom rarely leaves her cell on – if she did the battery would only die, and she has better things to do with her valuable time than charge phone batteries.

Ten rings.

Mom's landline has two extensions – one in her kitchen, and one in her bedroom. I have tried to get her to use the cordless phone I bought her, but she won't touch the thing. She insists the fidelity isn't as clear as it is on her *real* phone. And as always, Mom is absolutely right.

We were up to twelve rings now, and I noticed I hadn't taken a breath since ring number five. The customer outside was now tapping on the glass like a woodpecker on caffeine, and Stanley was looking up at me wondering if I had lost my hearing.

Finally, on the thirteenth ring, she picked up. She answered with her usual soft but no-nonsense, "Hello."

"Mom, you okay?"

She ignored my question to ask one of her own. She always does this. "Norris. What are you doing up? It's eight forty-five in the morning. Your pajamas catch fire?"

I started breathing again. "Mom, I just got the craziest phone call. It sounded like… well, like someone had kidnapped you."

"Kidnapped? Me?"

"Except he called you Amy."

Mom paused. She always does this too. It isn't that her mouth triggers slowly. She just likes to aim it carefully. "You've started drinking breakfast again, haven't you."

I ignored her ridiculous suggestion. She knows darn well I don't drink breakfast until noon. I said, "So, you're okay then. Nobody's tried to… I don't know… grab you or anything?"

"For Pete's sakes, son, cook yourself an egg. Or at least some toast. You know what alcohol does to an empty stomach."

I lowered my voice to a whisper. "Mom, if somebody is with you right now and you can't talk, say the word *bacon*. Try to work it into the—"

"Bacon? Why should I say bacon?"

Now I'd succeeded in confusing both of us. "So then… somebody… is… with you?"

"No, but I think somebody is with you. And his name is Jack Daniels."

I assured her I was perfectly sober. She, too, seemed in fine shape and in her usual top fighting form. I noticed the impatient customer outside had left. Stanley walked back to me to make sure I was alright. I gave him a reassuring pat and continued with Mom. We spoke for a few minutes, but because Mom and I had talked only two days previous, we really didn't have much news to swap. Except for the crazy call, that is. Satisfied all was well with Mom, I hung up and went about my business, opening up the shop for the day.

I unlocked the safe and counted out a cash float into the register. I then did a little sweeping, and as I worked I couldn't help replaying that crazy phone call over and over in my mind. Was it really what it sounded like? Had I just received a wrong-number ransom call?

And what was that shit about alpacas?

Frankly, I blame modern cell phone technology. The buttons are small. It's too easy to hit a wrong number, especially for people with stubby fingers. And from my considerable experience, kidnappers tend to have stubby fingers.

In a way, this whole misunderstanding was my own fault. The confused caller would have immediately realized his mistake if I had simply answered the phone the way I was supposed to answer it – *Lake*

Placid Paws 'n' Claws. But I wasn't thinking clearly. It was early, and I'm not a morning person.

And neither, it seemed, was this kidnapper.

Before unlatching the front door and flipping over the *Open* sign, I made one more phone call – this one to my buddies at the local New York State Police headquarters, Troop B in Ray Brook. I know the guys up there pretty well. You see, I didn't always run in the fast lane like this, selling kitty litter and answering misdialed ransom calls. I used to be a cop. Spent most of my career as a detective with the Buffalo Police Department's major crimes unit. And after that, I headed up a small municipal police department here in the Adirondacks. For reasons I'm not totally sure of, but am nevertheless quite happy with, I no longer chase bad guys. Instead, I sell flea collars and tick spray. Similar mission – different weapons.

When the young state trooper on the phone heard my name, he repeated it a couple of times, rolling it around on his tongue like he was trying to guess the vintage and grape variety. "Tanager... Tanager..." Finally, he had it. "Chief! *Chief* Tanager."

"Just Tanager now. Who am I talking to?"

"Trooper Carlisle, sir. You probably don't remember me. We met a couple summers ago." The trooper went on to explain that he and I had attended the scene of a traffic fatality together. I'm afraid I didn't remember this trooper, but I certainly remembered the traffic accident. A chipmunk had wiped out an entire family. The striped forest critter hadn't meant any mischief, of course. The little guy was just trying to cross the road when a family of four from Schenectady swerved to avoid him and ended up rolling their Winnebago down a forty-foot ravine. Sadly, the kind driver's self-sacrifice was in vain. Total body count was five. These sorts of well-meant but badly advised maneuvers are not uncommon on mountain roads. Certainly more common than wrong-numbered ransom calls.

I asked Trooper Carlisle if he would kindly check his latest Missing Persons Bulletin for me.

"Let's have a look, here," he muttered aloud to let me know he was scrolling through something pertinent on his computer. "Amy...

Amelia… Amanda… Don't see any missing persons by that name. Want me to check with the Feds?"

"Sounds like a good idea."

Trooper Carlisle reconsidered the whole exercise, "Of course, this could all just be somebody's idea of a joke."

"Could very well be."

"You want us to see if we can trace the call?"

"Whatever you think best, trooper. I just thought you guys ought to be informed, that's all." I didn't want to push. I'm not comfortable telling people how to do their jobs. If I were I'd probably have accepted my last promotion at the Buffalo P.D. instead of taking off to the mountains.

To end the call and get back to something more worthy of his valuable time and training, Trooper Carlisle thanked me sincerely for my concern. Before kissing me off, he offered to keep me updated on any further developments. I knew he had better things to do – so did I – but it was a nice gesture just the same.

For the rest of the day, apart from calling my mother a couple of times to check that she was still safe and sound, I didn't give much thought to that morning's crazy phone call. I was busy. It was Friday, early May, and that meant our little resort town was overrun with strung-out escapees from the city, many of whom had thoughtfully brought along their doggies to unwind with them. Happily for me and my business partner, Marlene, in their haste to have their pooches chill out, many of these harried urbanites forget to pack the kibble.

Despite the busy cash register, on Fridays I get to leave work early. It's part of my deal with Marlene. I open the shop and she closes it. This way I have time to spruce up before going to my regular Friday night gig playing electric bass at a local roadhouse. My band plays R&B, a bit of pop, and as much funk as we can pull off without frightening the moose or the dancers. Playing music is important to me. It keeps me sane. Well, saner than I would be if I didn't play.

On this particular Friday night, I badly needed something to restore that sanity, something to bring me back to reality. That morning's crazy phone call had rattled me more than it should have. But luckily, the guys in the band were in the mood to groove, and so was the audience. Pretty soon my brain pan had emptied itself of all concerns that did not involve four hard beats and three solid chords.

From the riser the bar manager likes to call a stage, I happily watched the dance floor burble before me, a foaming sea of city haircuts churning and bopping to the backbeat like a school of well-moussed porpoises. At first, the picture was hypnotic, like staring at a set of rapids. But pretty soon my mind started to drift. Next thing I knew, my churning thoughts broke loose and started floating downstream, headed toward white water, into dangerous torrents and spinning whirlpools. And before I could paddle them to calmer waters they got hung up on some sharp rocks.

That damn phone call. No matter what I did, the whole dumb conversation kept rising to the surface like a bloated corpse that hadn't been weighed down with enough cement. Finally, when the band took a break, I dragged the wet cadaver up onto the beach for a closer look. I left the stage and weaved my way through the tables to sit at the bar with a fellow named Yance Buckner.

An old-time regular here at the bar, Yance likes to get up with the band occasionally and blow blues harp. This is peachy fine with us because having a guy of Yance's vintage on the stand makes the rest of us fifty-somethings look young. Well, *feel* young, at least. Anyway, after buying Yance a beer, I turned to my grizzled, well-oiled drinking buddy and asked, "Yance, you know anyone in town named Amy? Might be a little older than you." I knew that Yance, who was born in the Adirondacks, had a pretty solid knowledge of the area and its older inhabitants.

Yance blew a slippery diatonic glissando on his harmonica before answering. "Knowed a few Amy's in my time. Don't recall ever fucking one, though."

"I don't mean *known* in the biblical sense."

"Oh, then I can't help you. I only remember the chicks I boink."

I challenged him on this bold statement, "You remember your sister, don't you?" Ha, ha. Funny joke. I thought I had him with that one.

But Yance just nodded matter-of-factly.

I decided not to pursue this line of questioning any further. And happily, neither did Yance. Instead he said, "There was an Amy down in Tupper. Worked the sawmill. Ran the big ripper. Not much to look at, but she gave the best three-fingered hand job in town." He took a swig from his mug of draft beer before continuing, "Then there was Amy with the profound hearing loss…"

Yance went on to profile a few more memorable ladies, most of whom, for some reason or other, had suffered various forms of physical disability. Yance eventually explained to me that he used to work at the local Social Security office as a disability claims assessor. For anyone hoping to get their claim approved, he was in a very powerful position, but he swore he never took advantage of that power. Sadly, he confessed, he never knew whether the bandaged and crutched female claimants were dating him for his own sweet self or for his vaunted civil service position.

I bought Yance another beer, assuring him that the gesture was for his very own sweet self. The fresh drink seemed to oil his mental gearbox enough to remember one more Amy for me.

"And then there's Amelia Tapin from Saranac," he said. "Never had nothin' going with her at all. That chick had near twenty years on me. Never boinked that Amy. No, sir. Never gave it a moment's thought."

"Too old for you, huh?"

"Hell, no. Nothin' wrong with the older ones." Vance winked and took another pull from his beer. "No, Amy Tapin had the clap." On the word *clap* he sprayed beer foam across the bar like a stuttering lawn sprinkler.

"I see." I grabbed a paper napkin and wiped the counter top. "So, you draw the line at STDs."

"Yeah, well, when you're young you can be picky. Weren't Amy's fault, though." Yance wiped his frothy lips with the back of his hand. "Einstein give it to her."

"Einstein?"

Yance burped a big *thumbs up*.

"*Albert* Einstein?" I asked.

"You know him?" Yance said this with some surprise.

"Well, sure. Everybody knows Albert Einstein."

"Yeah, that's usually how it happens."

Behind me I could hear Rodger tuning his guitar, but I had to get this thing straight before going on stage. "So, your lady friend told you Albert Einstein gave her an STD."

"A what?"

"Venereal disease."

"Don't be silly. Who'd go braggin' on something like that? No, no. It was written on her form. Her disability application. She tried to claim it as 'work-related.'"

"Work? Was Amy a hooker?"

"Well, she said she was the old dog's sailing instructor. But tomato, tomahto. Of course, there's no proof she actually got her disease off this Einstein fella. Amy was a popular girl." Hearing Rodger firing up his gear prompted Yance to ask, "We gonna start with *Shaky Ground?*" This was Yance's favorite song.

"Sure. Whatever you want." My mind was still on his story. I knew that Albert Einstein used to spend his summers up here, but that was a long, long time ago. I asked Yance, "This Amy… she still alive?"

"Ain't heard nothin' to the contrary." He stood up to walk to the stage.

I got to my feet. "If she dated Einstein she must really be getting on in years."

Yance picked up his bandoleer full of additional harmonicas. "Ninety if she's a day. Probably closing in on a hundred. I hear the old girl's mind is gone, though."

We walked together to the stage. "She in a nursing home?" I asked.

"Last I heard, she moved in with her son, Henry. The boy must be well into his sixties now. Lives somewhere in the hills outside Saranac. Middle of nowhere. All alone. Just him and his mother. Well, her and his fuckin' alpacas."

The word hit me cold. I stopped dead as if I'd suddenly seen an open manhole in front of me. "Alpacas?" I said.

"Cute little critters. But crazier 'n shit. The Tom Cruise of the camel world. From Bolivia or Columbia or some place. You know, like the good weed." Yance stepped up onto the stage where he proceeded to lay out his stained bedroll of tobacco-juiced harmonicas on top of my bass amp like he was setting up camp for the night.

And I just stood there. Frozen. In the middle of the dance floor. Mentally hitting the replay button on that crazy phone call.

Alpacas?

CHAPTER TWO

When I get home from a gig, I usually head straight to the refrigerator, but tonight I showed some restraint. I headed straight to my landline telephone. The hour was late, almost two o'clock, but I figured that wouldn't matter to the state police. Or at least, it shouldn't have.

Trooper Dan Garneau, who was manning the night desk, said he'd heard about my call earlier that day. Yeah, I'll bet he had. I imagine the boys in Ray Brook have been trading stories all day about this Norris Tanager character, the crazy ex-cop who thinks he received a wrong-number ransom call.

Trooper Garneau told me that no new developments had popped up regarding my mystery caller other than the discovery that the call had been made with a blocked number on a prepaid card. In other words, the caller's name is unknowable. I thought about mentioning the curious alpaca reference and the call's possible tie to some woman named Amy Tapin in Saranac Lake, but I decided to save that tenuous tidbit for someone at the station who knew me better and could attest to my sanity. Besides, Trooper Garneau had already made it clear to me that he was swamped with work and that I should call back later in the morning when the day-shift guys were on duty and the office wasn't so short-staffed and the moon wasn't so full and the bats were back in the church belfry and I hadn't maybe had so much to drink. *But thanks for your concern and please call anytime, ex-Chief Tanager.*

I couldn't blame the guy. The young trooper probably felt I was lonely and bored and missed being on the job. Why else would an ex-cop call at two in the morning? So I hung up and turned my attention to someone who was always happy to hear from me, no matter what the hour.

I grabbed Stanley's leash. He danced his usual dervish of delight, and we went out for a late-night sniff and tree irrigation. Stanley, a medium-sized mutt of indeterminate age, pedigree, and intelligence, sleeps most of the day. But once the sun goes down, his furry body and his furry brain shift into high gear and he's scratching at the screen door, itching to prove he can out-run and out-think any raccoon on the block. I know the feeling. Stanley and I are both night owls.

When I was a cop, this nocturnal peak was fine. But now that I'm working days and dragging Stanley to the store along with me, we've both had to reset our circadian rhythms. Every morning as we drive to work the pooch looks up at me from the passenger seat, blinks those sleepy black eyes, and, I suspect, seriously considers getting a job of his own so he can move out. It's all a bluff, of course. We both know there's not a lot of work in these mountains for anyone who doesn't cook, serve tables, or clean guest rooms.

When we first met, Stanley was gainfully employed as a watchdog at a meth lab. The owner of the lab was sentenced to five years in prison, and Stanley got life with me. I'm not sure which of the two perps got the sweeter deal, but I do know that the owner of the meth lab has already been paroled. Anyway, tonight after we finished our walk, and I had my usual snack of cheese and crackers with a chaser of single malt, Stanley and I went off to sleep. Eight hours later, I called the shop and explained to Marlene that I would be in a bit late. She was not happy.

"It's Saturday morning," she said.

"I just have something to do first."

She was on to me. "That stupid phone call?"

"I just have to check something out."

"Why?"

"I don't know... because somebody's life might be in danger."

"But why do *you* have to check it out?" Marlene punched the word *you* as if she'd just caught it stealing a French fry off her breakfast plate. "I thought you said you passed the incident along to Ray Brook." Marlene referred to the headquarters of the State Police as the town in which they were located because she, too, used to be in law enforcement. She was my admin assistant before the town of Glen Echo fired both of us.

"I filed a report, but I don't think the trooper is taking me or the call seriously."

"No, really? A wrong-number ransom call? Gee, I wonder why."

"I won't be long. Should be in by noon. I just want to look into a couple of things."

"Chief…" Marlene paused long enough to pop a French fry in her mouth. "You know you're not a cop anymore, right?"

"Then why do you still call me 'Chief'?"

"Because Norris is kind of a dorky name."

I couldn't argue with that, so I didn't. "I'll see you at ten."

Marlene didn't give up. "You know other people's troubles are no longer yours."

"Eleven at the latest."

"The world will survive just fine without your help."

"Maybe eleven-thirty."

"You're not wearing a badge anymore. No gun, either. And you now pay for your own gas."

"Noon, definitely."

"Noon? But we have that summer student to interview."

"Tell you what, if I'm not there by one, I'll buy you lunch."

"How you going to pay for lunch if you're not here?"

"Tell Kenny to put it on my tab. I'll see you real soon. Cross my heart. You know I would never leave you alone on a Saturday. See you no later than two." At the time, I honestly believed I would keep this promise. I really did.

I hung up and wolfed down a quick breakfast of a poached egg, a whole wheat English muffin, and an under-ripe banana while sitting at my desktop computer. The internet burped up two landline numbers for

Tapins residing in the Adirondacks. Unfortunately, neither of the numbers was anything close to my store's phone number, certainly not close enough to justify a misdial by a clumsy felon's finger.

The listing for the first Tapin did not include a street address, but the number was a Plattsburgh exchange, a town that's just an hour away from Lake Placid. I called the number and asked for Amy.

The woman, a Ms. Margaret Tapin, said no Amy lived in her household, but she'd heard of an Amy Tapin, unrelated, who apparently resided somewhere down here, maybe near Saranac Lake. I thanked her and dialed the second number that had appeared on my computer screen. This listing belonged to a G. L. Tapin in Tupper Lake, a town that wasn't far from the aforementioned Saranac Lake.

A woman answered, "Yes?" She sounded anxious. Like she'd been waiting for my call.

"Ms. Tapin?" I asked.

"Yes." She could be my age, maybe younger.

"My name's Tanager. You don't know me, but—"

"Please. Not now."

"But I—"

She hung up.

Thanks to telemarketers and other scam artists, modern-day detective inquiry has become impossible to initiate over the phone. Texting would be a weak alternative, if I had a cell number. But I didn't. All I had was a landline number. So I had no choice but to jot down this woman's listed home address and grab my car keys.

Before leaving the house I filled Stanley's bowl with fresh water. He knew what this meant. He looked up at me with those big dark eyes. I hated to leave the pooch alone, but as I had told Marlene, I honestly expected I wouldn't be gone long. Not long at all. So I patted his big furry head. "Be right back, pal. Just an hour. Maybe two."

He didn't buy my line any more than Marlene did. The pooch headed straight to the front door and stood at the ready, directly under the peg that held his leash. I'm a sucker for big brown eyes.

I hooked the leash onto his collar and laughed. It's probably a good thing I never had kids.

* * * * *

The town of Tupper Lake is an easy drive from the town of Lake Placid. Easy at this time of year, at least. No drive in the *'Dacks* is easy in winter. But this was early spring, so within half an hour I was in Tupper, standing in the outer lobby of a three-story, low-rise condo building. I pressed an intercom button that cuddled up close beside the Dymo-labelled name of *G. Tapin.*

And then I waited. And waited. The silence suggested there was nobody home, but I wasn't convinced. After all, just thirty minutes ago, she'd picked up the phone and promptly slammed it down on me. So I pressed the button again but this time held it down for an impolite half note rather than the previous quarter note. I considered pushing all the call buttons and mumbling my way into the building, but I hate to pull cheap crap like that unless I absolutely have to. Luckily I didn't have to. A smartly-dressed, middle-aged woman came scurrying out, giving me a chance to grab the door before it could lock itself shut again.

The departing lady stopped dead. She clearly did not approve of my slippery entrance. Smart woman. Gutsy, too, because before I could get away she said, "May I enquire as to whom you are visiting?" I noticed her hand reaching into her purse. If this were the city I'd expect her fingers were now wrapped around a 9mm. semi-automatic. But up here in the uncivilized back woods she was more likely clutching a small canister of bear spray.

"It's all right," I assured her. "I'm a…"

Whoops. Out of habit, I started to tell her I was a police officer. Shouldn't do that anymore. I amended my fib, "I have a delivery for Ms. Tapin." I pointed to my car, which was easily seen through the glass of the front entrance, parked in the circular drive. She took a good look at the vehicle. Stanley was lying low on the seat, so all the lady could see was the gold lettering on the door proudly announcing, *Lake Placid Paws 'n'*

Claws. Beneath that was our store's logo – a classic pose of a sly doggy and a sexy kitty dancing a tango. You can tell it's a tango because the doggy has a thin moustache.

"Gloria doesn't own any pets," the lady proclaimed, proud to have caught an obvious burglar in an obvious lie.

"She's considering purchasing one," I countered, adding for verisimilitude, "A puppy."

"A puppy?" The woman's face dropped. Probably a cat lady. She pulled her hand out of her purse so she could wave a loaded finger at me. "Nothing large, I trust. Tell her to check her lease. This building does not allow anything larger than twelve pounds."

"Twelve pounds?" I mumbled as I entered the inner hallway. "That's a load of *Shih-Tzu.*" Although my words may have sounded like something else.

Ignoring the waiting elevator, I scampered up the stairs to the second floor hallway. I soon found a door that boasted the numbers 208 in gleaming brass. I knocked. Waited. No answer. I could hear music playing from a TV or radio. I knocked again. The music stopped.

"Ms. Tapin?" I said softly, careful not to sound threatening. "May I speak with you? Just for a moment. I won't be long."

I heard a chain slide, either on or off. I waited to find out which. Soon the door opened. But only as far as the short chain would allow. Half a face peered out. It was a pretty half. One dark brown eye, almost black. A strong eyebrow, and a slightly freckled cheek bone that was iced with vanilla skin. Beneath that, a delicate, rather pointed jawline framed a pair of thin lips, made thinner as they clenched tight. I recognized this clench well. Any cop would. It's a look of defense. Suspicion. Fear.

I chose my opening words carefully. "I am *not* a police officer."

The door did not close. Nor did it open any farther. The narrow, one-eyed gaze traveled slowly down my shirt and over my belt buckle. From there it took the long two-lane highway down my chinos and finally came to rest on my feet. Here, the examination paused for a good study of my shoes. Smart woman. If the man standing before her with the cop's haircut and the cop's build and the cop's bad knees were actually a legitimate officer of the law, his footwear would give him away. Today, I was wearing my suede-topped Wallabies, the comfy ones with the translucent gum-rubber soles that no self-respecting law officer would be caught dead kicking down a door with.

As she checked me out, I did some observing of my own. From what little I could see, this lady was wearing a sweatshirt and shorts. They weren't tight shorts, more like the kind she might wear to go hiking. But more to my immediate interest, I could see she was in her early-to-mid-thirties. The math was easy, so I said, "You're worried about your grandmother, aren't you."

That single eyebrow rose. I presumed the other one did something similar. The tight lips softened. Then they parted. "Is… is she all right?"

"I honestly don't know. That's why I'm here. "

She didn't understand. of course. And neither did I. I continued, "Ms. Tapin, I'd like to help you. I'd like to help you find your Grandma Amy."

"And you're not a cop?"

"Nope. Not a reporter either. It's a long story. May I come in? For just a moment? We can leave the door wide open."

The door closed. The chain slid. The door swung back wide. And Gloria Tapin silently invited me into her world.

It was a small world but a nicely furnished one – good taste on a modest budget. A plush sofa and two matching chairs waited to give comfort after a tough day. A solid oak coffee table sat in the center of an oriental rug. At the far end of the room, a red cherry spinet piano cowered against the wall like a frightened puppy, no doubt afraid to give a playful bark for fear of complaint from the neighbor lady I'd met downstairs. On top of the piano, patiently waiting for the music to begin, stood an eager audience, each friend and family member framed in standard poses. Some of the photos included this woman I was now facing. In one photo she had her arm around a young boy, but I saw no evidence of a child recently having occupied this room. I also noticed there were no photographs of this woman posed with any man who was close to her own age. If that young boy was indeed her son, he likely now lived with his father. I happened to notice one particular man, around sixty years old, whom I vaguely recognized. But I couldn't recall from where.

Okay, this was no time for small talk. I simply jumped right in and told Ms. Gloria Tapin who I was and why I was here. I explained about the puzzling phone call, including my conversation last night with Yance, and of course, the strange reference to alpacas. I left out the rumor about Grandma Amy having a quick fling with Einstein. There'd be plenty of time to insult granny's youthful morals later.

Until now, I had done all the talking. So I finished with something to finally prompt a reaction from her. "How long has your grandmother been missing?"

Gloria didn't answer, of course. So I tried another one: "Have the kidnappers been in touch with you?"

Still no answer. And I think I understood why.

"Honest, Gloria, I'm not a police officer. Or a reporter."

"How do I know you won't go to the police? Or post something on the internet?"

I answered her truthfully. "You don't. But if I did, what would it matter? Nobody would believe my story. Not even on the internet. And as far as the police go, I've already spoken with them, and they think I'm—"

"You what?" Gloria's dark brown eyes widened like pools of spilled coffee. Her slender hand flitted to her mouth to stifle a choked cry. My news about alerting the police had sparked sheer terror. It was like Goldilocks was watching her granny get chewed up by the wolf right before her very eyes.

"I'm sorry," I said. "But it's always best. I know these people. They try to scare you. They threaten. They tell you not to go to the authorities. But they have no way of knowing if you really—"

"Daddy…"

I didn't understand. "Who?"

"They'll kill him." She hurried to the sofa and picked up a cordless phone that was lying on a throw pillow. "They'll kill my father."

"But your grandmother…" I said. "I thought they had your Grandma Amy."

She pressed a button on her phone. As she waited for the speed dial to finish chirping its ironically cheery tones she said to me, "They won't hurt Grandma. They need her. They don't need Daddy."

I still didn't get it. So I did something smart. I shut up and listened.

She waited a dozen rings or so. No answer. So she dropped the phone back onto the sofa and proceeded to the front door. From a small table, she grabbed a wallet and a set of keys. She shoved the wallet into the pocket of her shorts, opened the front door and held it open for me. Her unspoken message was clear. Meeting over. Time to leave. The idiot with the big mouth, first.

As she locked the door behind us, I said, "That was your father?"

"Must have his cell turned off."

"No landline?"

"Not anymore." Gloria tested the door handle to make sure it was locked. "Nowadays, he uses his cell at the cabin."

I followed her down the hallway, toward the stairs. "How far to his cabin?"

She gave me a puzzled look, as if to say *What makes you think I would go off with you, a perfect stranger?* Then she voiced her concern more concretely, "Who the hell are you anyway? You say you sell pets."

"Pet *supplies*. No live animals. I used to be a police officer."

At this news bulletin, she stopped dead. "*Used* to be?"

"*Used* to be," I assured her.

"But not anymore."

"I'm trying to quit," I said. "But it seems someone has other plans."

She understood. This was a smart lady. "You don't think the ransom call was really a wrong number?"

"I honestly don't know." We were at the stairs. I held the steel fire door open for her, and we entered the stairwell. My next words echoed off the concrete walls and metal staircase giving them far more gravity than they deserved. "You aren't allergic to dogs, are you?"

"No…"

"Good. Then we'll take my car."

She stopped. "Are you insane? What the… How do I know you are who and what you say you are?"

"You'll know when you smell my car."

CHAPTER THREE

Stanley liked her. But then, he likes all women, especially when they're wearing shorts.

I pulled his wet nose away from her bare knees, apologized for his rude behavior, and exiled him to the back seat. Gloria didn't say anything. She just got into the front seat taking little notice of the furry pervert behind her – she had more important things on her mind.

The drive to her father's cabin took well over an hour. Geographically, it wasn't really that far, but once we turned off Route 30 and onto the secondary mountain road, my foot was on the brake almost as much as it was on the gas. This time of year, with the last vestiges of snow barely gone, these back roads can be muddy murder, especially for an eight-year-old Nissan with all the ground clearance of a toboggan. On the plus side, the long drive gave us time to talk, something which Gloria was finally willing to do. She started out by explaining her Granny's link to Albert Einstein.

As I already knew, back in the nineteen-forties and fifties, when the great man worked at Princeton University, he spent his summers here in the Adirondacks, sailing on our beautiful lakes. Unfortunately, the old boy was not as handy with a mast and tiller as he was with a pencil and slide rule. He claimed he did his best thinking while out on the water – he even may have developed his Theory of Relativity while bouncing over the waves back in Germany – but little of that thought involved compass directions or weather reports.

Enter Amy Tapin.

According to Gloria, one day, during a violent thunderstorm, Grandma Amy saw the scrambled egghead out on the lake, floundering helplessly with his two-handed dinghy. Young Amy jumped into her dad's motorboat and towed the great smarty pants to safety. From there, a friendship quickly developed, and pretty soon the great genius was parking his dinghy in Amy's cove on a regular basis. Gloria didn't say whether her grandmother actually had a sexual relationship with Einstein or not, but I doubt it. Sure, we've all heard that the old boy had an eye for the ladies, but would he have had a fling with someone who was that much his junior, a girl who was barely out of her teens? There's no evidence he was like that.

Either way, after a few more summers their relationship cooled off and died. And eventually, so did Albert Einstein. Amy went on to marry a local boy with whom she had one child, a son named Henry. That son, in turn, had one child – a daughter named Gloria – the thirty-something-year-old lady who was presently sitting beside me, fiddling with my radio dial. Reception in these hills stinks, so I offered her my binder of CD's to thumb through. She thumbed, discovered it was all jazz and blues, and soon went back to messing with the radio dial. Meanwhile, I questioned her about the mountain cabin we were bouncing toward.

Originally just a hunting and fishing retreat, the building has since been winterized and now serves as the principal residence of Gloria's father, Henry Tapin. Turns out he is also the man I vaguely recognized in those photos on Gloria's piano, but I still couldn't remember from where. According to Gloria, her father moved into the old cabin a few years ago after losing his town home in a divorce settlement. Henry now shares the cabin with his ninety-five-year-old mother, Amy Tapin.

"And this is where the kidnappers snatched her?" I asked.

"Looks like."

"But why her? I mean, does your father have money?"

"Daddy?" For the first time on our drive, Gloria laughed. "Hardly."

"What about your grandmother? Might she have some put away?"

"Not that I know of, but…" Gloria sat back in her seat to carefully ponder her next words. "There was this thing. Couple months ago. Daddy and Grandma arrived home from a trip to town. Daddy found the cabin had been broken into. An absolute mess. Everything thrown everywhere. Like, completely ransacked."

"Did your father report it?"

"Why bother?" Gloria opened her empty palms to the heavens. "I mean, nothing had been taken. Shit, there was nothing worth taking. Daddy had long since sold or pawned anything of value to pay fees at Grandma's nursing home. So no – he didn't report the break-in. He figured it was just some kids. You know… looking for cash. Liquor. Whatever."

She was probably right. Vandalism is a common problem with these secluded hideaways, especially between seasons. I could sense there was more to her story, so I nudged her along just as I was nudging this car along, up and over this rough mountain road. "So the place was busted into… but nothing stolen."

"A couple weeks later, a man drops by the cabin. Out of the blue. Said he was looking for something. Wanted to purchase it."

"But you say your father had sold everything of value."

Gloria shook her head like she was trying to clear the sour notes of a bad song from the corners. "It was, like, nuts." She turned to look at me directly as she said, "The man said he wanted to buy the violin."

"Violin?"

"*Einstein's* violin."

"Oh, yeah…" I nodded. "Einstein used to play violin. Not well, I hear. Probably as well as he sailed."

"Daddy had no idea what the man was talking about. Thought he was crazy and told him so. But the man wouldn't listen. He thought my father was lying, holding out for more money. The man said he'd give Daddy ten thousand dollars for the thing."

"And you think this was the person who broke into the place."

"Who else?" Gloria turned her face ahead to address the oncoming trees and empty road. "But there was no violin. *Is* no violin." Gloria opened her arms wide like a magician demonstrating she had nothing up her sleeve. "Never *has* been. Shit, if Grandma had kept something of Albert Einstein's, wouldn't we know? Daddy says he's never seen a damn thing of Einstein's. No notes. No letters. No mementos. And certainly not any musical instruments."

"And your grandmother… did you ask her about the violin?"

Gloria slumped her shoulders in despair. "Why? She wouldn't know. She gets mixed up. Her mind… it's not good. Sometimes she doesn't know who Daddy is." Gloria's voice drifted off to a sad whisper. "Or who I am."

I took my eyes off the sad, rumpled road long enough to glance at my sad, rumpled passenger. She turned away from me, a hand going to her eye. She sniffed, then said to the passing trees, "Daddy and I both told the man to leave us alone. There is no stupid violin. But the guy wouldn't believe us. They, they never do."

"*They?*"

Gloria sniffed again and glanced around the car. "Got any tissues in this thing?"

I flipped open the center console, yanked out a facial tissue, and handed it to her. As usual, the sound of the tissue box got Stanley excited. He sat up and stuck his head between the seats. I pushed his nose back, "Settle down, buddy. She doesn't need your help."

Gloria turned and, for the first time, gave Stanley's head a pat. "Why *Stanley?*"

"It's the name of a bass player I like." I got back to the subject at hand. "You said something about *'they never believe us.'*"

"It's Grandma. She's not the most discreet person. Even when her mind was okay. She liked to talk."

"About her relationship with Albert Einstein?"

"Always going on. Stuff they did together. Games they played. Apparently he liked cards." Gloria kept patting Stanley. "Its so sad. Poor Grandma can't remember what she ate for breakfast, but she can tell you exactly what hand she was holding the last time she beat Einstein at poker.”

“Beat Albert Einstein… that would be something to brag about.”

“Not really. Apparently, he was bad at cards.”

“Yeah,” I said. “I always heard he couldn’t remember his own phone number.”

“The older Grandma got, the more she liked to talk about the past. Next thing we knew, rumors started spreading. Rumors about all sorts of things Einstein supposedly left behind. Violins, books, suitcases, clothes, tackle boxes… Would you believe one guy contacted us because he’d heard Grandma had kept Einstein’s truss?”

“Albert Einstein had a hernia?”

Gloria ignored my irrelevant interest for a more trenchant observation of her own. “These Einstein people… they’re worse than Elvis fans. They’ll do anything to connect with their hero.”

“When did your father last hear from this guy? This violin guy.”

“The man contacted Daddy a couple more times. Always by phone. Upping his bid every time. Last offer was fifty thousand.”

Fifty grand was indeed the amount the mystery man on the phone had told me he had offered. I took my eyes off the winding road long enough to look at Gloria, “You say your grandmother was last seen two days ago.”

“Daddy never leaves Grandma alone, but sometimes he just has to. Not for long. Just see to some chore. Tend to his garden. Feed the animals. This time, he just slipped off for an hour’s fishing. Grandma was taking her afternoon nap, so he thought he was safe. But…” Gloria stared out the front window, straight ahead, as if she were looking into the past. “When he got back, she was gone. Daddy was frantic. Then he found the note.”

“A ransom note,” I said.

“A piece of paper tucked under the jigsaw puzzle, the same puzzle Grandma has been doing over and over for the past two years. Of course, to Grandma it’s always a new puzzle. Every day. Every hour. A new puzzle.”

I said, "And the note ended with the warning: *Go to the cops and your mother is dead.*"

Gloria corrected me. "The *police*, not the *cops*. The man always speaks very proper English." Gloria wiped her eyes and looked at me. "I don't get it. How can my father give this man what he wants if it doesn't exist?"

Good question. And as we bounced along the mountain road, the car shook a hundred more good questions loose from my brain. But for now I decided to keep ninety-nine of them to myself. I had just one question that needed an answer right now. "You say the kidnapper kept calling your father to raise the offer. What phone did he call to? Your dad's cell?"

"He called Daddy at work. There's a land line."

"Work? Where's that?"

"You know… the music store. Tupper Lake." She said this as if I should have known. I didn't. And then I did.

A light bulb flashed on in my mind. Well, a whole string of bulbs, actually. They were blinking sequentially as they marched in single file around a cluttered storefront window, a dirty window filled with dusty old guitars and sun-bleached books of sheet music.

"Your father… he's Crazy Henry." I didn't mean any disrespect. That's what the sign over his store said.

"That's my Daddy," she said with mock pride.

"Crazy Henry's Music Emporium," I said. "Of course. I know your father. Not well. But I've met him a few times. Jammed with him once. A monster keyboard player. Big ears. Chops up the wazoo." Then I explained, "I play bass."

Gloria didn't feel it necessary to thank me for my compliments about her father's prodigious talents. She just gazed straight ahead, watching the oncoming roadway narrow, squeezing us tight between steep hills. Meanwhile, my own thoughts funneled to the man we were on our way to visit.

Until now, I had never known his last name. But his first two names were the stuff of musical legend in these hills. I had jammed with Crazy Henry only that one time, but it was enough to tell me I wanted to hook up with the guy again. But when I mentioned him to the guys in my band, with the suggestion that we use him on an upcoming gig at a local rib festival, the guys told me to forget it. According to them, Henry, the keyboard player extraordinaire and owner of Crazy Henry's Music Emporium And Coin Laundry, was not the most reliable guy to book for an important gig like a rib festival. Apparently, the *Crazy* nickname was more than just a catchy sales moniker. Sure, the guy can play up a storm. And yes, he can plink, pluck, strum, or blow the hell out of just about any musical instrument left unattended. But good luck getting the man out for a specific date. Henry might show, might not. You never knew. The guy was undependable. True, Henry was a bit older than we were, but his age or health weren't the problem. He was just a jerk.

Now that I knew who he was, I had to ask Gloria, "What does your father do with your grandmother when he goes to work at the store?"

"Takes Grandma with him. He fixed up a room for her. One of the teaching studios." She pointed to the road ahead. "Here's the turnoff."

I made a tight right turn off the cruddy gravel onto a cruddier dirt road. We didn't go far before we stopped at a heavy tubular steel gate onto which a wooden sign had been bolted warning hunters that they will be prosecuted to the full extent of the law should they even think about dropping by for tea and cookies. The sign, of course, was liberally peppered with bullet holes.

While Gloria jumped out of the car to unhook the gate's combination padlock, I glanced skywards, up into the leafy green spring canopy. I noticed an electric feeder line branching off from the road's main service line. There was no telephone line, just as Gloria had said.

Gloria hopped back into the car, and for the next quarter mile, rocks and exposed tree roots kicked the shit out of my rims, oil pan, and gas tank. But I pressed onward, largely because I had no choice – the road was too narrow for a U-turn. No room for a sober second thought. Someday I'd love to move out west, to Montana or Wyoming, where a man can see what's waiting for him on the far horizon and say, *Screw this – I'm turning back.*

As we snaked around each bend and tip-toed up over each blind hill, the woods funneled us in tighter and tighter, squeezing us forward like an intestine trying to get rid of a bad meal. I prayed that Mother Nature's high fiber diet would keep this passageway clear of oncoming traffic.

As it turned out, the old gal had been eating her whole grains, and we soon found ourselves plopped unceremoniously onto a large clearing overlooking a lake, a small cabin, and a few outbuildings. As I inched the car over hard-packed sand, Gloria scanned the property. Her gaze stopped on the open door of a wooden garage. "Truck's gone," she said.

"Must be out," I said, maintaining my usual firm grasp of the obvious.

"No, he isn't." Her eyes were now locked on the front door of the cabin. It was open wide. Would her father drive off the property without closing his front door? Gloria obviously didn't think so, because without waiting for me to stop, she leapt out of the car.

"Hold on!" I shouted with no effect.

I shut the engine off, opened my door, and yelled, "Don't go in there." From the back seat, Stanley barked a repeat of my warning as I reached across the center console and unlatched the glove compartment. I found my service revolver buried under a pile of antacids, breath mints, and condoms. Of the lot, only the antacids see any regular use. The unloaded gun lay beside a small box of cartridges. I thought for an instant but decided to leave the weapon where it was. I'm not crazy about running around the woods with a firearm jammed under my waistband unless I'm pretty darn sure I'm going to be frightening someone with it.

"Stay here, pal," I said. And I closed the car door behind me.

Gloria was already inside the cabin, but I rapped on the doorjamb anyway and gave out a *Hello* as I stepped into the gloom. I wanted to shout, *Police officer*. But I didn't. I really must get out of that habit.

Gloria had described the cabin as basic. Turns out she was being generous. Dominating the open living space was a simple pine kitchen table on which lay the sad remains of a half-completed jigsaw puzzle. The box top showed a picture of a Scottish castle, an ancient stone building that probably took less time to complete than this futile endeavor. Placed next to the puzzle were two diner plates, two drinking glasses, and some cutlery, all spotlessly clean. I understood this setting. Anyone who lives alone knows there's no point in putting dishes back into the cupboard between meals.

Gathered round the table, three hard pine chairs dating back at least two generations sat waiting for a third generation of bottoms to numb. The chairs and table rested on an oval jute rug that tried its best to cover scratched and worn wooden flooring but failed like a bad toupee. The only other piece of furniture was a three-cushion sofa, placed in the open to differentiate this living space from the cooking area.

From down a short hallway, I could hear Gloria fumbling through some rooms. I couldn't see yet how many rooms were down there — despite the time of day, the cabin's interior was fairly dark, brightened only by trickles of daylight sifting through faded curtains covering small windows. These draperies hung, not from brass or aluminum curtain rods, but from wooden broomstick doweling. I saw no evidence of a television set, but I did notice a vintage stereo hi-fi system complete with analog tuner, turntable, and cassette tape player.

Okay, so the place was modest and austere, maybe even shabby, but it was not dirty. In fact, as my eyes grew more accustomed to the gloom, I could see there wasn't a speck of dust in the place. This impressed me. After all, here was a man living with his elderly mother alone in the middle of the woods, no visitors expected and none invited, and yet the guy kept his floors swept and his table dusted. That says something about him. I don't know what, but something.

Gloria came out of the hallway to announce everything looked fine in the two bedrooms and the bathroom — no signs of foul play. But of course, she added, this doesn't mean her father isn't lying dead out there in the woods somewhere. She hurried out the front door. I followed her. I didn't run. She did. She headed up hill toward a couple of out-buildings.

As I stepped off the porch and walked across the yard, I noticed, down at the waterfront, a cedar strip canoe resting upside down on a small dock. I called out to Gloria, "That the only boat?"

"No motors allowed on the lake," she said as she disappeared inside the first of the two outbuildings, a structure that could best be described as a large shed or a small barn. I picked up my pace and followed her like a hungry puppy.

That hunger didn't last long. The stink, alone, made my stomach lurch. Then her scream brought my breakfast halfway up my throat. By the time I reached her side, I faced a sight that pretty much completed the meal's bitter ascent.

We were standing over two dead creatures which I assumed to be alpacas. I say *assume* because, first, I had never seen an alpaca close up before, and second, because neither of these deceased animals had a head – just long, graceful necks that ended in bloody stumps.

I took hold of Gloria's trembling shoulders, not so much to comfort her as to keep her from collapsing onto the blood-soaked hay on the plank floor. I tried to guide her back to the doorway, back to fresh air. But she wouldn't have it. Her eyes stayed fixed on the horror in disbelief.

"I… I don't understand," she said. "Why?"

I didn't have an answer. Neither did the flies swarming the fresh carnage. I brushed the devils away from my eyes and looked deeper into the dark corners of the stall. And pretty soon, vivid visuals started to develop out of the gloom. Visuals with a message.

At first, I thought the marks and streaks on the plastered wall were simply random shadows, patterns painted in fluid strokes with a brush dipped in sunlight, mud, and alpaca shit. But slowly the brush strokes took on a more distinct form and purpose. They became letters of the alphabet. And one numeral. And then I realized the sick memo wasn't painted with dirt after all. It was painted with blood. And framing this mad graffiti, on either side of the sprawled message, were two faces. Sweet, gentle faces. Eyes wide open, tongues hanging out.

The two alpaca heads had been spiked atop a rake handle and the tines of a pitchfork. Both faces had been carefully posed to face sideways so that their glazed eyes seemed to be directed at the message written on the wall. As if they were reading it, pondering its profound, now-famous declaration.

$E=MC^2$.

CHAPTER FOUR

I hurried out the door and gulped the fresh morning air. "We have to call."

"No, no," Gloria pleaded. "Can't you see? That's exactly what they're telling us not to do. This…" She pointed toward the dark open throat of the barn behind us, "This is a warning."

She had followed me out, but not too close. She hung back a bit, stayed in the shadows, beyond my reach. This should have alerted me to what was coming next, but it didn't. I continued on my way down the hill.

When I reached my car, I slowly opened my door, careful not to let Stanley out. He'd gotten excited by all the fuss. And noise. And smell. I held his collar with one hand, popped open the center console between the front seats with the other, and reached inside for my cell phone.

It wasn't there.

This made no sense. I knew I'd brought it along. I did the math. I turned toward Gloria. "Okay," I said. "Hand it over." She must have pocketed the phone sometime while we were driving in.

"You promised," she said. "No police."

I started toward her, my hand out. "Gloria, these people are playing hardball."

She backed away. But not toward the barn, nor toward the cabin. She was inching her way toward the lake. "Don't you get it?" she said. "The kidnapper knows we've called the police. *You've* called the police. He's telling us not to do it again."

"Gloria, the phone."

She reached into the large, deep pocket of her hiking shorts and slid my cell phone out. She looked at the device for a moment, pondering what to do. She looked up at me. Considered what I might do. Finally, she made her decision. She turned toward the lake.

Now it was my turn to plead. "No… no, you don't." But I might as well have been talking to those severed alpaca heads.

I must say, for a slim woman, she had a strong pitching arm. Must have played sports in school or something. She was a good fifty feet from the shoreline, yet she had no trouble whipping my cell well out into the deep water. Under-handed. Must have played softball.

I opened my arms to the surrounding forest and announced to the chipmunks and squirrels, "That's great. That's just fucking brilliant." Okay, I'm usually better with my sarcasm, but I was truly pissed. That phone had a lot of valuable numbers on it, a few of which had required substantial sweet talk and considerable purchases of alcohol to obtain.

I walked to the water. No intention of wading into it. I just wanted to pay my last respects to my phone's watery grave. I was trying my best to be understanding. I knew I wasn't seeing this lady at her best. The poor woman was out of her mind with worry about her father and her grandmother. She had every right to be upset. So I said to her gently, "Give me yours. I know you have a phone."

"Not here. In my car. Remember? You insisted we take yours?"

Great, now this was all my fault. "Come on," I said, turning back toward my car. "We'll go find a neighbor. Someone will have a phone."

For a moment, I heard her footsteps walking behind me. Then they stopped. I kept walking. I had no time for this. Sure, she was afraid to defy the kidnapper's orders. I understood that. But somebody has to take control of this situation. We need to hand this mess over to the police. The state. Maybe even the feds. So I continued across the yard, over the patches of spring grass, and up onto the packed dirt of the driveway.

I had just about reached my car when I heard the shot ring out. I threw myself to the ground, rolled until I was behind my vehicle. From there, I carefully peered up over the hood. My ears told me where the bullet had come from, and I can't say I was surprised.

Gloria had the pistol clutched tight in both her hands. The gun was small, so small it looked like the wisp of white smoke was rising from between her fingers. She must have had the weapon hidden away in those loose shorts, somewhere in those giant pockets.

I watched with relief as she slowly swung the barrel of the weapon just a hair to the left so it was no longer pointed at my head. My relief didn't last long. She closed one eye and carefully aimed the gun at my car.

"Don't!" I screamed. "You'll hit Stanley!"

I scrambled to my feet just in time to see my tire take the hit. Helpless, I stood and watched my poor, sad vehicle lean down to favor its injured hind leg.

From inside the car, Stanley's muffled bark asked, "What the fuck does that chick with the tasty knees think she's doing out there?"

"Are you crazy?" I cried as I bent down to inspect the damage. "These tires… they're brand new. Barely have a hundred miles on them." I crouched down to massage the soft, fresh rubber of the pancaked tire. "Look! Feel that tread. Like butter."

With gun still in hand, she said, "You're not going to the police. I can't let you." She was trying her best to look tough – eyes narrowed, jaw set tight – but I wasn't buying it. The woman's right hand, now holding the gun on its own, was trembling like the last remaining leaf on a winter birch.

I walked toward her, my hand extended. "Gloria, just give me the gun."

She moved away, stepping backwards into the tall grass. I hoped she didn't trip – the gun was pointed at me. "I'm serious," she warned. "I'll shoot you."

I believed I knew what was really troubling her, and I felt it was time to bring the subject up. "Look, if you're worried about your father being found out, I think he's got bigger problems right now."

My comment caught her by surprise. She didn't know how to react. What did I know? What had I seen? Should she feign ignorance? Try to bullshit me further? I didn't wait for her to make up her mind.

"How'd he get started?" I asked. "Just growing a little taste for himself, I'll bet. A home garden project. Maybe give a little surplus away to a neighbor now and then. Like extra tomatoes in August. But no roadside stands. No dealing. Not at first, anyway. But then your grandma got sick. He needed money. He owed the nursing home. Doctors, drugs, medical expenses."

She held tight to the gun and to her story. "I don't know what you're talking about."

I looked up toward the second, smaller barn farther up the hill – the barn we hadn't searched yet, the one with the heavy 200 amp electric service wires running to it. Back in the cabin I'd noticed a newly replaced junction box. It was a lot more amperage than a little place like this would ever need.

I pointed to the closed barn door with the heavy padlock on it. "So, that where he starts the plants? Where he gets the seedlings fired up?"

Gloria's shoulders lowered. She knew she was beat. There was no point in continuing her bluff. "My father already has one conviction. Twenty years ago. Possession. Seeing as how it was his first offence, the judge went easy. But if Daddy gets caught again…"

She didn't finish the thought. She didn't need to. Possession is one thing – production, something else. Henry would definitely see time. Real time. And that wouldn't be easy for a guy who owns a canoe. Especially a cedar strip.

I stepped closer to her. And this time I easily took the small Colt .380 from her hand. "Got a permit?" I asked, mostly out of habit.

"It was in Daddy's night stand. He's never been much for filling out forms."

I clicked the safety on and pocketed the little weapon. Then I turned away and walked up the pathway toward that second shed which we hadn't searched yet. This time, Gloria stuck close by my heels.

The old plank door held a shiny new padlock that matched the new combination lock on the steel gate at the entrance to the driveway. That heavy gate and new padlock had been my first clue – nobody goes to that much trouble to guard a thirty-year-old hi-fi system and a couple of weird critters that look like small camels but smell like large camels.

I held out the padlock for Gloria to work her magic on. While she fiddled with the combination, I asked, "So what's with the alpacas? Money laundry? A way to explain the new income to the tax man? An excuse for the electric upgrades?"

"A little like that. But Daddy really hoped they'd work out. Make more alpacas."

"But no luck?"

She popped the lock and swung the door open. "He figures one of them is gay."

"That's the problem these days. We're not allowed to ask." I went inside.

There were no surprises waiting for me, just a big empty room the size of a rather tall, three-car garage that smelled of soil and mildew. The room had been thoroughly cleaned out, and unless you were actually looking for it, you would find no evidence of illicit activity. Three long wooden trestle tables sat in the middle of the dirt floor, but they could be used for anything. The only indication of agricultural pursuits were a few garden implements and a stack of fiber seedling pots sitting on the end of a table. I looked up into the rafters. The beams above my head held hooks from which light fixtures must have been hung. I pointed to the two exhaust fans that had been recently installed into the two end walls. I had noticed their vents when we first drove in. "Those are a bit of a giveaway," I said.

"If anyone ever asked he was going to say they're for more alpacas when… you know, the herd starts up. Same for the water pump."

I finished surveying the room. This was clearly a small operation, geared only towards getting the plants started during the winter. Come spring they'd have to be finished outdoors, which is why this shed was now empty.

"So where are the plants now?" I said.

With a wave of her arm, Gloria tossed my question out the door as if she were casting nuts to the squirrels. "Somewhere in the hills. I don't really know. Does it matter?"

"This man who's been hounding your father…"

"No way." Gloria was ahead of me on this one. "He has no interest in this."

"Did he know about it?"

"If he did, he never mentioned it." Gloria walked out the doorway.

There was nothing more to see inside this shed, so I followed her out into the warm, morning sunshine. "So maybe that's where your dad is now – out tending his crop."

"As far as I know, there's nothing to do yet. He's finished planting. Wanted to do it before the black flies get bad."

"Smart man." I said, swatting a tiny black fly away from my face. "Not biting yet, though."

"They will."

She had a point. Black flies take flight and then reconnoiter the buffet table for a couple of days without causing any trouble. But once they get hungry, watch out. Somehow, a black fly is the only creature whose teeth are bigger than his head.

I walked alongside Gloria down the hill, back into the cabin. I headed straight to the fridge. Along with medicine cabinets, you can learn a lot from poking around a man's fridge.

Nothing seemed unusual about Henry's stock of perishables except a lack of beer. Gloria said that her father wasn't much of a beer drinker. She grabbed a jug of ice water and poured us a couple of glasses. As she served, I said, as casually as possible, "Gloria, I don't think your father is being totally straight with you."

"You mean about the kidnapping?" She looked into my eyes, something she hadn't done much of so far. She seemed to have settled down somewhat. Softened a bit.

"About this violin of Einstein's," I said. "Your father claims he doesn't know anything about it. I have trouble with that. Especially considering the trouble this kidnapper is going to."

"My father's lying? Daddy wouldn't do that. Not to me."

I wandered to the table, looked down at poor Amy's unfinished jigsaw puzzle, it's cardboard pieces scattered like confetti with nothing to celebrate, their worn and tattered edges testifying to endless efforts to restore order over and over again with no success. I was through screwing around. I said, "I'll have the state boys check his call records. Have them drop by the store. There's more going on here than we know." I put my empty glass in the sink, left it for someone else to wash later, and headed for the front door.

This time, Gloria didn't get excited with my plans. She had clearly softened – somewhat. "Do we really have to?" she said. "You used to be a cop – can't you check? Like, on your own? I'll pay you."

I ignored her. I stepped out onto the porch and glanced up toward the empty garage. "Can you get me the make and plate number of the missing truck?" I then walked down the porch steps, headed across the yard. I had a flat tire to fix.

Gloria kept up with me. "It's an F-150. Black. I don't remember what year. But I can find out. He keeps all that stuff at the store."

"Fine." I kept walking to my car. "I'll tell them to look through his files."

"Good idea." Gloria's shoulders rose. This new tune of hers was now sung in a brighter key. "I'll wait here. In case he comes back."

"Wait for your father? Forget it." I opened my trunk and started clearing the junk out so I could get to the spare. "I can't leave you here. Not alone. You don't even have a phone."

"I'll have the gun."

"Sorry." I patted my pocket. "This is staying with me." I lifted out the car's jack and dropped it beside the mortally wounded tire. Using the jack handle wrench, I started loosening the lug nuts on the wheel.

Meanwhile, Gloria kept pitching, "You go find a phone. There's a place just past where we turned off. Turn right instead of left. There should be somebody home. They're full-timers, not summer people."

I slid the wrench handle's socket over a lug nut and started twisting. But it was tight. The thing wouldn't budge. I braced my legs for another try.

Meanwhile Gloria continued. "I'm not having my father discover those poor dead creatures on his own. It's just too sad. Daddy doesn't have a lot of use for people, but he loves animals. I have to be here." And with that, she turned and walked back to the cabin.

I gave the jack handle a good hefty shove, put everything I had behind it. But the wrench slipped off the nut, smashing my thumb hard against the wheel well. "Goddamn fucking hell," I explained as I buried my throbbing thumb into my armpit in a pointless attempt to… well, bury my thumb into my armpit.

From his place inside the car, Stanley barked. Or maybe laughed. With him it's had to tell.

I pulled my throbbing thumb out and inspected the damage. Yup. Looked like I was going to lose the nail. And it was my right thumb, too – one of the two most important thumbs for a bass player. Especially a funk player.

Gloria heard the cussing, but she didn't run over to kiss anything better. She just called out, "I didn't ask you to help, you know." And with those kind words she stepped into the cabin and closed the door.

On the plus side, the troublesome nut was now loose.

I should have taken that as an omen.

CHAPTER FIVE

While I was busy changing the flat tire, Gloria locked herself inside the cabin. I considered busting down the door and dragging her out, but I decided she'd be all right for the few minutes it should take me to get to a neighbor's phone and come back. Just to be safe, I passed her father's little pistol back to her through the open window so she'd have some protection just in case the alpaca killer returned. Of course I could have left Stanley with her, but he isn't much of a guard dog. He's a licker, not a biter.

According to Gloria, the closest residence belonged to a couple named the Brennans. Apparently, the trip shouldn't take more than fifteen minutes each way. As I bounced along the rutted cow path I could understand why Crazy Henry was considered unreliable for showing up at gigs. This angry python of a road was tough enough to handle in broad daylight, I'd hate to have to wrestle it to submission after dark just to get to some saloon that paid in free beer. Especially considering he doesn't drink beer.

I found the Brennan's cottage exactly where Gloria had told me it would be. I knocked, waited. Then I tried the door. Many families out here don't bother locking their places. Unfortunately, this family wasn't one of them. In more of an emergency situation, I would have broken into the place to use the phone. But this was not an emergency. As far as I could tell, no life was in immediate danger except maybe my own if I was caught by a passerby breaking into a home.

I got back into my car and headed off to see if there was another residence down the road. Ten-minutes later I got my answer in the form of a fish. It was one of those mailboxes where you yank your birthday cards and restaurant menus out of the throat of a large mouth bass. I turned into the driveway, and a few hundred yards up stream I came to a house. This place, much like the previous abode, wasn't much of a building. More of a mobile home, really. Gloria had mentioned that the expensive real estate was on the far side of the lake, nearer the state highway. But this house had one encouraging sign – a car parked in the driveway. Of course, out here that doesn't necessarily mean much. In the city, a single vehicle in a laneway means chances are fifty-fifty somebody's home. Two cars means chances are almost a hundred percent. But out here there can be a dozen cars, a snowmobile, two semi-trailers, and a yellow school bus parked on the front lawn and all it means is the lady of the house, when she does come home, will probably smell of diesel oil.

I parked. Stepped out of my car. Heard a noise. Stepped back into my car. Closed the door and rolled up the window. From the safety of my front seat I watched a large barking dog, or a small barking moose, come galloping around the corner of the building, his wake turbulence almost sucking the aluminum siding off the wall. The animal, apparently a Rottweiler/cougar mix, was drooling like he'd just heard that Walmart had squirrels on for half price.

Stanley casually stood up, looked out the window, saw the crazy dog, and lay back down again. He looked at me as if to say, *What's that idiot so worked up about?* In these situations I can never figure out whether Stanley is Mr. Cool or just deaf.

I opened my window a bit – not all the way – and honked my horn. This was a needless exercise, of course, considering my arrival was already being clearly announced.

I kept my eyes on the house. The front door opened, and a young boy, about ten years old, stepped out onto the small porch. He shielded his eyes and squinted to see what size bear his doggie was currently chewing up.

"Hello, there," I called out, trying to fit my friendly words in between angry barks and the open crack of my window. "Your mom or dad home?"

The boy stepped off the porch and approached my car. "Not supposed to say."

"Good boy," I said. "Your mommy taught you well." I looked down at the slobbering hound that was looking straight back at me and licking the back of his own head with his giant tongue. "Uh… any chance you can call off your doggy?"

"Yes, sir."

I waited. Then I realized my mistake. "Would you please call off your doggy?"

"Not supposed to do that either."

Man, this was one obedient kid. I tried another approach. "My name's Tanager. What's yours?"

"That your first name?"

"No, it's my last name."

"Last? You mean you're never going to get another?" The kid smiled at his joke.

I laughed, "That's a good one." I rolled my window down a bit farther and rested my elbow on the window. The dog lunged.

"Holy mother-humper," I exclaimed, pulling my elbow back in.

The kid instructed his dog, "Down, Cooper. Sit."

Cooper sat.

I said, "He probably smells my dog."

"What dog?"

I looked back and saw Stanley was lying sprawled out on the back seat pretending to be a throw cushion. I turned back to the kid. "Tell me, son, do you have a phone?"

"Nope."

"No phone? Really?" I looked out the windshield at the telephone pole by the driveway and clearly saw three wires, one of which was a phone line feeding into the house. "You wouldn't lie to me, now, would you?"

"No, sir." The kid smiled again. "My parents have a phone, though."

I'd hate to go up against this kid in court.

While Cooper put his front paws up on my door and started using my outside mirror as a tooth whitener, I said to the boy, "I don't suppose it's a cordless phone?"

The kid understood. "You want me to bring it out to you?"

"Would you? That would be great."

"How do I know you won't steal it?"

"Cross my heart I won't. I just need it to call the police. Right away."

At this news, the kid looked genuinely concerned. But still suspicious. "You in some sort of trouble, Mr. Tanager?"

"No, but one of your neighbors is. And he doesn't have a telephone."

"No phone? You must be talking about Mr. Tapin."

"Yes. Yes, I am. You know Mr. Tapin?"

"Yes, sir."

"Have you seen him lately?"

"No, sir."

"Well, we need to get the police out to his place, right away."

"I'll go call 911," said the kid. And with that, he turned and ran toward the house.

I called out to his departing heels, "Tell them to hurry. Tell them there's been a kidnapping." Okay, it might be a slight stretch, but I didn't want to have to wait around all day for a minor crimes unit or a bored traffic cop to respond.

The kid turned back to me, his eyes open wide "A kidnapping?"

"More or less."

"Holy motherhumper." The kid turned and ran into the house.

I smiled. It always feels good to make an impression on a youngster.

* * * * *

Knowing that the cavalry was on its way, made my return trip to the cabin seem smoother – the wrinkles had been ironed out by the knowledge that I had indeed done the correct thing, right from the very start. In situations like this it's always best to call in the authorities. I had done my duty, and now I can get back to selling kitty litter. But first, I'll sit with Gloria until the police arrive.

I pulled onto the property and honked my horn. Knowing she had that Colt .380 loaded and ready, I didn't want to startle her, so as I stepped out of the car I sang out to the trees and chipmunks, "Hey, Gloria. It's only me."

No immediate answer from Gloria nor from the Colt .380. Stanley, however did start grumbling about needing a squirt, so I clipped his leash to his collar and let him jump out. I'd like to have forgone the leash, but I didn't want to chance losing him to a passing squirrel.

While Stanley watered a handy birch, I again called out a cheerful, "Yoo-hoo, Gloria."

No answer. But that didn't worry me. Not yet. After all, it was a large property, Gloria could be anywhere. Still, I must admit to a cold lump starting to crystalize in my stomach. I was over-reacting, of course. Gloria was probably busy inside the cabin. Or in one of the sheds. Or maybe she'd gone off into the trees to check on her old man's crop of weed. Hell, there could be a hundred reasons why the woman hadn't come running out, arms open wide to greet me.

I walked Stanley across to the cabin. As I neared the building, I called out, "Found a telephone. Some kid down the road. Nice boy. Taught him a new word."

Still no answer. The cold lump started to grow from a small frozen pea to an ice-wine grape. Had to be my guilt just working overtime. I obviously felt bad about leaving Gloria alone here, or about pushing myself into her private affairs when she'd pleaded with me to mind my own business.

I climbed the steps onto the porch and tried the front door. It opened. It had been locked when I'd left here.

The cold grape was now an icy lemon. Before further entering the cabin, I tied Stanley's leash to the porch railing – I couldn't risk having him contaminate any evidence inside the residence.

I went in. Had a good look around. Everything seemed fine. The cabin's main room looked pretty much the same as it had when I'd left.

But no Gloria. I checked the two bedrooms. Then the bathroom. Nope, no sign of her, but no sign of any trouble either. Meanwhile, Stanley had started barking. I'll bet Gloria is roaming around out there.

I hurried out. "What is it, fella?" I looked around, surveyed the property's ragged rim of bushes and scrub trees. Meanwhile, Stanley kept barking at the yard. Or at the forest. Hey, maybe at those dead alpacas. That outbuilding had smelled bad to me, it must really stink to Stanley. "Stay here, pal." And I continued on, up the hill to inspect the alpaca shed.

The site was still horrid, but nothing had changed. Two rotting alpaca carcasses, two severed heads, a cloud of flies, and a fog of stench. But no Gloria. I left the shed and continued on farther up the hill to Henry's second outbuilding – the one he'd used as a grow-op.

No sign of her there either, so I walked back outside. From here, atop the rise, I had a good view of the grounds. And the lakeshore. And that's where something caught my eye. Or more correctly, *didn't* catch my eye. The canoe. It was gone. And now so was that cold lump in my stomach. That's where she's gone. Mystery solved. She's taken the canoe out. Probably searching the shoreline for her father. Good idea. Smart woman. I'll just wait for her, here.

Meanwhile, Stanley was still barking from the cabin's front porch. I called out to him, "It's okay, buddy. No problem. She's just gone for a paddle." I walked down to the lake to have a closer look, see if I could spot her out on the water.

The small dock comprised cedar boards bolted to a tubular frame mounted on four posts that stood in about two or three feet of water – not deep enough for an outboard, but fine for a canoe.

Across the lake, I could see a few cottages sprinkled along the shore, but I couldn't make out any signs of human activity. No smoke. The offshore midday breeze was stirring up a slight chop on the water. Not exactly ideal conditions for a canoe ride, but I suppose Gloria could handle herself. After all, she was raised in these mountains.

A short ways down shore, a large crow, sitting high atop a yellow birch, scolded me. He was clearly pissed about something. I like crows. Some people say they're as smart as dogs. Apparently, the omnivorous black scavengers can recognize individual people. I'm sure this guy and I had never met, but he was clearly telling me something. Maybe he was inviting me to come share lunch – or warning me to keep the hell away from his. I could see another crow feeding at something lying in the grass at the base of the tree. I squinted for a better look. My eyesight is pretty good, but from here, fifty yards from the tree, I couldn't quite tell what it was.

Suddenly, Stanley came running across the yard. He was dragging his leash and a stick of wood behind him. My fault. I had noticed that wooden railing looked kind of rotted when I tied him to it.

The pooch, still barking his head off, was not running to me – he was running toward that tree with the crow in it. Or the lump of grass at the bottom. "What ya after, pal?"

From the dock, I couldn't walk along the shoreline, too many bushes, and rocks. So I circled up and wound my way through the trees. Meanwhile, high overhead, that crow, now pissed at the dog, kept cawing louder and faster than ever.

As I neared his perch, the bird up top took off, his surveillance duty done. I was close enough to the birch now to recognize a few colors woven into that tall grass. Colors that shouldn't be there. Like blue. And pink.

Like sneakers. And legs.

I called out, "Gloria?" I got no reply. A few leaps and I was by her side.

She was lying face down. After the horror scene with the alpacas I was actually afraid to turn her over. Stanley had stopped barking. His job complete, he looked up at me, *Now it's your turn.* Ever so gently, I rolled her over. As I lifted her, Gloria's lovely head stayed exactly where it was supposed to stay. Still attached. Her upper torso looked fine. But a large crimson stain on the front of her shorts indicated a wound to her abdomen. A few bright red drops of blood dropped onto the dandelions, suggesting that she might still be bleeding freely. I watched her stomach. Yes, she was still breathing.

I slid one arm under her legs, my other arm under her shoulders and lifted. I carried her back through the long grass, across the yard, and up the steps into the cabin. Stanley followed me into to the bedroom where I placed her onto her father's bed. Throughout the painful trek, she didn't groan – she stayed mercifully unconscious.

I found some first-aid supplies in the bathroom cabinet – gauze, tape, a bottle of hydrogen peroxide . I cleaned the entrance wound as best I could. No exit wound. This was not good. I just hoped the bullet had been stopped by her pelvis and not by her spine.

I managed to slow down the bleeding, but I couldn't stop it completely. How do I apply pressure to a soft belly? I didn't know. I didn't bother feeling for a pulse – she was clearly still breathing. I gently opened a closed eyelid. Her pupil was dilated. Must be in shock. The woman needed help, and she needed it fast. I have attended enough traffic accidents to know that gut wounds unleash a herd of demons that have to be corralled immediately if the victim is to have any hope of survival.

I had a decision to make. Stay or go. If that young boy up the road has done his job, the police should be on their way. But what if the kid didn't call? And even if he did call, cops are not paramedics. The troopers will have no more medical expertise than I have, which isn't a whole lot. So what is the point in my waiting?

Decision made.

I picked up Gloria and carried her out to my car. I laid her flat as possible in my back seat, careful to keep her feet propped up so that whatever warm blood was still sloshing around inside her will be kept circulating to her brain. I covered her with a blanket from the cabin, placed Stanley into the front passenger seat, and climbed behind the wheel. The pooch has a sense about these things. He knew playtime was over. He kept his wet nose to himself. Like that crow, he had done his duty.

We headed out onto the dirt road. I drove as fast as I could. Seemed every time I attacked this damned trail I had a new reason to hate it and a new reason to increase my speed. This time I had stronger motivation than ever for breaking my previous time, which meant a greater risk of busting a tire or axle. But it was a risk I had to take. If Gloria didn't get medical attention soon she might as well not get any at all. Sure, it was a small wound and maybe I'd stopped a lot of the bleeding, but inside that gut some ugly stuff was now spilling out of torn intestines and mixing up a fatal concoction. It was only a matter of time before her heart called the whole game quits on account of contaminations, infections, and internal blood loss. As I say, gut wounds are the worst.

And so was this road. Despite what we hear in pop songs, country roads are nothing to sing about. Give me the mean streets of the inner city anytime. Cab drivers may be stubborn but they're not as hard-headed as granite. Nor are pedestrians as deaf as pine trees. On these roads you can honk your horn all you like, nothing is stepping out of your way. Still, in hindsight, I should have been honking that thing. Especially when I crested that last blind hill.

As I approached that final steep grade, I recognized many of the features I had passed coming in, so I knew I was almost at the main highway. I was pleased with the excellent progress. I knew it should be smooth driving from here, once I was over the top.

Confidence triggers bold moves. I was now going like hell, clutching the bucking wheel with both hands, taking reckless delight in the knowledge that I was only a few hundred yards from the flat asphalt of the county highway. So I gunned it up the hill. Even though, at this point, the hill was still basically one lane.

The other poor bastard never had a chance.

No tires squealed, but plenty of dirt and gravel flew. With no room for either of us to swerve to safety, we crunched left eye to left eye. Happily, by the time we had hit we'd both slowed to a speed that destroyed only our grills and our spirts, not our skulls. I don't know legally whose fault the accident was – after all, the other guy should have been honking, too – but liability didn't matter. Never does when the car you hit is a police car.

"Step out of your vehicle," the New York State trooper called out. He had moved fast. He was already out of his car. He had already drawn his gun. And he was already crouching behind the open door of his injured cruiser, even before I had opened my door. He finished his instructions, "Clasp your hands over your head."

It's hard to open a car door with your hands clasped on top of your head, but somehow I kicked open the door of my hissing car. "Trooper," I said as I emerged. "I have an injured woman here. She needs medical attention, fast."

Our cars were jammed nose to nose, like two rutting moose. Steam was snorting from the nostrils of my busted radiator. Tears were dripping from his. The trooper stepped out from behind his vehicle's dark blue door with the smart gold lettering and snazzy state crest emblazoned on it. He was young. "Place your hands on the side of your vehicle, sir. And spread your legs."

I complied, careful to keep my face away from the hot steam that geysered from under my crumpled hood. As the young trooper patted me down I again drew his attention to the injured woman lying in my back seat. "She's been shot," I said. "Your radio still working?"

He took a quick look at my passenger's unconscious body. Her blanket had been knocked off by the crash, and he could see the blood seeping through her bandages. He also noted the dog sitting quietly in my front seat.

"Don't worry," I said. "He's friendly." Then I added, "You want to call for medical?"

The trooper pondered his choices, then announced, "Sir, you're under arrest."

He pulled out his cuffs while reciting my Miranda rights. I didn't give him any grief. Frankly, if I had caught a maniac driving through the woods with a half-dead woman lying in the back of his vehicle, I'd have done the same thing.

Wouldn't have cuffed my arms around that tree, though.

CHAPTER SIX

The good news was we had smashed up our cars very near a wide spot on the county highway that was clear enough for the Life Flight helicopter to land and whisk Gloria off to the trauma center in Saranac Lake. The bad news was that the young Trooper Scott wouldn't let me accompany her. But then, I couldn't really expect him to let me off the hook. After all, I was now the prime suspect in the shooting.

I had explained that I was an ex-cop. I had even managed to show Trooper Scott an old photo I.D. from my days in law enforcement. But I'm afraid the Buffalo Police Benevolent Association membership isn't the *Get Out Of Jail Free* card it once was.

When the young trooper first cuffed my arms rather intimately around that white pine tree, I suggested to him that I, his prisoner, might be just as securely locked up in the back seat of his patrol car. But he declined my suggestion, pointing out that his injured cruiser, which was steaming and possibly leaking gasoline onto its hot exhaust system, was not deemed safe for prisoner confinement. So he left me where I was, for my own good. The trooper may have had a point, but personally, I think the guy was just cheesed off about my crunching up his snazzy vehicle. Happily, I didn't have to wait too long before a pair of more sympathetic ears arrived on scene. Big fat ears that matched a big fat face.

I heard him coming long before I saw him. Smelled him, too. We always do. "Hey," Lieutenant Manny Manwaring shouted to the trees. "Somebody pass me a camera. I think I've found my Christmas card."

Chewing pine bark as I was, I couldn't look Lieutenant Manwaring in the eye, so I just spoke into the tree. "I smell garlic. Either Manwaring is here or there's a moose eating Kielbasa."

Manwaring gave me a hearty slap on the back. "What's wrong, Sweetcheeks? Get your dick stuck in a knothole again?" Manwaring turned to young Trooper Scott. "Let this be a lesson, trooper. A man can get mighty lonely in these woods."

I knew Manny from when we were both in Buffalo. I was in homicide, he worked vice. He claims that the experience left him with a twisted outlook on sex. Frankly, I doubt he needed the excuse.

Lieutenant Manwaring addressed Trooper Scott again, "You can unlock Woody Woodpecker now. Don't worry, if he tries to fly, I'll shoot him."

Once the cuffs were off, the first thing I did was take a leak. Rather ironic being cuffed to a tree and not being able to squirt on it, but to do it right, a guy really does need at least one hand free. After I zipped up, I went to my car and let Stanley out do his business. Then I joined Manwaring in his car. At this time of year, fly season, we try to stay in our cars as much as possible.

As quickly as I could, I explained the where, how, and why of what had happened to poor Gloria Tapin, who was reportedly now at the hospital. Just as quickly, I also suggested that Manwaring jump on the radio and order roadblocks on all highways leading away from this area. I described what I knew of Henry's missing truck, which wasn't much other than the make, color, and approximate year. Manny took my advice and also called for an aerial unit to fly over the lake and search for Henry's missing canoe. Manny knows me well enough to give my words some weight.

By this time, a tow truck had cleared both my car and Trooper Scott's disabled cruiser from the dirt secondary road so Manny and his team could now proceed to the crime scene, Henry Tapin's cabin. Manny didn't mind me tagging along to assist, but he made me leave Stanley with one of his troopers.

As Manny drove, he let me use his cell phone so I could call Marlene and explain that I wouldn't be in to the store for the rest of the day. She understood. Sort of.

"You do know you're not a cop anymore, right?"

"So I've heard," I said. "But according to those who still do wear badges, I seem to be the closest thing they have to a witness." Manwaring turned his head and gave me a look. I got the message and amended my statement, "And a suspect." Satisfied with my amendment, Manny turned his eyes back to the road.

"*Suspect?*" Marlene was justifiably shocked.

"I'll explain later. I just want to let you know I'll be a bit late today." Manny looked at me again. "*Very* late," I corrected. Manny looked back at the road.

Marlene paused briefly to let me know that, while she wasn't totally buying my excuse for slacking off, she knew there was nothing more to be said about the subject. So, she returned to more immediate matters. "Shipment of aspen shavings finally came in."

"That's good," I said. "A lot of hamsters will be happy to hear that."

Another pause, then she said, "Caught Sandra Bissonette slipping a couple of canary perches into her handbag. Didn't call her on it, though."

"Wooden perches?"

"Pumice."

"Right," I said. "She's been worried about Petey's claws."

"Sandra must still be out of work." Marlene said.

"I think she retired. Wants to stay at home, be a full-time podcaster."

Marlene thought this over. "That's just dumb."

"I don't think Petey's too thrilled with it either."

Another pause. Finally, she said, "You coming in tomorrow?"

"Yes. Definitely. Of course, I'll be in tomorrow." I didn't look to Manny for his take on this. I didn't need any more bad news. I said to Marlene, "So why don't you take tomorrow off. You've earned it. I'll handle things by myself."

"Okay. That's nice of—" Then she remembered, "Hey, tomorrow's Sunday."

"Oh, yeah. Well, I'll cover for you Monday then." I looked over at Manwaring and added for his benefit, "Unless, of course, I'm in jail." I chuckled at the very thought. Manny did not.

I thanked Marlene again. Then I signed off with a big, *Thanks, babe, you're the best.* And I meant it. Marlene is a great pal, and I suppose she thinks I'm all right too. So far we've kept our relationship platonic, and that's fine with me. She's about ten years younger than I am. She's also about twenty pounds heavier, but that's not the problem. We just don't want to mess up a good friendship and a profitable partnership. Besides, these days I seem to have a girlfriend. Sort of. I mean, we're not exclusive or anything, but… well, Marlene's just too young for me.

"Not much to look at is she?"

"Huh?"

"A bit of a fixer upper."

I now realized Manwaring was talking about the property we were pulling into. "Oh, yeah," I said. "I think the real estate agent would call it *rustic.*"

"*Shit-hole* would be another choice," Manny said.

We pulled up to Henry's porch. Behind us, followed a parade of three police cruisers plus a second unmarked car like this one. More crime scene units were on their way, and their vehicles will be followed by media hounds from Plattsburgh and Watertown, maybe even a few from Albany and Rochester. A shooting in the middle of nowhere like this doesn't normally attract a whole lot of attention. Once the story gets out, however, about the kidnapping and the mysterious connection to Albert Einstein's mystery violin, the alpaca poop will likely hit the fan. All great fodder for *Details at eleven.*

With some pain, I climbed out of Manwaring's car. Funny how being wrapped around a tree for a length of time like that can stiffen a guy up. Manwaring started to lead the way into the cabin, but I redirected him down toward the lake, to the spot on the shoreline where I'd found

Gloria's wounded body. I wanted Manny to see it while the evidence was still fresh.

The blood on the patch of dandelions had turned to dark rust, but apart from that, everything was as I'd left it. While I pointed out the more obvious highlights concerning the scene, Manwaring's young pal, Trooper Scott, busied himself festooning the area with yellow crime scene tape as if he was decorating the gym for the big dance. Manny took notice of Scott's youthful enthusiasm and told the trooper to go easy with the stuff. Considering how far off the beaten track we were, the only function the tape was going to serve was to make life difficult for the older, less athletic investigators to limbo under. After we'd finished at the shoreline, I walked Manwaring up the hill to inspect the interior of the cabin.

In Henry's bedroom, I pointed out the nightstand where Gloria had found her father's handgun, the little Colt Mustang with which she had shot out my tire. I explained to Manny that I had left her armed with this particular weapon back when I first went to call the police. I also explained that, when I'd returned and discovered her injured body, I hadn't had time to go looking for the weapon, so Manwaring's team should have a look for it now. I added that I doubt they'll find it on dry land. If, as I suspected, this particular weapon was the gun with which she had been shot, it is probably now lying in the bottom of the lake along with my cell phone. I suggested Manwaring order up the SCUBA team as soon as possible. Manwaring had enough self-confidence to take my suggestions in the spirit with which they were given. He called in the request for the divers and also ordered a drone unit to come help look for that missing canoe.

When we were finished checking out the cabin, I took Manwaring up the hill to see the dead alpacas. After a cursory inspection, which is all our noses could take, we stepped outside and gulped a few lungsful of fresh air. We then proceeded on to the second outbuilding.

On first glance, Manwaring didn't notice anything suspicious about this large empty shed. so, I ratted on Henry. I told how Gloria's father used the room to start marijuana seedlings before planting them somewhere out in the hills. I stressed that Gloria felt the illicit crop was in no way linked to her Grandma Amy's kidnapping nor to the alpaca deaths.

Of course, whether this was true or not was up to Manny and his team to determine – my part here was done. Fini. Complete.

As a good citizen, I'd seen my duty and I'd done it. And now all I wanted was for some nice policeman to drive me back to town so I could pick up my dog, rent or borrow a working vehicle, and get on with my simple life of selling chew toys and playing with my band. It had been a long day, sure, but there was still part of it left, and it was the best part – the part that included beer and blues music. This is one of the nice things about being a civilian again. Saturday nights are my very own. No distractions. No beepers. No cell phones. And no having to watch my alcohol intake. Hell, nobody cares what a pet store owner's breath smells like at two in the morning. It's a shame high school guidance counselors don't stress this advice on Career Day.

I felt I had done all I could do here, so I asked Manwaring if he could kindly ask one of his lovely staff to give me a lift to town. Manny was fine with this, and he was just about to send me on my way when things took an ugly turn. And once again, it was Trooper Scott who forced my happy plan off the road and into the ditch.

Manwaring and I were crossing the grounds, on our way to find a driver for me, when Trooper Scott came running up from the lake shore. Out of breath with excitement, the uniformed trooper was clutching something in his trembling hand. As he neared, I saw he had a clear plastic evidence bag, the kind of bag Scott's mother probably wraps his sandwiches in. Except, instead of containing a nice baloney and processed cheese on white, this bag held something downright unhealthy. Grinning like a kid bringing home his first goldfish from the fair, the young trooper held out his prize for us to see.

It was a handgun. And it looked familiar. I mean, really, really familiar.

The trooper explained in breathless detail how his keen eye had noticed sunlight glinting off a shiny metal object where it lay in the tall grass just beyond the spot where I had found Gloria's injured body.

I lifted the bag from Trooper Scott's sweaty hand so I could take a closer look. The trooper didn't seem to mind my aggressive action. He was too impressed with his own actions to take offense at anyone else's.

Meanwhile, Lieutenant Manwaring stood by, waiting patiently for my expert analysis of the weapon.

Of course, we all knew that no fingerprints had been lifted from this gun and that the caliber, a nine millimeter Browning, hadn't yet been matched to the bullet that was presently resting deep inside poor Gloria Tapin's torn abdomen. Nor had the gun's serial number yet been traced to any particular owner. But it was obvious to both Trooper Scott and to Lieutenant Manwaring that this weapon must have been the gun used to shoot Gloria. And it was equally obvious to me that it was my gun. My old service revolver. The gun I'd last seen a couple of hours ago when I checked for it in the glove compartment of my car. I had decided to leave the weapon there, safely buried under the antacids, condoms, and breath mints. And yet here it is, somehow resting in a plastic bag, presented as the obvious murder weapon.

I had no choice. I immediately volunteered the incriminating information. Hell, I even offered to open the bag and point out the minty smell that would clearly identify the weapon as being from my own personal glove compartment.

Trooper Scott could barely contain his delight at my confession. After all, I, ex-cop Norris Tanager – from here on referred to as *the suspect* – was his collar. Young Trooper Scott had caught me all by his lonesome, in the middle of the forest, by cleverly ramming his car into my vehicle, thereby halting my escape from the crime scene. Trooper Scott's day is just getting better and better. I'm sure the young, handsome, square-jawed trooper was already picturing the headlines and photos and official announcements of his impending promotion.

Manwaring, however, was a little more reserved. "You sure it's yours, Tanager?" For once he didn't call me *Sweetcheeks*.

"See that scrape?" I pointed to a scratch on the base of the handle. "That's a tooth mark."

Scott found this surprising. "You chew your gun?"

Manning got it. "His dog."

I said, "I never transport it loaded." I took hold of the bagged weapon again. "Somebody must have grabbed this out of my car. Or maybe Gloria took it. Like I told you, she'd already snatched my cell phone."

"The phone she tossed in the lake," said Manny.

"Yes."

"But this isn't the weapon she drew on you."

"No, no. That was her father's little three-eighty."

Now it was Trooper Scott's turn. "But if she'd already removed your gun from your car, why did she pull a different weapon on you?"

It was a damn good question. Too bad I didn't have an answer of equal quality. "You got me. All I can say is, the last time I saw this weapon it was sitting in my glove compartment."

"Locked?" said Manwaring.

I couldn't help acting sheepish on this one. "Well… normally, I always keep that compartment locked. But this morning, when we got here, I opened it. I wanted to make sure the weapon was available. I guess, now that I think of it, I might not have… you know, not locked it up again."

"Leaving a weapon unsecured…" Manwaring shook his big head with big concern. "That's not like you, Tanager."

He was right. It wasn't. And I wasn't proud of it. So I changed the direction of our discussion. "Look, have your people go over my vehicle for prints. You've got mine and Marlene's on file. You'll find our prints plus Gloria Tapin's prints in that car. And maybe Nina's. She's a girl I've been dating. That's everybody that's been in the vehicle over the last month. Any others and you've got the perp who took that weapon. Oh, and Stanley's prints, of course."

"Stanley?" asked Scott.

Manny answered for me, "His dog."

Then I remembered one other person who had recently been in my vehicle. I wish I hadn't remembered her, but I did. "Oh, and a girl named Madison. A waitress at Blues and Cues. Sometimes tends bar. But that's everyone. Any other prints will belong to—"

"Madison?" the young Trooper interrupted. "Madison Scott?"

"Yeah, you know——?" Oh, shit. Me and my big mouth. Tentatively, I asked, "Sister?"

"Mother," said Trooper Scott, looking both surprised and angry. It was a look I recognized from when I'd pranged into his squad car coming over that hill. This had indeed been a busy day for both young Trooper Scott and his face.

"Nice, nice lady," I stammered, trying desperately to soften that hard face back to its original freshness. "I give her a lift home from work occasionally. You know, when my band plays. I don't like to see the girls walk home alone. Late. At night. In the dark. *Women*, I mean. Not girls. Nice, nice lady."

"Mom has her own car."

"Yeah, well, I think she's been having trouble with it." This was a lie of course. Truth was, when at work, Madison likes to sample the drinks as she mixes them. That's the real reason I drive her home. Damn, I didn't know Madison had any kids at all, let alone a son with the state police. Or that she was *old* enough to have a son who was with the state police. She told me she'd just turned forty, and I believed her. I mean, what woman over forty is named *Madison*?

I expected my friend Lieutenant Manwaring to make a crack about this awkward situation, but he didn't. He wasn't even smiling. Instead of riding me, he said, quite seriously, "No plans to travel, I trust."

"Aww, Manny…"

"If you were anyone else, Tanager, I'd be slapping the cuffs on those hairy bass-playing wrists right now, and you know it."

He was right, of course. These police officers have only my word that I was on my way to the hospital with Gloria. And now it turns out the victim was very likely shot with my own personal firearm. This was not good. Until Gloria regains consciousness and can testify on my behalf, it will be just my word against…

My frightening thoughts were interrupted by a highly distinct cell phone ring. It was the theme from *Gilligan's Island*. Made sense. We used to call Manwaring *The Skipper*.

Manwaring slipped his cell out of his pants pocket and muttered, "Yeah…" He looked out across the lake as he listened. Then he said, "On arrival, huh…" His eyes turned to me, "Yes. I'll tell him. He did his best, I'm sure."

I didn't need to hear any more. Didn't want to. I just turned away and walked down to the lake. I'm sure Manny and Trooper Scott kept their eyes on me. But they didn't bother to follow.

I stopped to pick up a couple of stones and continued out onto the cedar dock. The breeze had strengthened enough to lug in some heavy clouds in from the south east. I could smell ozone. Rain was on its way. I cast my eyes downward into the shallows and watched a school of minnows dart in and out of the seaweeds. A storm was definitely on its way. The promise of blustery weather often makes the little fish frisky and skittish. Gloria Tapin kind of moved like this. She was small and tended to dart about. I had known her for only a few hours, and they obviously weren't her best hours, but she seemed like an energetic sort. Ballsy as all hell. Other than that, I knew very little about the woman. I never did find out if she had any children. Or a husband. Or a boyfriend. No time to discuss what she did for a living. Or what her hobbies were. She didn't care much for funk music, I know that. But she also disliked Broadway show tunes. I liked that.

As I watched the minnows chasing each other, playing tag amongst the pickerelweed, I noticed a larger fish, a northern pike, lying quietly at the edge of the lily bed. He was watching. Waiting for a tasty little thing to swim by. I lobbed a stone his way. In a flash of silver the sharp-toothed perp was gone and the little fish were safe once again.

Too bad it isn't always that easy.

CHAPTER SEVEN

Lots of familiar faces at the Troop B police headquarters in Ray Brook. But no smiles. They knew why I was there.

Lieutenant Manwaring took it easy on me. He could have cuffed me. He could have made me stick around for a judge to issue a material witness order on me. But no, the good Lieutenant simply took an official statement and accepted my promise not to leave the area. Trooper Scott didn't like this. He wasn't at all happy with such kind and understanding treatment of a prime suspect who was his collar. If it were up to Scott, I'd have been surrendering my belt and shoe laces and enjoying a nice cold delousing shower. The young trooper was still pissed about my banging up his car. And maybe his mother.

But the decision was up to Manwaring, so he sent me home with the strong recommendation that I stop playing cop until I regain my sanity and start carrying a badge again. Until then, I should stick to playing music and selling hamster cages. I was happy to comply with Manny's suggestion. All I wanted now was to find my dog. Word had it he was roaming around the station.

We located Stanley in the lunch room where he was conning a lady trooper into feeding him some luncheon meat by-product which no self-respecting dog, nor cop, should eat. I would have said something to her about proper doggie nutrition, but the pooch had also conned her into driving us home, so I let it go.

I live in a nearby town called Glen Echo, a place where, until about a year ago, I was Chief of Police. It's a quiet community. Too quiet. So the mayor decided the town didn't need a police force anymore. When my contract was up, he let the entire department go – both of us. Marlene, my administrative assistant at the time, said it was all my fault for doing such a good job. According to her, I should have left a few shop lifters, graffiti artists, and assorted perverts on the streets to keep things brewing. Kinda like sourdough starter. But no, I cleaned up the town well enough to make our jobs redundant.

At that point, I could have returned to my old gig in Buffalo, but I'd grown to like the mountains, the people, and their dogs. So when I saw that Stanley's favorite pet store in Lake Placid was up for sale, I bought it. I thought it would be a nice opportunity to see what life was like with comfortable shoes on and evenings off. Marlene, who already had some retail experience, was happy to come join me. Meanwhile, I kept the little two-bedroom house I'd been renting in Glen Echo, just a short commute from Lake Placid.

After Manwaring's nice lady trooper dropped Stanley and me off at the house, I took Stanley for a walk. Then I grabbed a quick shower and phoned for a taxi. I planned to rent a car soon, but for now I'll just enjoy being able to drink as much as I want with dinner and not worry about the drive home. Earlier, at the state police station, I had made a date to meet a lady friend at the Albion Tavern for dinner.

As I left the house, I assured Stanley I'd be back soon. I take him most everywhere with me, but not to places where there's a live band. There's no point in both of us having to watch Columbo reruns with close captioning on.

At the Albion Tavern I ordered something deep-fried and served in a basket. My date had warned me she would be late and to go ahead without her. I like women who take charge. Especially when I'm hungry. I was still eating and still alone when the band showed up. It wasn't my band but some friends I knew from Plattsburg. Their drummer, Mike Shumpka, immediately headed over to my table and asked me if I wanted to sit in. I answered by showing him my freshly bruised, blue thumb, the one that I'd smashed changing that tire.

Mike wouldn't accept my refusal. "C'mon, man. Just a couple tunes."

"Sorry. With this thumb I'd sound like shit."

"Then you'll fit right in." Mike leaned in close so the musicians setting up on stage wouldn't hear. "We need ya, man. This new guy couldn't find the groove with a GPS."

"Sorry, but I—"

"Smack dab on the beat. That's where he drops every fucking sloppy note. Plop. Splat. It just lies there, man. Like a fresh cow pie."

I didn't want Mike to continue trashing a fellow bass player who might overhear, so I gave him the real reason I didn't want to join him on stage. "Sorry," I said. "But after what went down today, it just wouldn't be right."

Mike leaned back. He understood. "Gloria Tapin, huh?" He bowed his head and looked deep into my basket of fries. "Heard about her. That's a drag. Nice chick." He snatched a French fry.

"You knew her?"

"My wife works with her. Or *worked* with her. Beechgrove Elementary."

"Oh, right. She mentioned something about teaching."

"Never met her. Knew her father, though."

"Henry?"

"Took a few drum lessons from the guy."

"Henry teaches drums? I thought he was just a piano player."

"That dude can play anything. Can't teach it for shit. But he can play it." Mike helped himself to another French fry. "Second lesson he tells me to pack it in, save my money. Says I'll never be a drummer. I'm too stupid."

"Too stupid?"

"Can you believe it?" He dipped his fry in my ketchup.

"That's crazy."

"That's what I thought. Too stupid to play *drums*?"

"No, I mean you're a damn good drummer. And you're plenty smart."

"Yeah, well, not compared to him, I guess. I learned my lesson. Never go to a teacher who's brighter than you. They expect everyone to catch on as quick as they did. It's a life lesson. Take my advice, man. Stay away from brainiacs. Hang with idiots." Mike helped himself to another French fry. "That way you'll keep your self-esteem."

"And your French fries," I said. "I don't suppose you've kept in touch with Henry."

"Hell, no. Why? If I want somebody to tell me I'm an idiot, I have a wife and two kids."

At this point, Casey the waitress dropped by with a bottle of beer for Mike. He took the opportunity to recruit her support in urging me to join him on stage. "Hey, Case, you're a socially sensitive chick. You don't see anything inappropriate with our boy, here, getting on stage, having a little fun, and in turn, bringing some joy and sunshine to an otherwise drab evening?"

Casey, a lovely woman with a figure that could stop a bull moose for a second glance, looked down at me. "You're feeling down about that Tapin chic."

I wasn't surprised that the news had gotten around. I said, "Well… I *was* the last to see her alive."

Casey put a reassuring hand on my shoulder. "Did you shoot her?"

"No, but…"

She smacked the back of my head. "Then get your ass up there and give us all a break. This new guy plays bass about as well as my twat shuffles cards." And with that, she walked away before I could suggest a round or two of bridge.

Mike grabbed his bottle and stood up to lead me to the stage. "C'mon. I'll introduce you as a special guest. Just a couple of tunes. Kevin won't mind. You can use his axe."

But I stayed right where I was, my ass glued to the chair. What did Mike expect me to do – insult this poor Kevin guy? Worse than that, what if a friend of Gloria Tapin's should drop by and see me up on stage having a ball, grinnin' and groovin' mere hours after I had left her mortally injured body? So I remained where I was and ordered another beer. Hell, I wasn't driving.

By the time I was into my fourth beer, and the band was into their third tune, my date showed up. Nina is a food and beverage manager at a large resort just outside Lake Placid. She and I have been seeing each other for just a couple of months. She sat down but didn't undo her coat. Not even the top button. I wasn't surprised. Nina doesn't like neighborhood pubs, which is odd, considering her job. Of course, maybe she just doesn't like live music. She rarely comes out to hear my band.

I shouted over the screaming guitar riffs, "What can I get you? Beer? Wine? Ear protection?"

She cupped her ear. "Wha—?"

I held my beer bottle up and gave her the international sign for, *Care to destroy your liver with me?*

She silently declined my generous offer and cocked her head toward the front door, giving me the international sign for, *Let's get the fuck out of this shit hole.*

The air outside was cool enough for me to see her steamy breath as she merrily announced what she thought would be good news. "Guess what," she bubbled. "I managed to get that week off. We can take Brianna to Branson."

Brianna was a nine-year-old girl known for resenting any man who tried to make a move on her mommy. Branson was a town in Missouri known for its clean, wholesome family entertainment. If Nina was waiting for me to shout, *Yippee,* I hope she brought a lunch.

I didn't answer right away. After about thirty seconds of listening to the spring peepers chirp in the dark swamp that rims the bar's parking lot, Nina reloaded and fired again. "June sixth. Business up here should still be slow – Marlene should have no prob covering the shop for you, so we should be good to go."

Nina used phrases like *good to go* a lot. That's one of the reasons why our relationship has never been good to go.

Nina unlocked her car, but before getting in, I asked her, "You *have* heard about the incident this afternoon, right? The homicide?" I knew darn well she had heard about it – I had given her a quick rundown of the whole tragic episode over the phone.

To her credit, Nina realized her error. "I'm sorry. Of course. Are you all right? What a thing. That must have been horrible, just horrible. That… that poor woman. Did you know her?"

"No. Kinda know her father, though. He's going to be pretty broken up."

"I'm sure. Poor man. So sad." Nina got into her car. Since it was her vehicle and I had been drinking, she sat behind the wheel – although frankly, she generally prefers to sit behind the wheel no matter what the circumstances.

She buckled her seat belt tight. Then she jabbed the ignition button. With her middle finger. Hard. Like a badly paid urologist. "So, shall I have Carol book our flight? Web site says Tag Purvis will be there for the whole month."

Carol was Nina's executive assistant at the resort. Tag Purvis was a wholesome, family-friendly, middle-aged country music performer famous for smashing up trucks, guitars, and girlfriends.

"Gee, I'm sorry, but…"

Nina was ready for this. "You don't want to go. You hate country music."

"No, it isn't that. I don't mind the music. It's just that I…" Suddenly a brilliant excuse occurred to me. A legitimate, honest excuse. "I can't travel."

"Can't travel?" Nina's face fell faster than Tag Purvis's flagging career.

"Can't leave the state," I said. "I'm real sorry." I tried my best to look disappointed, but in truth, I was never so happy to be a homicide suspect.

"But you said you're just a witness. They haven't arrested you, have they?"

"Well, no… not yet. But the chief investigating officer asked me to stick around. He might need my help."

"I knew it…" Nina's grip on the steering wheel tightened. "Once a cop always a cop." Nina has never bought the story that I am really through with law enforcement. She thinks it's crazy, a young stud like me, quitting at the height of a brilliant career as a star police detective. Okay, maybe she doesn't use those exact words, but I could see it in her eyes.

Nina let go of the wheel and sat back. The car's engine was running, but she wasn't ready to shift into gear yet. Staring straight ahead, out the windshield into the swampy darkness, she said, "It's Brianna, isn't it."

"What do you mean?"

"You never liked her."

"What are you talking about? I like Brianna. She's a lovely little girl."

"It's the nose thing. You never forgave her for the nose thing."

Okay, a bit of background, here: When I'd first met Nina's daughter the kid made a crack about all the hair growing out of my nose. Apparently Brianna's father, Nina's most recent ex-husband, had sported spiffy bald nostrils. So smooth, so empty, that when Nina yelled at him she heard an echo. From what she tells me, the guy shaved head-to-foot. Not a stray follicle on his entire body. Clean as a whistle. Crabs could toboggan off this guy's nuts. A guy like this is a hard act to follow.

"Don't be silly," I said. "This has nothing to do with Brianna. I just have to stick around for a while, that's all. We'll go to Branson. But not quite yet. Okay?"

Nina jammed her lever into gear. And for the next twenty minutes we had a very quiet drive which turned out to be a darn good thing because if we had been laughin' and scratchin' and having a gay old time I probably would never have noticed the vehicle following us.

"Slow down," I said. "Let's see if he passes."

We did. He didn't.

"Okay, speed up."

We picked up the tempo. So did he. I didn't know who the driver thought he was fooling. Tailing somebody at night on a rural highway like this is impossible without being made.

I pointed to a spot on the shoulder ahead. "Pull over. See what he does."

We stopped. He sailed by. His vehicle was a mid-sized SUV. I could only assume the driver was male – the windows were tinted, so I couldn't tell for sure. Couldn't make out the license number either, other than confirming it was a New York plate.

We waited and watched him disappear round the bend. After a moment, I instructed Nina to edge our tires back onto the asphalt. We continued on, but slowly, all the while keeping an eye out for any place where the driver might have turned off. For several minutes we didn't see him, nor did we see anyone else. At this time of the year, there's not much traffic on these roads.

I was just starting to feel that we'd lost him and that I had over-reacted about this whole thing, when I noticed his SUV pull up behind us. "Must have been hiding off road with his lights off," I said.

Nina stepped hard on the gas. She's that sort of gal. I am not.

"What are you doing?" I asked. Or maybe squealed.

"We can lose him, easy."

As we rounded a tight curve, I grabbed the roof strap. "There's no need to lose him. Let him follow if he wants."

But she gave the engine more gas. "This thing corners like it's on rails. He'll never keep up."

"I don't care. Please, slow down." I kept my eyes on the ribbon of asphalt unwinding ahead of us and said, "This time of night these roads are full of drunks. And moose."

"Oh, grow a pair. I thought you used to be a cop."

"Yes. A live cop. And I stayed that way by respecting dark, winding roads.

A few moments and tight curves later, she looked into her mirror. "I think we've lost him."

"Congratulations. You won. Now slow down. I've already crunched up enough vehicles for one day."

She slowed up. "So who is this guy?"

"Not sure. But I have my suspicions." We continued along at a nice, sane speed through the cool, black night. We were headed to the hotel where Nina worked, just outside of Lake Placid. As we reached town, we found ourselves stopped at one of the town's few traffic lights. As we sat, Nina's patience with the slow light wore thin. "Will you get your panties in a knot if I creep through? There are no cops around."

"I wouldn't be too sure of that," I said. And sure enough, our mystery pursuer's SUV pulled up behind us.

"You think he's a cop?"

"Let's find out." I opened the door and hopped out.

As I'd expected, the vehicle was an unmarked Ford Explorer, a CITE car, which is police talk for Concealed Identity Traffic Enforcement. The young trooper behind the wheel was wearing plain clothes so he wouldn't be made, but the disguise was pointless considering his choice of vehicle and haircut.

To my surprise, the driver wasn't Trooper Scott as I'd expected. Scott was probably at home now, telling his mother, Madison, how he had run into an old friend of hers in the woods this afternoon.

"Look, pal," I said as I approached the SUV's open window. "My girlfriend and I are on our way to Pinehurst Inn where we plan to find ourselves an empty room and fill it with moans, groans, and giggles." This wasn't true, but the narrative fit my plan for this guy. "Now, I don't last as long as I used to, but you should still have time for a coffee and a quick bite. Maybe a sandwich. Hell, if I'm on top of my game you might even have time for dessert. Pie would be appropriate." I smiled. He did not. I checked my watch. "It's just past ten. Room service should still be open, so if you'd like to park near the front entrance I'll have them bring the snack out to your car. Okay?" I slapped the roof of his pursuit car and headed back to Nina's Lexus.

Until now, the young trooper had remained steadfastly silent. But just as I slid into Nina's vehicle, I heard him call to me, "Lemon meringue, if they have it."

I stuck my arm out the window and gave him a big *thumbs up*. Good choice. Lemon meringue is my favorite, too.

* * * * *

The Pinehurst Inn Resort and Conference Center boasts a grand Georgian-style entrance whose ornate columns owe much to ancient Rome but little to the modern-day Adirondack mountains. Nina pulled her Lexus into the elegant drop-off circular driveway with the trooper's SUV tagging along close behind us. As we entered the revolving front door, I gave the trooper a quick wave to let him know I hadn't forgotten him.

The two front desk night clerks stiffened slightly at the sight of their boss lady walking in. Nina nodded hello to both of them and headed on straight for the hotel's kitchen. I waited out in the lobby while she placed the order for the trooper's late-night snack, complete with instructions to give him curb-side service. We then got down to our own personal business – business which, sadly, had nothing to do with the fantasy sex romp I'd outlined to the trooper.

At my request, Nina had called ahead and arranged for me to pick up a car from the resort's on-site rental agency. From here I planned to go straight home. To bed. Alone. By myself. This separation wasn't my choice. It was Nina's. You see, we haven't slept together yet. Although she's divorced, as am I, she hasn't really gotten used to single life yet. Nina says that, after practicing marital fidelity for so long, she is now having trouble with the idea of easy, casual sex with the first idiot who comes along. And I respect those feelings. I didn't share them, but I respect them.

So after a quick coffee in the lobby bar, I grabbed the rental car keys at the front desk and continued with Nina out a rear door of the building to my rented sedan. Nina will stall here for a half hour or so before she exits the hotel's front entrance alone, thereby leaving the young trooper to wonder where the hell I had ended up. Had I rented a room at the hotel for the night? He won't know. I wasn't being intentionally deceitful just to screw with the poor trooper. I was doing it to screw with Manwaring. Frankly, I resented his distrust of me. When I say I won't leave an area, I mean it. He didn't have to put a tail on me.

So I kissed Nina goodnight in the rear entrance. No, that doesn't sound right. Anyway, I thanked her for all her trouble and promised her I'd speak to Lieutenant Manwaring about cutting me enough slack to go away with her. But I had to warn her that I probably wouldn't regain that freedom until I was off the hook for Gloria's homicide. Or maybe until somebody corroborated my story about Amy Tapin's kidnapping. After all, that crazy ransom call was what started all this. And frankly, the only person who can back me up on that tale will be Amy Tapin's son – Gloria's father, Henry Tapin.

"Then you must find this Henry Tapin fellow very soon," Nina whispered into my ear with a juicy wet flick of her tongue. Then she kissed my neck and whispered, "Because I want to run away and make mad, passionate love to you. In beautiful, downtown Branson, Missouri."

I was more than a little surprised. "You, uh… you feel you're ready?"

"You have no idea what Tag Purvis does to me." And with that she gave my ear another lick, slid her hand down the front of my chinos, and gave my package a little squeeze.

Okay. Until this very moment, I had never really cared much for country music. But maybe a trip to Branson would be an eye opener. I mean, how bad can a stage full of boots, cowboy hats, and steel guitars be?

Of course, if Nina's flirtatious and skillful ball handling was intended to give me incentive to clear my name for travel, she needn't have bothered. I had no intention of remaining number one on Manwaring's list of suspects for long. I had to locate Henry Tapin. He is the one person who can corroborate my story about the crazy ransom call and the supposed kidnapping, the one person who can explain why I was found at the scene of his daughter's homicide. Sure, Manny's team was looking for Henry Tapin. But in locating this mystery man, I had an advantage that the New York State Bureau of Investigation did not have.

And first thing tomorrow morning, I plan to use it.

CHAPTER EIGHT

Like me, Stanley is not a morning dog. He likes to sleep in, and the squirrels know it. They count on having the yard to themselves until at least nine, which is plenty of time to raid my bird feeder and practice their Cirque du Soleil routines on the branches of the sugar maple. So they weren't at all happy when I put Stanley out at seven for his morning toilette. Neither was Lieutenant Manwaring thrilled when I called him during his morning dump. How was I to know the man takes his phone into the bathroom with him?

"Yeah?" he answered with a ceramic-tiled echo.

Out of respect for his seated mission, I skipped the small talk. "You found Henry yet?"

Manwaring ignored my query for one of his own. "So what happened last night, lover boy? You get stuck in the Jacuzzi? My man says your girlfriend came out quick, but you stayed in the hotel all night. In fact, according to Trooper Hooper, you are still inside the place at this very minute, which is odd considering my call display indicates you are presently phoning from your landline in Glen Echo."

"*Trooper Hooper?*"

"Yeah, we all got our cross to bear." Manny returned to the subject at hand: "Why the games, Tanager?"

"Why the tail, Manny? I thought you trusted me."

"I do. But Trooper Scott does not."

"Scott? Since when does a rookie trooper have the juice to order surveillance?"

"Since his mother started banging the assistant D.A."

Oh, right. Now I remembered. Madison had told me she was dating a lawyer from Elizabethtown. Nice to see things were working out for her. I got back to my original concern. "So, have you found Henry Tapin yet?"

"No, I have not. And the press is riding my adorable, hairy ass to let them publish the vic's name."

"That's appalling. You don't shave your ass?"

"Shit, if I ever started shaving my ass my wife would kill me. It's a tell. Like going on a diet or joining a gym. When a husband starts shaving his ass, he might as well hang a sign on his balls – *Honey, I'm fucking the babysitter.*"

I tried steering this runaway train back onto the track. "How about Gloria's mother? Any sign of her?"

"We've called, left a ton of messages. According to the vic's address book, her mother lives down state."

"Yeah, Gloria said her mom and dad split quite a while ago."

"Her father hasn't returned our calls either. He follow social media?"

"I doubt it. He's not the type. Too smart. Too old."

"How old? We got photos, but we can't tell when they were taken."

"Older than I am. Hell, even older than you. I don't know… maybe mid-sixties?"

"And you say the vic didn't mention any boyfriends."

"Not to me." As Manny seemed to have no news for me and I was anxious to make more calls, I wrapped things up, "Listen, if there's anything I can do…"

"For starters you can quit jerking my troopers around."

"Sorry, but I hate to see you wasting your talented, highly paid manpower tailing poor innocent local retailers."

"Some people don't consider it a waste, Tanager. Once this story gets traction, it's going to take off. Young schoolteacher shot in the woods, mystery violin that may have belonged to Einstein, an old lady gone missing… If she really is missing."

"Oh, she's missing all right."

"You sure? How do we know she isn't with her son, this Crazy Henry guy?"

"We don't. That's why you have to find him."

"People are asking why our prime suspect is still walking the streets, playing his guitar and selling kitty litter."

"It's not a guitar – it's a bass guitar. And don't you worry, I'll keep in touch."

"You picked up a new phone yet?"

"I'm on my way."

"Don't take it far. I'd hate to have to clamp an ankle bracelet on you."

I laughed at his little joke. Manny did not. He just bid me a somber goodbye. And I got on to my next call.

I scrolled through my address books, both paper and digital, looking for anyone who might possibly know Henry Tapin. For this task, I had an advantage over the police. Henry Tapin and I were both members of the same small, exclusive club. Well, maybe *exclusive* isn't the best word, but it is a club. And it's small. We're local bar musicians, a tight community who stick together and fight to keep from going extinct like passenger pigeons and prop comics. So for the next hour, I sat at my desk making calls. Not texts, but actual old-school, voice-to-voice phone calls. It was early morning, a good time to catch people while they were in. Being that it was Sunday morning, I was confident that most of my friends would be home. I was not confident, however, that they would be conscious. For bar musicians, the freeway going from Saturday night to Sunday morning can have smooth on-ramps but bumpy off-ramps.

By nine o'clock, I had managed to get ahold of a dozen or so musicians, none of whom knew any more about Henry Tapin than I did. All were in agreement that the man was an extraordinary musician and that it is amazing how such a fellow can live and work in a small community like ours and yet still remain a total mystery. But frankly, that's one of the attractions that lures some people to the Adirondacks. The pine-blanketed hills and deep, dark valleys provide good cover for any man who wants to tuck himself away from society.

It wasn't until nine-thirty that I finally reached a man who actually felt he knew Henry Tapin. Or at least, he thought he did.

Milo Gauci is a keyboard player I used to play with but haven't seen all winter. He is an excellent musician, but a heavy stoner. As a result, his tempos tend to speed up or slow down depending on which drug he has recently ingested. Milo answered on the eighth ring, although he probably thought it was the second. He sounded quite wide awake probably because he hadn't yet gone to bed. After reminding him who I was and where we had last met, I asked him about our possible mutual acquaintance, Henry Tapin.

"Hey, me and Henry are like *that*." There was a pause, then he added. "You can't see this, but I am entwining my fingers in a serpentine fashion." Milo's speaking tempo slowed up indicating either sadness or good weed. "Geez, man… bummer 'bout what happened to his daughter, uh… Oh, shit… Don't tell me…"

"Gloria."

"Shit, I told ya not to tell me."

"Sorry. Just trying to help."

"Gloria. Nice chick. A bummer, real bummer."

"You've heard about the homicide then."

"Sure. Hasn't everyone?"

"Not quite," I said. "For instance, Henry hasn't."

"You're kidding. The dude doesn't know his own daughter's dead? Shit, that's not right. You'd think the cops would have told the guy by now. Fuckin' pigs, eh? You light up a doobie on the chair-lift and they're waiting for you at the top. Somebody caps your daughter and they don't bother to pick up the fucking phone. Cops…"

I was starting to realize why Milo was so intimately familiar with Henry Tapin – Milo wasn't just an acquaintance of Henry's, he was a customer. Maybe he even helps with the grow op. I said, "Milo, you have any idea where I might find Henry?"

"Why? You got a gig?"

I tried my best to be patient. "No, I just want to tell him about his daughter. You know, about Gloria."

"Good idea, man. Somebody ought to tell him. Now, let me think…"

The line went quiet. I waited. I didn't want to yank Milo's mental reigns too hard. Something might snap. So I waited. And as I waited, my mind played black and white footage of tumbleweeds rolling down a deserted street. A blacksmith's sign creaking in the wind. Somewhere, a dog barked. Eventually, my patience was rewarded. Milo's stagecoach rumbled to a sudden halt. "The Town Council," he announced with pride.

"Town council? Which town council? Tupper Lake? Glen Echo?"

"Cold River. He hangs with the Cold River Town Council. 'Cept it's not, like, a real town council. They just call it that. I think they're just being, like, uh…"

"Sarcastic?"

"I was going to say ironic. Is there a difference?"

"Ironically, yes. So, what's this *Town Council* all about? Sounds like a booze can."

"No. It's just like a club."

"You mean, like the Lions? Masons. Shriners."

"Sort of. But no funny hats. At least, I don't think so. You gotta understand, man, I've been there only the once. Henry took me. Didn't like it, though. Not my kind of crowd. That shit's not for me."

"You're not a joiner, huh?"

"Couldn't if I wanted. It's just for guys like Henry."

"Like Henry? You mean, you're too young?"

"Too dumb. They're all brainiacs. Intellectoids. Smarty pants."

"You mean, it's like *Mensa*?"

"Do they wear funny hats?"

"I doubt it. Their heads are too big."

"Henry just calls it The Town Council. Noah's Town Council."

"Noah? Like the Ark?"

"I think it's another Noah."

This rang a bell. I actually thought I was starting to understand. I said, "Where is this Cold River Town Council?"

"Cold River, I guess."

"Do they have a regular meeting place?" I said.

But I had pushed my luck too far. Milo's mind was now leaving the main drag to take a side street. "Hey, man, don't you run like a pet store somewhere?"

"Lake Placid."

"Yeah, right, I thought so. You know anything about ferrets?"

"Not much."

"Think they could carry herpes?"

"You been French kissing your ferret again?"

"My girlfriend. She lets the little fucker lick her face, right on the lips. So I was hoping maybe I could tell her that's where she, like… you know… picked up the cold sore."

It was time for me to get this wagon out of the mud and back onto the road. "Milo… this meeting place… the Town Council…"

"You know Long Lake?"

"Sure."

"You know the causeway bridge?"

"Uh, huh."

"There's a bar there. Like, a café. In fact, that's what it's called. Noah J's Café. Small. Too small for a band. Not a four-piece, at least."

"I think I know the place."

Milo's wagon had hit another rut. "So you playing anywhere these days?"

"Blues 'N' Cues. Fridays."

"Tony still with you?"

"Yup." Tony is our regular keyboard player. But I threw Milo a bone, "But hey, if we ever need a sub…"

"You got my number?"

"I just called you."

"Oh, yeah, right. You like porridge?"

"Not particularly."

"I hate the shit, but Francine says it's supposed to be good for me."

I had no idea who Francine was, nor did I ask. I just thanked Milo, wished him and Francine all the best with their lip eruptions, and let him get back to his heart-healthy breakfast. Ten minutes later, Stanley, and I were scooting up Highway 3 to the town of Saranac Lake to buy a new phone. From there, I returned down through Tupper and along Highway 30, headed for the lovely little community of Long Lake, home of Noah J's Café.

*****

The rental car that Nina had loaned me last night, a big Chrysler, rode smooth as a hovercraft, but it handled curves like a river barge. I imagine the vehicle was popular with the older resort guests who came to the mountains for the golf greens rather than for the hiking trails. When I turned on the radio, I wasn't surprised to find all the presets tuned to news stations and Public Radio.

Forty information-filled minutes of highway later, Stanley and I crossed the causeway bridge into the little town of Long Lake. This hamlet, chiseled as it was into the hillsides that rimmed a long narrow stretch of water that looks more like a river than like a lake, has an almost European feel to it, like something you'd find along the German Rhine, except with fewer accordions and more twelve-string guitars. The village is quite nice, if you like that sort of thing. Personally, I need a bit more going on in my hamlets. I mean, what can you say about a community whose most notable historical resident is a shut-in, a long-since-deceased hermit? When Milo Gauci told me that the name of Henry Tapin's favorite hangout was Noah John's Café – N.J.'s for short – I had clued in.

Noah John Rondeau was a famed hermit who, back in the nineteen-forties, lived deep in the woods at Cold River, twelve miles north of Long Lake. This Rondeau guy referred to himself as The Mayor of Cold River, population 1, and called his cabin The Town Hall. Big joke, I guess, if you're a hermit. Apparently, Noah Rondeau lived alone – which I suppose is one of the few prerequisites for status as a hermit – but eventually became known for his letters and editorials that were published in local newspapers. His fame spread and eventually Noah John Rondeau bought a toothbrush and booked himself on national lecture tours in theaters and concert halls, where he spoke about the ills of modern society and the virtues of leading a back-to-nature existence without electricity, running water, or five-bladed razors.

Sadly, Noah's stint in the spotlight did not last long. Seems, while his woodsy tales were quite popular, his woodsy smell was not. According to reports, old Noah never shed the nasty habit of smearing himself in bear grease before joining the ladies for tea in the parlor. With the novelty of his act wearing thin but the stink lingering thick, Noah eventually found himself back in the Adirondacks working menial gigs like playing Santa Claus at a local North Pole tourist attraction. When the kiddies complained of the smell, I imagine Santa Noah blamed Rudolph.

Ironically, Noah John Rondeau, the gun-toting libertarian hermit who gained fame by rallying against the evils of taxes, socialism, and tooth whitener, spent his final years begging from tourists on the streets of Saranac Lake and sponging off the government welfare system. Quite a waste considering Noah's considerable intellectual talents. They say, despite his having only an eighth-grade education, Noah was well-read, articulate, and exceptionally bright.

Despite his impoverished ending, Noah left a legacy of sorts. Back in the 1950's when his fame was at its peak, Long Lake became a Mecca for two-bit Noah-wannabees – intellectuals of independent spirit who wanted to leave society, responsibility, and shower gel far behind. And though there is no Noah Rondeau Waterpark in these mountains yet, some local merchants do continue to capitalize on the name and the legend. Which brings us to Noah John's Cafe. According to Milo, this is the place where Henry Tapin likes to hang with a crew of fellow smarty pants called *The Cold River Town Council.*

Sort of a plaid flannel-shirted version of the *Algonquin Roundtable*, these guys like to play three-dimensional chess while pickling their impressive brain cells in cheap beer and stale coffee. Rumor has it, to become a member, one must perform some sort of outstanding mental feat, like solving a Rubik's cube while blindfolded, completing the New York Times Crossword on an Etch-a-Sketch, or explaining how the game of curling somehow got into the Olympics. While these guys might not be my first choice to spend my spare time with, they sounded like just the sort to attract an anti-social intellectual like Henry Tapin.

I navigated my Chrysler across the rolling sea of sand and gravel that served as parking for N.J.'s Café. The lot was full – Sunday brunch must be popular here. As soon as I shut off the engine, Stanley sat up and started wagging his tail in eager anticipation of meeting new friends. I patted his head and explained that the restaurant didn't allow dogs. Stanley takes bad news well. That's the difference between dogs and cats. Cats get pissed off at the drop of a hat. Dogs just happily chew the hat. I got out of the car, being careful to leave a window cracked for my understanding pal.

As the screen door slammed shut behind me, a few eyes turned to see who was blocking the sunlight. Not heads or faces, just eyes. They soon turned away, vowing, I'm sure, never to reveal such a blatant display of curiosity again.

The place was indeed busy. But it didn't sound busy, probably because of the acoustic dampening of the barn board paneling that gave the large room a cozy cabin feel. The walls were decorated with framed pictures, mostly old black and white photographs, and mostly of an elderly bearded man camping alone in the woods. Alone, I guess, except for a handy photographer. In one of the pictures, the subject, Noah John Rondeau, was sitting by a campfire, playing a violin. I guess Albert Einstein wasn't the only wild-haired genius around here to pack a fiddle in his knapsack.

I headed for a vacant stool at the bar. Unlike Noah John Rondeau, I didn't come here for solitude. I came here to mingle.

The woman behind the counter was not what Hollywood would cast as a counter gal in a roadside cafe – she was too young, too thin, and too quiet. She took my order without comment, although she did raise an eyebrow when I requested that my toasted western be made with whole wheat. While she poured my coffee, I managed to mention that I live in Lake Placid where I run a pet shop. I intentionally spoke up loud and clear so that my fellow counter mates would overhear. I find that people are always happy to chat with a guy who owns a pet store – it gives them a chance to brag about their own beloved cats, dogs, and ferrets. In this respect, pet owners are a like grandparents, except pet owners know their animal's correct age.

The good folk of Long Lake did not let me down, and pretty soon I had three new chums – two men who owned dogs and the counter gal who owned a cat. Happily, probably because I was not in uniform, none of them recognized me as once being police chief of Glen Echo.

We talked pets for a bit, and by the time I was chomping down on my sandwich, I felt it safe to leave the subject of fleas, ticks and seasonal skin allergies and approach the real reason I had piloted my giant Chrysler here. I picked up the menu for a look at the dessert selection and casually but distinctly said to the counter gal, "I'm told the pies here are pretty good. My buddy Henry Tapin is always going on about the banana cream."

Well, you'd think I had just farted Flight of the Bumblebee in a tough key. Conversation on either side of me halted and three sets of eyes – five actual eyeballs, since the guy on my left was as walleyed as a trout – turned my way. The trout was the one who spoke first.

"You know Henry?"

"Not well," I said. "But we jam occasionally. I'm a musician."

"You play an instrument?" another man asked. It was obvious to me that none of these guys at the counter were members of the elite club of geniuses that supposedly hang out here.

"Bass guitar," I said.

"I thought you ran a pet store." This man seemed to be accusing me of lying.

"I'm one versatile fella." I smiled to let them know I was joking. I don't think the message made it very far down the counter.

"You look familiar," the walleyed man said.

Should I admit I used to be a cop? I decided not to. Instead, I jumped back to my original line of thought, "Haven't seen ol' Henry in quite a while, though."

"Henry who?" asked the third guy down the line.

"Henry Tapin," the counter lady said with some impatience, trying to bring everybody back on page. The gal behind the counter turned back to me and said, very tentatively, "You, uh… you heard about his daughter, I guess."

I nodded. "Terrible. Just terrible. Poor kid. What a tragedy." I poured a small dollop of ketchup on my plate and then dropped a large splat of surprise on my new friends. "I was with her."

Everybody was understandably impressed. The walleyed man was first to take the bait, "You… you were with Gloria?"

I bowed my head and gazed down into my pile of French fries. "Yesterday. At the cabin."

"You mean…" This was the fellow on the other side now. "When she got herself shot?"

Letting the suspense build, I dragged a corner of my sandwich through my blood-red pool of condiment. As I chewed I could feel the curiosity rising like the uncooked onions in my western omelet. I said, "Not supposed to talk about it, though. Cops' orders."

The counter waitress edged herself closer. "Not heard much on the radio."

And from my left, "Won't even give her name. Just say a woman from Tupper."

Then from my right, "Don't know who the hell they think they're foolin'. Gunshot victim gets airlifted to the hospital, they think word ain't going to get out?"

I wiped my mouth with my paper napkin. "I imagine they're waiting till her father can be notified."

"Henry don't know?" This came from a surprised male voice somewhere farther down the counter.

"Not yet, he doesn't." I took a bite of sandwich and let this news sink in for a moment or two. When I had first walked in here, I had noticed an old upright piano tucked away in a back corner. I had not seen any evidence of a piano at Henry's cabin, which was odd considering Henry was a piano player. So, I asked the counter waitress, "That Henry's piano?"

"Dumped it here last December. Last thing I needed. But he said he needed some cash. So what the hell – give him fifty bucks for it."

The waitress went on to say that Henry could really make the instrument sing. Trouble was, he would never play her favorite tune, *Your Cheatin' Heart*. And even when he did break down and play the song, halfway through he might suddenly flip out and go into something completely different, like maybe a classical piece. Or worse, jazz. Nevertheless, she thought Henry was basically a nice fellow, which was more than she could say for the rest of his "genius friends." I told her I'd heard about the Cold River Town Council and asked if any of the members happened to be in here this morning.

The walleyed man pointed to a fellow sitting alone at a back table, his head buried in a newspaper.

I took a good look. "Think he might be willing to talk to me?"

"You kidding?" The man to my right said. "For the price of a cup of coffee he'll sing the entire score of *Lion King* to you."

I thought about Stanley waiting for me out in the car. He'd had a pee just before we left the house, so he should be good for a few minutes yet. So I stood up and said to the counter lady, "Mind making the introductions?"

She walked from behind the counter and led the way. As we neared, she lowered her voice and whispered a word of advice to me. "Best not to look too close."

I could see what she was referring to. The guy was sporting a hairpiece that looked like it might not be dead yet. I said to the counter lady, "You mean his rug?"

"No," she said. "His table manners."

The lady introduced us by explaining to the bearded gentleman, a Mr. Bosley Piltch, that I was trying to locate Henry Tapin in order to pass along the tragic news about the death of his daughter, Gloria. Bosley Pitch already knew to what the counter gal was referring, proving once again that news spreads fast in these hills. Even among hermits.

The counter lady, her matchmaking finished, didn't stick around to see how I and my new pal hit it off. She skedaddled, and I understood why. This guy smelled like last month's meatloaf. I pulled up a chair and sat down. Meanwhile, Bosley went back to his newspaper. I noticed now that he wasn't reading the thing – he was doing the daily Sudoku puzzle. In pen. This gave me a good chance to show some humility.

"I finished one of those once," I said. "If I live long enough I hope to finish another. I'm not good with math."

He spoke without taking his eyes off the puzzle. "Mathematics has nothing to do with it. Sudoku is a game of simple logic. The numbers are mere symbols, as meaningless as our lives. As pointless as our words. And as insignificant as our very existence."

I pointed to his newspaper. "You finished with the comic section yet?"

With a flourish, Bosley completed the last three squares of the puzzle and popped the cap onto his fountain pen. He then looked up and, for the first time since I'd arrived, took a good long look at me. He then announced, "You, sir, play drums."

I don't. I play electric bass. But I wasn't here to quibble details. "Wow," I gasped. "That's incredible. How'd you guess?"

Bosley Piltch, a corpulent man in his late thirties whose pudgy face was jammed tight between a pure white beard and a jet black hair piece, sat back in his chair and said, "I did not guess." He then went on to explain his conjurer's trick with understated self-satisfaction, "You, sir, are an acquaintance of Henry Tapin's, so chances are you are a fellow musician. You have passed by the piano twice so far without trying the instrument out, so you are likely not a keyboardist. I see no callouses on your finger tips that would indicate abuse from guitar strings. When you came in you did not walk with the slight but tell-tale limp that indicates the inevitable hernia commonly associated with years of blowing a brass or a reed instrument. Ergo…"

"…I must be a drummer." I laughed aloud. "Very good. Can I buy you a drink?"

"A little early for consumable spirits, but…" He lifted his empty coffee cup. "A refill might be in order."

"And how about some apple pie to go with it?"

"With cheddar cheese, please."

"I would have it no other way." I called the counter lady over and placed the order, and few minutes later I had two things not to stare at –

Bosley's matted toupee and Bosley's greasy moustache as he gobbled through the pie. I didn't know if this guy was technically a hermit or not, but he certainly had the eating habits of a man who was used to dining alone.

I found it curious that someone so visually unattractive should bother sporting a rug. Maybe it was a gift. Or something he'd trapped behind the outhouse. On the plus side, Bosley turned out to be a burbling mountain spring of information – an expert on just about any topic I threw his way, including the subject of Henry Tapin. By the time Bosley had tunneled halfway through his second piece of pie, I had mined up enough information on Henry to fill a wheelbarrow with valuable ore. The tailings and slag of this motherlode included the names of several friends of Henry's, the most interesting of which was a fellow-smarty-pants member of the Cold River Council – a woman whom Henry had recently met here at the café during chess night and was now dating.

But Bosley saved the most interesting nugget of Henry Tapin lore for the last forkful. Quite offhandedly, as he scraped the plate clean, Bosley said, "You know Henry is a direct descendant of Big Al's."

"Big Al?"

"Big Al Jones."

I didn't get it. Sounded like the name of an athlete. Or maybe an old blues musician. From the puzzled look on my non-genius face, Bosley figured that an explanation was in order. He spoke slowly, as if he were talking to a rather dull five-year-old. ""Albert Einstein. Princeton University. Students called him Big Al Jones."

"Really?" I said. "I didn't know that."

"What didn't you know? That Einstein taught at Princeton? That he was nicknamed Big Al Jones? Or that Henry Tapin is related to him?"

"Take your pick."

"Well, according to Henry, he is Albert Einstein's love child." At this notion, Bosley snickered. But it was a forced snicker. Followed by an insincere scoff. The envy that dripped from Bosley's lips was as thick and as oily as the melted cheddar that speckled his beard. The poorly masked jealousy made sense. After all, if you're trying to dazzle your brainiac pals during a crazy night of three-dimensional Yahtzee, it would be hard to outshine a guy who claims to have a direct genetic lineage to the genius of all geniuses.

"Could happen," I said, defending the idea so proposed. "Rumor has it Henry's mother, Amy, did have a relationship with Einstein."

"Platonic," Bosley stated in no uncertain terms. He then licked his fork clean and waved it at me. "Had to be. Einstein was an old man."

Bosley's own vintage was tough to guess, his face being hidden behind all those whiskers and pastry crumbs. I wondered what age he considered to be old. I said, "Don't some old guys keep firing live ammo well into their seventies? You know, like Mick Jagger. Al Pacino. Billy Joel. Tony Randal. Rupert Murdoch."

Bosley countered with. "My guess is the supposed offspring of those gentlemen bore strong resemblance to mommy's Pilates instructor." Bosley picked up his cup of coffee.

I expected my next question to be a waste of breath, but I asked it anyway. "Tell me, Bosley, have you ever heard Henry Tapin mention anything about a violin?"

About to take a slip of coffee, Bosley paused in mid-slurp. "Violin?"

"Supposedly belonged to Einstein."

Bosley Piltch gently put the cup down. And for the first time in our short relationship, the man showed more interest in my tasty face than in his tasty pie. "Is that what this is all about?" he said. "The violin? Is that why Gloria was murdered?"

"So, there is such a thing?"

On hearing my admission of ignorance on the matter, Bosley's brief interest in my handsome face melted away faster than that cheddar cheese on his hot pie. He picked up his newspaper and waved it at me. "If you want a mystery to solve, Mr. Tanager, I suggest you stick to these things." He pointed to the Sudoku puzzle. "They're equally pointless and far less dangerous." He then flipped the newspaper to a new page and buried his cheddared face in it, thereby dismissing all further discourse and telling me our meeting was finished. *You may leave now, Mr. Tanager. After all, two pieces of pie are worth only so much. Even with cheese.*

I was happy to leave. This over-brained under-socialized garden gnome had given me a couple of good leads which I was anxious to pursue. More important, my pooch was waiting in the car, probably overdue for a bathroom break.

When I got to my car, I clipped Stanley's leash to his collar and escorted him to an unsuspecting patch of dandelions. As always, I turned my back to offer him some privacy. It may be my imagination, but I think Stanley has a shy colon. Don't laugh, but sometimes it even helps if I whistle. Okay, you can laugh now.

While Stanley squatted and I stood whistling the opening tune to *The Andy Griffith Show*, I watched the cloud shadows drift over the lake and climb the green hills on the far side. The overcast briefly tarnished the waters of Long Lake from sparkling silver to dull pewter. Looked like rain. Smelled like it, too. Unfortunately, I'd left my windbreaker back in my own, personal car – the vehicle that was presently in the police garage in Albany being dusted, groped, and otherwise molested for incriminating evidence regarding Gloria's homicide. No doubt young Trooper Scott was anxious to make sure all the blood that stained my back seat matched only Gloria Tapin's DNA and that I hadn't also shot up a schoolyard full of children on my own time.

Stanley was finishing up his business now, so I reached into my pants pocket for the, uh… Oh, oh, I'd left my doggie poop bags in the pocket of my windbreaker back in my own car. And now Stanley has proudly downloaded a spiral pyramid large enough to entomb a poodle. A standard, not a toy.

Well, what's done is done. You can't put toothpaste back in the tube, so to speak. Only thing I can do now is turn my back on the evidence and hope nobody has witnessed my crime. *Our* crime. Only trouble is, Stanley is a creature of habit. So when I yanked his leash to encourage a quick getaway, the furry idiot wouldn't budge. He knows I always pick up after him. *What's wrong?* he seemed to be saying as he turned his big black eyes up to my eyes and then down to the poop and then back again to me. *Get the picture, dumb ass? Did you notice what I just did here?*

"C'mon, pal," I muttered. "We gotta go." And I yanked again. But no luck. It was like his ass was now glued to the grass. I glanced down the street. In the distance, a half-block away, an elderly woman was watching us from her front porch. So this time I bent down, slipped my fingers under his collar and pulled. If this didn't work I'd have to physically lift the pooch. But he got the message. He knows I have a bad back. So he followed me to the car.

As we drove off, we had to pass that elderly lady's porch. She squinted at me, probably taking note of my license number. Just my luck. If the police can't grab me for Gloria's homicide, they'll nail me for failure to stoop and scoop.

Once we had successfully fled the scene, I picked up my brand new cell phone and checked it. No messages waiting for me. On the plus side, this meant I was still a free man – the D.A. was not yet requesting my presence. But on the down side, it meant they hadn't located Henry Tapin yet – Lieutenant Manwaring had promised to call me the minute Gloria's father was found. I placed my new phone back onto its wireless charger and aimed my giant Chrysler north.

I was headed to Lake Placid where I hoped to locate the woman who Bosley Piltch says Henry Tapin has been dating. She, like both Henry and Bosley, is supposedly a smarty pants member of the Cold River Council. But unlike the other brain-burdened members, she is apparently not trying to escape from society. Bosley says this woman is socially and financially functional. She even holds down a regular nine-to-five job. In Lake Placid. At a spa. Where she works as a masseuse.

Smart man, Henry. Maybe you really are Albert Einstein's son.

CHAPTER NINE

The road from Long Lake to Lake Placid blows straight through the town of Tupper Lake and in so doing hums within a half-block of Crazy Henry's Music Store, so it was no big deal for me to stop in for a quick look.

The curb out front was occupied by a pickup truck and a fire hydrant. The truck didn't match the description of Henry's vehicle. I pulled down a narrow laneway beside the building and into a small lot behind. The lot was empty, but that doesn't mean Henry hasn't parked somewhere else on the street.

No rain yet, so I left my Chrysler's windows open wide for Stanley's comfort. I then walked to the front of the building. I didn't bother trying the store's back fire door – if Henry was inside, a rattling doorknob might spook him. The structure itself, was a single story, brick duplex with Crazy Henry's Music Emporium jammed into one half and a laundromat/laundry stuffed into the other half. The sign on the laundry advertised on-site folding, pressing, and ironing. Of course, each businesses had its own sign, but the careless way in which the two signs were placed made it look like Crazy Henry's was a darn good place to get the creases out of your accordion.

I tried the front door. No luck. Locked tight. I rapped on the glass. Didn't expect an answer, didn't get one. I cupped my eyes to the glass. It was dark in there. No electric lights had been left on. From what I could see, everything in the store was just as I remembered it. When I last visited this place, a couple of years ago, I had no idea who Henry Tapin was, so I didn't pay much attention to the quiet fellow sitting beside the cash register. I learned later that this is the preferred method of dealing with the man. During that previous visit, there was nothing inside the dusty little shop that particularly interested me. But today was different. Today I'd like to take a walk around, maybe stroll through the receipt ledger, tiptoe through an address book. But how do I get inside? I retraced my steps to the rear parking lot.

A quick glance into the Chrysler told me Stanley was happily asleep on the back seat. I wasn't surprised – today had been an early morning for both of us. I continued on to that steel clad fire exit of the store.

The door was formidable, but that's understandable. Guitars and amplifiers are easy to steal and even easier to fence. For the hell of it, I gave the knob a try. And for the hell of it, the thing turned. This was sloppy. Some distracted cop on Manwaring's team must have slipped up. Last guy out, either this morning or last night, probably didn't realize he was the last guy out.

I eased open the door a crack and called out a meek greeting to the gloom, "Uh, hello. Knock, knock. Yoo-hoo. Anybody home?" Man, I sure missed being able to boldly announce, *Police officer. Stay where you are.*

Getting no answer to my gentle howdy, I stepped farther inside. I didn't flick on the lights, though. No point in attracting attention from out on that front sidewalk. You never know who might be watching this place. Sure, Lieutenant Manwaring might understand my nosing around uninvited, but a local patrol cop might easily get worked up about an intruder screwing around. I continued on into the store. Happily, there was enough daylight filtering through that front window to keep me from bumping into the furniture.

The store's fixtures were in much the same condition as the furniture inside Henry's cabin – old and worn out, but clean. Along the back wall, a table of wooden bins sat like coffins, each individual bin straining under the dead weight of old, yellowed sheet music and instruction books, all neatly filed and categorized under cardboard tombstones that testified to the instrument or musical style buried herein.

On another wall, cheap guitars, both solid and hollow-bodied, hung by their long skinny necks like gutted ducks in a Chinese butcher shop. Beside them, a further line of carcasses seemed spiced with dull smudges of brass which turned out to be tarnished wind instruments that hadn't felt a warm breath since they were born and probably never will. Along the wood floor, assorted-sizes of amplifiers and speaker cabinets stood guard, shoulder to shoulder, like the silent watchers at Easter Island, each ready to scream its grill-covered lungs out for the first kid with three chords and grandma's birthday money.

I threaded my way through the dusty graveyard and up to the cashier's pulpit near the front of the store. I opened a drawer, rifled through some loose papers. I was hoping for address books or personal phone directories, but I seemed to be too late. If Henry did keep such analog documents, and I'm sure he did, Manwaring's investigators must have already taken them in their effort to contact the man. And judging by the empty phone jack on a wall's baseboard, they took the landline phone, as well. Same for the computer tower that must have sat on the desk where a disconnected keyboard, mouse, and printer now sat in quiet impotence. I looked around for a Wi-Fi router, but I couldn't find one. Had this guy actually been trying to carry on business without Internet service? If so, it's a wonder the place has lasted this long.

I left the desk and walked to an interior doorway at the back, near the door where I'd come in. It led down to the basement which, I assumed, is where the teaching studios must be. I understand Henry teaches several instruments plus general music theory. I've heard he used to rent out studios to other teachers as well, back before the market for musical education transferred to the internet.

Rather than tackle the steep, wooden staircase in the dark, I felt around for a light switch. Couldn't find one. I could go get my flashlight from the car. But that's okay – I'll go slow and feel my way down. There's got to be a switch at the bottom somewhere.

Holding tight to the wooden banister, I made my way down just fine. At the bottom, like a ballet dancer executing a perfect pirouette, I lifted my toe off the last wooden step and congratulated myself on a move well executed. But as my graceful foot touched down onto the painted concrete floor, my crepe-soled shoe glided on something wet and slippery and my heel flew out from under me. I went crashing on my ass.

I lay still for a moment. Got my breath. I banged my elbow pretty badly. Hurt like hell. But I don't think I broke anything. Carefully, I picked myself up and stood stiff-legged in the darkness like a kid on his first roller skates. I slowly ran my hand along the wall to find a switch. Better to light a candle, they say, than to curse the darkness.

Turns out they're full of shit. When I found the switch and flipped on the lights, I cursed, but not the darkness. What I had slipped on was a pool of blood. Somehow, I had missed stepping on the body.

Unlike the last shooting victim I saw, which was lying face-down in soft weeds and grass, this one greeted me face-up from hard concrete. His eyes were shut. One leg rested on a step. The other leg lay pretzeled beneath his body. It wasn't a position a man holds for long. Not if he has a conscious choice in the matter.

Henry Tapin no longer had any choice in this or any other matter.

In the harsh light of the sixty-watt bulb hanging above my head, I could see he was wearing black chinos and a light gray fleece sweatshirt with a picture of a black man's face printed on it. I recognized the face as that of jazz pianist Art Tatum, probably the greatest genius to ever sit at a piano. A bullet had torn through the center of Tatum's forehead and continued straight into Henry Tapin's heart. This was probably not the sort of link to musical brilliance Henry would have preferred. I knelt down and placed my finger tips on Henry's carotid artery. I waited to begin counting. But there was nothing to count.

I stood up to get a better look at the man. He seemed younger than the sixty-something years of age I knew him to be. How long had he been lying here? I had no idea. But it couldn't be long. He was still warm. And that pool of blood was bright red. And from the way the knuckle of his little finger flexed when I raised that talented right hand, rigor had not commenced. This was a fresh death. A fresh homicide. Frighteningly fresh.

I held my breath. And listened.

I turned slowly, kept my ears tuned for any creaks. Any scuffles. Shit, any breathing. And as I listened, I peered down the short, dark, narrow hallway.

The walls were paneled in fake wood. Like a fifties rec room. Two doors, both closed, were labelled A and B. Teaching studios. At the far end of the hall, a third door was partially open. Pale light from the hallway bulb revealed it to be a furnace and utility room.

I turned to the closest room, Studio A, and groped the wall for a light switch. When I flicked it, I was rewarded with the sight of a standard teaching studio complete with a cheap electronic keyboard, a stool and chair, a couple of music stands, and a desk with an old portable CD/tape player boom box sitting on it. I continued on to the next dark room.

Once again, I stuck my hand in to feel for the light switch. Never quite got to it, though. A hand grabbed mine. A strong hand. It yanked me into the black void. Rather than resist, as I'm sure he expected, I flung myself forward against him, driving both of us farther into the darkness. The room was small, and I immediately had him jammed up against a wall. I heard a clatter as something metallic hit the concrete floor. I couldn't see my assailant, but I could see the silver metal object that was now lying at his feet. We both scrambled for it. I won.

Still bent low, and now head-to-head with my assailant, I grabbed the gun's handle and stuck my finger in the trigger guard. I started to straighten up. But I never quite made it. He had the advantage on me — he was still in the dark, and I was silhouetted against the light of the open doorway. This helped his foot find its target. With one swift kick, like a lumberjack felling an oak with a size twelve axe, he chopped me right between my sturdiest branches. I doubled over in pain, my free hand clutching my aching groin. But I didn't lose my grip on that gun. Didn't matter much, though. While I was doubled over with pain, he hit me in the base of my skull with something heavy and solid.

The room spun. I reached out for something to grab. My flailing hand found the only piece of furniture in the room, a piano. A real one, not a dumb digital synth. As my legs folded beneath me, my desperate fingers mashed down a cluster of keys. I remember noting that the instrument was badly of tune, which surprised me. I would have expected a fine musician like Henry to show an acoustic instrument more respect than that.

The sour notes of the piano sustained, providing a menacing background score for my attacker's footsteps as they clattered across the concrete floor, down the hall, and up the wooden staircase. And then I faded out.

I dreamed of piano keys. Except they weren't piano keys anymore. They were the sharp white teeth of a giant chipmunk who was gnawing at my scrotum while laughing about how I couldn't do a Sudoku in ink. I was just about to blow the little rodent's brains out with the gun I held in my right hand when, luckily for all concerned, I woke up. Then I sat up. And finally, I threw up.

I had no idea how long I'd been out. Couldn't have been long, though. The throbbing ache in my nuts was garden fresh. My legs seemed to work now. So I ran, or hobbled, along the lighted hallway. I stepped over the dead body of Henry Tapin, making sure not to slip in the blood again, and I climbed the steps. Two at a time.

When I reached the top, I had to stop. The pain in my head had suddenly caught up with the throb in my groin. I grabbed hold of the door frame to keep from tumbling backwards down the stairs. When I got my breath, I turned to my right and headed to the rear exit.

The back door was wide open – my attacker had not bothered to close it. Everything in the rear parking lot looked precisely as it had when I'd left it, confirming that I'd been out cold for only a moment or two. The shadows had not lengthened. My car was still there. And no new vehicles had arrived. The only new additions to the scene were a couple of squirrels that were doing a high-wire act high above my head, scurrying along the telephone line like furry circus performers. I'll bet Stanley has been barking his head off at them. He usually does.

Funny, though. I don't hear him barking now.

I looked toward the car, my eyes straining to search the Chrysler's cavernous interior. No sign of him. But that doesn't mean he's not there. Stanley was not a big dog. Just a medium sized mutt. He could still be lying low. Or on the floor. I ran, calling his name.

But the car was empty. Totally and utterly empty.

And suddenly, my head no longer hurt. My groin no longer ached. All the pain had transferred to my soft, dumb heart. But hey, maybe I just left the window open too wide and he jumped out. Maybe he's off chasing a squirrel. Then I thought of something I hadn't checked on. I opened the car door and checked the back seat. His leash was gone. Earlier, I had unclipped it from his collar, and now it was gone. This could mean only one thing.

I ran down the laneway and out onto the front sidewalk. Hadn't there been a pickup truck parked out here at the curb, close by the store's front entrance? About ten feet from the water hydrant? It was green. Fairly new. A Chevy, I think. I remembered it had a bumper sticker on it. The word *Experimental* had caught my eye. The rest of the sticker's message had been obliterated by dried mud, but I had noted that word and had wondered what it might refer to.

But the truck was gone now. Or at least, I think it was gone. Maybe it was never here. To tell the truth, that hit on the head had left me a little wonky.

I stood looking at the empty curb, trying to focus, trying to get my scrambled brain into gear. Yes, this is definitely where the truck had been. Just moments ago. I'm sure. Or was that a dream?

I finally tore my eyes away from the black void of asphalt nothingness lying under my feet to look down the street. No dogs. No movement at all except for one or two shoppers out for a noontime stroll. Maybe they saw something. Maybe one of them had noticed a man getting into that missing green truck. Or walking quickly, leading a dog away. Stanley wouldn't have put up a struggle. He'd have gone off with anyone. Stanley's a people person, not a guard dog.

I stood on the sidewalk, my head swiveling like a hungry barn owl searching for a careless mouse. But this was Sunday afternoon. Rain was threatening. All the mice were tucked away in their homes. I noticed an elderly man. About half a block down. His back to me. He was walking a dog. Not my dog. A little one. A Yorkie. I ran to him.

"Excuse me, sir," I called out, far too loud. He turned, curious to see who was about to mug him. "You didn't just see somebody with a dog, did you? Dark brown. Medium-sized. Lab mix."

The man said nothing. But his eyes spoke volumes. They widened. He seemed frightened. Had I scared him? No, that couldn't be it. I hadn't yelled that loud.

I touched my head. And my fingers came away smeared with blood. I looked farther down and noticed I had blood on my shoes. Henry's blood. And now it was mixing with drips of my own. No wonder the poor man hadn't said anything. I tried to explain, "I, uh, had a bit of a tumble. I'm okay. It looks worse than it is. So, have you seen my dog? Lab cross. Not big. About twenty times the size of your little puppy here."

The man's silent concern for my welfare suddenly did a one-eighty. He came to life. My remark had clearly offended him. "Why does everybody assume just because a dog is small he's a puppy. He's not, you know. Finnegan is fifteen. In dog years that makes him older than you and I combined."

"Of course. I can see that now." I bent down. "How ya doing, Finnegan? Cute little fella." The dog snarled at me. I straightened up. "Must smell my dog. So, did you happen to see—?"

"No, I did not."

"Well, thank you." I turned to hurry back to the store. But after a couple of steps, I heard the man call to me, "Why don't you ask them?"

Huh? He was pointing down the street toward a dark blue sedan that was turning a corner and heading this way. I recognized the vehicle. So did the man. The gold lettering and the light bar on top identified it as a state police Interceptor.

The cop car was not in a hurry, just coasting along at a leisurely Sunday patrol pace. But my mind was racing. I had a decision to make, and I had about five seconds in which to make it. Do I flag down the car and tell the troopers about the dead body currently resting on the basement floor of the town's music shop? Of course, I do. That's a no-brainer. Then the police can immediately start searching for my assailant and, more importantly, retrieve my stolen dog. Trouble is, this is not what will happen. I know cops. Oh, they'll go through the motions, of course. They'll issue a bulletin on the possible missing truck that this crazy ex-cop with a concussion has reported. But seriously, how hard are they going to search when they have their homicide suspect already in custody – standing right here, making up a tall tale about his kidnapped dog. And a kidnapped old lady.

I had to face it. I'm the idiot with the victim's blood on my shoe. I'm the idiot whose fingerprints are conveniently embossed in blood on the murder weapon that is presently lying on that store's basement floor. I'm the one whose handprints are smeared all over that wooden stair banister that leads from the murder scene.

I didn't have a chance. Hell, even *I* wouldn't let me walk – and I was a pretty reasonable cop. And as far as my tale about Henry Tapin's elderly kidnapped mother, that story sounded suspicious from the start. The detectives will assume I killed the old gal, dumped her somewhere, and I am now finishing off the rest of the family. And why did I do it? Who knows? Who cares? I know police detectives. Motive is a minor detail the D.A.'s office can work on later while I'm rotting in jail awaiting trial. No, I had to face it. I don't have a hope.

But that wasn't what really made me look away as the dark blue Dodge Charger approached. Frankly, I could have lived with the inconvenience of doing a little time until a good lawyer sprung me on bail, if it weren't for one thing: While everybody is wasting time with me, nobody will be out looking for my dog. I had no idea why this maniac has taken my furry pal. Is the man planning to use Stanley as some sort of bargaining chip? If so, what could the idiot possibly bargain with me for? I have no money – I run a damn pet supply store. Nor do I wield power or influence – I run a damn pet supply store.

Okay, my five seconds were up. The police car is passing by. As casually as possible, I held my hand up to my face to try and cover the blood on my forehead. But I needn't have worried. The two cops in the car had all their attention focused on the front window of Crazy Henry's Music Emporium across the street. The store that still appeared uninhabited. Completely undisturbed. Just as it had the last time their patrol drove by. No signs of life. No signs of trouble. No signs of Henry Tapin.

The two cops continued on to more important tasks.

And so did I.

CHAPTER TEN

The drive from Tupper Lake to my home in Glen Echo took thirty minutes. I could have shortened that, but I didn't want to give any eager trooper a reason to stop me and ask questions like, *How'd you get that blood on your shoes?*

A block from my house, I slowed to a crawl so I could reconnoiter the scene. Everything looked okay. No police keeping an eye on the place. So I pulled into my driveway. Paranoia isn't really so bad once you learn not to be afraid of it.

When I opened the door, the pain hit me. No, not another kick to the nuts. Nothing physical at all. This slap was purely emotional. For a few years now, I have been a spoiled man, always receiving a ridiculously gleeful *Yippee, you're home! Love, love, love. My dull doggie life is complete again!* The reception always made me feel like the most important thing on two legs. But not today. Today, the house was quiet. Empty. Funny how a dinky little two-bedroom bungalow can suddenly seem too large. I don't know how hermits like Noah Rondeau can stand being the only heartbeat in the cabin. If he were as smart as they say he was, Rondeau would surely have found himself a dog.

I had to hurry. I couldn't stick around waiting for Manwaring to come lock me up. So I threw a few things into a suitcase and tossed them into the Chrysler. Before closing up my house, I used my land line to phone

Manwaring's office. He didn't answer, but that was just fine. I wasn't looking for a two-way conversation.

"Hey, Manny," I said after the beep. "Look, I just remembered something very important. There's this vehicle you should be on the lookout for. A truck." From here, I told Manwaring a little white lie: "When Gloria and I were driving into her father's cabin yesterday, we passed it on the road. It's a light duty pickup. Green. Four by four. Might be an extended cab. Late model. Maybe a Chevy. It had a sticker. Rear bumper. I couldn't make out much of it – the thing was covered with mud – but I could clearly make out the word *Experimental*. I don't think this referred to the actual vehicle itself – it was more like a logo. Maybe some group or organization. Sounds scientific, huh? Anyway, the vehicle is definitely connected to Gloria Tapin's homicide. If you come up with anything, please give me a call. You got my cell number. Thanks, buddy. I'll keep in touch."

I hung up. If Manny does find that truck, I doubt he'll bother calling me, but that didn't matter. I just wanted a bulletin issued on the vehicle without my admitting I had been in Henry Tapin's shop.

The final thing I did before leaving my house was clean up a few scratches and take a couple of over-the-counter pain pills. Every muscle in my body ached from the beating I'd taken in Henry's basement. What I could use now was a good massage.

Oddly enough, I was headed to just the right place for such an item.

* * * * *

The Greenbrook Day Spa and Esthetics Salon was not for the ticklish. The menu of services, which was posted beside the front door, offered an oily handful of therapeutic delights, including reiki, shiatsu, reflexology, aromatherapy, hot stone massage, waxing, sugaring, and all the assorted exfoliation treatments needed to dissolve, pluck, or rip away all unwanted hair and excess cash. The exterior of the building was clad in vinyl siding. Too bad they couldn't just do that with the customers. I grabbed hold of the oily brass doorknob and somehow managed to turn it.

The young woman at the front desk gave me a big slippery smile. I asked her if a woman named Cheyenne was working today.

"Do you have an appointment?" she asked, knowing full well that I did not. Otherwise, why would I have asked if Cheyenne was here?

"No, I'd just like to have a word with her if I may. I won't keep her long."

"I'm sorry," she pouted with all the sympathy of a bouncer three times her weight. "I can't disturb Miss Cheyenne while she's administering a treatment."

At this point, I must confess I honestly didn't know what to do next. This style of investigation was new to me. I'm used to flashing a badge and getting immediate respect. Or at least fear. Now, all I have to flash is my dazzling smile. And that just doesn't have the effect on twenty-year-old receptionists that it used to have. I would have preferred to interview this Cheyenne woman at her home, of course, but Bosley, the pastry-eating genius who could recite pi to twenty-seven digits between mouthfuls, couldn't remember Cheyenne's phone number. Nor her address. Nor her last name. He knew only that she worked at a ritzy spa on Mirror Lake in Lake Placid.

"When will Miss Cheyenne be finished?" I asked. "Maybe I can have a quick chat with her between appointments." I added with honest sincerity, "It's very important."

The young woman flipped open a gilded leather appointment book and ran her gilded fingernail down the page. Her face lighted up. "Awesome," she exclaimed, which sounded promising. "There's been a cancellation. Cheyenne will be free at two forty-five." The receptionist's wide-eyed gaze then bounced up to the wall clock. "That's in half an hour. Shall I pencil you in?"

I certainly didn't need a whole appointment's worth of time, however long that may be, but it sounded like this will be the only way I get to interview this woman. "Yes, sure." I said. "Pencil away."

Since I prefer the aroma of coffee and baked goods to that of lavender oil and talcum powder, I left the spa and killed some time in a donut shop down the street where I could feel like a cop again. Thirty caffeine-filled minutes later, I was back at the spa, following the pretty receptionist's slim rear end to a darkened studio.

"Miss Cheyenne will be right with you."

The room looked like a doctor's examination room if the doctor were moonlighting as a Japanese Geisha. The sink, counter, and massage table gave the place a clinical feel, and the bamboo plants, tea candles, and Oriental prints added the Far Eastern touches. From a small bookshelf speaker with absolutely no bass response, Chopin was playing one of his latest hits which he had, apparently, recorded beside a waterfall while someone was feeding a flock of seagulls.

Before she abandoned me, the receptionist lit a couple of the candles and handed me a terry cloth robe. My intention, of course, was simply to talk with this Cheyenne woman about her boyfriend, Henry Tapin, and see if she could shed any light on his whereabouts. But now that I was sitting here with this plush cotton robe in my sore hand, with the incense burning and Frederic Chopin playing his romantic heart out, I must confess a massage was starting to sound like a nice idea. After all, I wasn't a cop anymore. I was here on my own nickel. But would she resent my trying to pry information from her under such slippery circumstances? My guess is, I shouldn't push my luck. So I draped the robe over a vacant chair, planted my sore, stiff butt on the edge of the massage table, and waited, fully dressed.

Moments later, with a quick knock on the door, a female voice asked if I was robed and ready.

"Come on in," I invited.

She was older than I expected. By *older*, I mean older than the receptionist, closer to my age, mid to late forties. Quite attractive too. She had big luxuriant hair and a figure to match… I think. Frankly, it was hard to tell what was going on beneath that white laboratory smock that draped down from wide shoulders and a robust shelf of breasts. The smock was unbelted, but I suspected she had a fairly slim waist. What hinted at such a trim superstructure was her willowy neck that was so long and so graceful she could probably wear an alpaca sweater straight off the alpaca.

Seeing that I still had all my clothes on, including my shoes, Miss Cheyenne immediately spun a one-eighty to go back out the door. "Sorry," she said. "I thought I'd given you enough time."

I immediately slid off the table to my feet. "No, no, no. Please, stay. It's all right."

She paused to think this over. Did this pervert want her to watch him take his clothes off?

I said, "I'm just here to talk."

Now I really had her confused. She stayed close to the open door, one hand still on the handle, the other hand clutching the frame. I didn't blame her.

"Don't worry." I said. "I'll still pay you for your time. I'd just like to ask you a few questions."

She smiled. It was a warm, welcoming smile. Now she understood it all. She was no dummy. Like Bosley had told me, she was a member of the genius club. She released her grip from the door handle and said, "First time, huh? It won't hurt. I promise." She dimmed the lights even further.

"No, no, that's not it. You see—"

"You guys can be such babies. Tell you what – I'll give you a lollypop when we're finished."

It now dawned on me that we had our oily signals crossed. I said, "You're not talking about a massage, are you."

She pointed out the door. "Kaitlin said you were here for a waxing."

"A waxing?" Holy shit, that was a close one. "No, no, no," I sputtered, "I'm sorry. Except for what's up my nose and ears, I'm thrilled to pieces with almost every follicle I've got." I extended my hand. "Name's Tanager."

"Tanager…" Rather than shake my hand she put a slender finger to her lips. "I know that name."

"I run a store here in town. The—"

"The pet store." She snapped her fingers. Very loud. Like she was summoning a waiter. A rather deaf waiter. "That's where I know you from. It was driving me crazy."

"You have a pet?" I said, my keen detective mind showing off to its full potential.

"No. No. Can't. I'm not home enough. It wouldn't be fair. No, I just needed a dog collar once and—"

"Dog collar? But you said you don't have any…"

She continued, "Eight and a half months ago. I was in your store. October fourteenth. A Tuesday."

"You remember the date? And the day?"

"Sorry. Numbers are sort of a thing with me. A bit OCD, I guess." She returned to her reminiscence. "Norris Tanager… So how do you like running a pet store? Do you miss law enforcement? Quite a change in lifestyles, I should imagine."

Holy shit, this woman was as smart as she was attractive. She went on to explain how she had read a story last year about a homicide in nearby Franklin County. She'd remembered how one of the cops on that case, a Chief Norris Tanager of the Glen Echo Police Department, had subsequently quit law enforcement to open a pet supply store. She went on to outline several details of that homicide case and of my part in solving it. I'd have been flattered by such keen interest in li'l ol' me and my career if she hadn't also remembered the name of every other player in that case, including the name of Lieutenant Manny Manwaring. She went on to explain that she had no special interest in that particular case nor in most local crime tales, she just has a good memory. She remembers most everything she reads.

As she spoke, I must admit, I thought about how this woman did not look like a genius. But then, who does? I mean, if Albert Einstein's reputation hadn't preceded him, would anyone trust that guy to hook up their Wi-Fi?

Anyway, now that she was totally relaxed and assured that I was not the pervert I first appeared to be, Cheyenne shut the door. She wheeled over a stool, but she didn't sit down yet. She just asked what was up.

I perched my butt back onto the edge of the massage table. "I was given your name from some people at N.J.'s Café."

"Long Lake."

"Right. I'm trying to find out what I can about a man named Henry Tapin. I'm told you know him."

For a moment she said nothing. The name of Henry Tapin just hung there, heavy as a rain cloud. The room darkened as her bright smile melted away. "So, it's true," she finally uttered.

"You know? About Gloria?" I was testing the waters.

She nodded. "The radio isn't giving any names, but…"

I finished for her, "It's a small community."

"How's Henry?" she said.

"You haven't talked with him?" I said.

"Henry can be tough to get hold of. He rarely leaves his cell on. My God, the poor man must be devastated." She stepped closer and rested her hand on my arm. "I really must see him. He'll need a friend. He doesn't have many. Where is he? The cabin?"

"The police haven't talked to you?"

"The police…" She waved her hand in frustration like she was swatting away a pesky fly. A uniformed fly. "I tried them, too. They won't tell me anything."

"Did you tell them who you were? That you know him?"

"They didn't give me a chance. I think they thought I was a reporter."

"If you don't mind my asking," I said. "How well do you know Henry?"

Apparently, she did mind. She ignored my question and asked one of her own, "What's your interest in this, Mr. Tanager? You're not a law officer anymore. Are you helping the police?"

"Kind of."

She examined my face carefully, like she was getting ready to give my eyebrows a good plucking. She surveyed. She examined. She analyzed. Then she announced her findings, "Nobody has told Henry yet, have they. Henry doesn't know about his daughter's murder. Correct?"

I suggested she sit down. I had a lot to tell her. I warned her it was going to be a long story. She said she didn't mind. She had already slotted me in for an hour's worth of hair removal.

* * * * *

She caught on quick. In less than ten minutes I had explained the whole mess, from the misdialed ransom call at my store through to the visit at Henry's cabin and Gloria's murder. I left out one important event, though. I didn't tell her about this morning's homicide, the death of her friend Henry. I felt lousy about keeping the news from her, but I had no choice. If I told her about my finding Henry's body on those steps she would go straight to the police, and my days of freedom would be over. I also kept quiet about the kidnapping of my pooch. Given the circumstances, a stolen dog might sound trivial.

According to Cheyenne Chartrand, whose friends call C.C., Henry has not mentioned anything to her about his mother going missing. Cheyenne did admit, however, that Henry had been acting strange lately. Or at least, stranger than usual. But then, she hasn't known the man for long – just sixteen weeks, two days, and seventeen hours. Apparently, she and Henry see each other just a couple of times a week, usually to play chess or something equally egg-headed and boring. Those were her words, not mine. She admires his intellect and personal integrity, but apart from that, there's not a lot going on romantically. He's a little old for her to get hot and sweaty over. Those are my words.

In answer to my final query, no, Cheyenne has never heard Henry mention anything about Einstein memorabilia, including a violin. If such an instrument does exist, she'd have made note because she plays several instruments herself, including violin and piano. Interest in music is something else she has in common with Henry Tapin.

I was wrapping things up, giving her my cell number in case she thought of any further leads for me, when Cheyenne turned to me and said, as a simple statement of fact, "You aren't here strictly out of the goodness of your heart, just to help Henry."

"No," I said with some shame. "I'm afraid not."

"As far as the police see it, you are a Person Of Interest in Gloria's murder."

I had to laugh. Man, this woman was bright. "Yes, my ass is currently hanging over the proverbial coals."

"And the police think you've made up this whole crazy story about a kidnapping just to save that hot ass of yours."

Hot ass? I didn't know whether she was being complimentary or just riding the metaphor along with me. I had to ask her, "How did you figure all that out?"

"Because if the police actually believed your story, Lieutenant Manwaring would be sitting here grilling me instead of you."

"I'm sure Manny will contact you soon."

"But he hasn't. You have." She jumped up from her chrome stool as if someone had just plugged it into the wall. She now seemed to be on a mission. "And you did the right thing. I'll make some calls. You can help me run through my address book, if you'd like."

I hadn't expected this, but I certainly didn't object. She may not have known him long, but she is the first person I have found who knew anything at all about Crazy Henry. And she's definitely the smartest. But before we left the privacy of the massage room I had one more question for her. And befitting the room's tactile purpose, it was a rather touchy subject. "Cheyenne, do you know anything about Henry's gardening activities?"

She did. "He promises this will be his last crop, but I'll believe that when I see it. Once a person gets used to easy money it's hard to stop. Real hard." She punched those last words as if she was speaking from personal experience. The way I might say, *It's tough to make a loveless marriage work.* Or, *It's always a long night when you're playing in a polka band.*

Cheyenne turned and left the room. I followed her. She stopped at the receptionist's desk to make arrangements for another staff member to take over her scheduled appointments for the day, and I continued outside for some fresh air. I much prefer the scent of pine and clover to the stink of waxing gels, exfoliating creams, and other forms of furniture stripper.

When Cheyenne emerged from the spa, with gym bag in hand, she had shed the white lab coat in favor of jeans and a sweatshirt. Neither piece of apparel was a tight fit. In fact, now that I think of it, nothing about this woman was tight. I had the feeling she would stay loose and relaxed through any crisis.

I walked with her across the parking lot to a vintage Oldsmobile Cutlass where she tossed her gym bag into the back seat. "You know The Book Nook?" she asked.

"Main street," I said.

"Park round back. Up the alley. I'm on the second floor." While she slid, or more correctly, bounced, into her car, I hurried over to my rented Chrysler. By the time I had buckled up and shifted into gear she had already glided her Oldsmobile out of the lot and was quickly disappearing down the highway.

I had no idea how Henry Tapin ever kept up with this woman. But I understood why he might try.

CHAPTER ELEVEN

I was not surprised by the mess, only by the apology.

"Excuse the boxes," Cheyenne said as we entered her living room. "Not been here long, just one year, two months, and six days. No chance to unpack yet." She added that she hoped to paint the place and replace some broken trim real soon, but… and then she changed the subject.

The cluttered apartment for which Cheyenne was making lame excuses sat above a charming little book store on the main drag of Lake Placid. She said she owned the entire building, including the book store, but she lets someone else manage the store for her. I asked her, as diplomatically as I could, why she didn't work the store herself instead of driving across town to wax, pluck, and thin out unwanted thatch.

"I'm a people person," she said with a big giant smile that left me wondering whether she was kidding or not. She then pointed toward the kitchen. "Crack us a couple of cold ones while I see if I can find my address book." With that, she headed for the stack of cardboard boxes under her dining table and started digging through papers.

The fridge was loaded with beer, mostly imported. I grabbed a couple of bottles that had pictures of the Alps on them and brought them back to the living room by which time, Cheyenne was seated in a big comfy chair with a cordless landline phone balanced on a padded arm. The chair's padded arm, not Cheyenne's. *Comfy* was the word for this place. It was also a pretty good word for Cheyenne. I handed her a bottle and took my beer for a stroll around the room.

Lots of framed photographs. No pictures of Henry Tapin, but I did note a few other men of various ages on display. There also seemed to be a couple of children in the mix, although I didn't see any signs of kids presently living in this place. Maybe they were nieces and nephews.

Meanwhile, Cheyenne made a call. Getting no answer, she clicked off and went on to punch in the next number. Again, she struck out – no live person. She didn't have any of these numbers programmed into her speed dial. And on all these calls, I noticed she did not consult her book for the numbers, just the names – the book was used just to make sure she didn't overlook any likely contact. This lady had quite the memory for numbers.

While Cheyenne continued working her phone, I sat down on a plush sofa and started rummaging through a pile of books and magazines that were splayed out on the coffee table. I wasn't surprised to see that the hardcover books were all high-forehead stuff – titles you might see on a university syllabus. But the glossy magazines were mostly celebrity gossip rags – the kind of junk you see at the checkout that nobody admits to buying. On closer examination, I found that the magazines all carried a mailing label addressed to the Greenbrook Day Spa.

On about her tenth try, Cheyenne finally reached her first live person. After minimal small talk, she got down to business. "Trying to find Henry… I'd rather not say. I'm just trying to get in touch with him… No, he's not at home. Not at the store either." Then, "You haven't, huh? How about… Nobody? When were you last at NJ's?… No?… Okay. Well thanks anyway."

She went on to her next call, and I went on to my next supermarket magazine. I noticed that, in some of these fan mags, somebody had used a felt pen to doodle bushy Brillo curls of hair onto the celebrities' brows, chins, and underarms.

Cheyenne noticed what I was looking at. She covered the handset with her palm and whispered to me, "I occasionally like to give some back." She winked, then she returned to her calls. Was she joking? No idea.

By four o-clock that afternoon, I had learned plenty about who was doing what to whom in Hollywood, but precious little about Henry Tapin's social activities here in upstate New York. Out of a couple dozen calls, Cheyenne had reached only five people live, in person. Of those live people, four said they hadn't seen Henry within the last few weeks. One woman, however, said she had run into him quite recently. After she hung up, Cheyenne summarized the woman's story for me.

Seems Carmela Pasinato, a hairstylist and aesthetician from Cheyenne's spa, volunteers her tonsorial talents one day a week to spruce up shut-ins at local seniors care facilities. During one of these visits, to The Lake Placid Villa seniors home, Carmela had run into Henry. This place was the nursing home where, until a few months ago, Amy Tapin used to reside. Henry told Carmela he was there to settle up some details regarding his mother's outstanding account. Carmela then enquired as to how Henry's elderly mother was now doing at his cabin. Henry said she was doing just fine, thank you. But when Carmela then offered to come out to the cabin and give dear old Amy a cut and rinse, at no charge, Henry suddenly changed his tune. He became rather agitated and said his mother wasn't well enough to receive visitors. Carmela found Henry's abrupt and dramatic change in tone rather unsettling.

After Cheyenne was through talking with Carmela, she checked her watch and officially proclaimed Cocktail Hour. While Cheyenne searched her kitchen cupboards for vermouth, I asked her if she could tell me more about Henry's mother.

"Amy Tapin… now, there's a fascinating lady," Cheyenne said. "A totally unfulfilled woman. Bright as a new penny. Or at least, she used to be. What a shame."

"Alzheimer's is a cruel disease."

"Sure is, but that's not what I'm talking about. Can you believe, when Amy was a kid her father pulled her out of school when she was barely fifteen because he didn't believe in higher education for girls. This despite straight-A grades."

"Different time, different world," I said, eager to display my firm grasp of the obvious.

"No wonder she was hot for Einstein," Cheyenne said. "He was probably the first man to treat her like she had a brain."

"I heard he was a boob man."

"Aha!" Cheyenne found the vermouth. She offered a shot to me, "Last chance before the turnpike."

"No, thanks. I've really got to get going."

Ignoring my attempt to adjourn our meeting, Cheyenne poured gin into a couple of lowball glasses and added just enough vermouth to call them martinis. "You gotta understand Henry," she said. "He's a lone wolf. He doesn't trust people. He doesn't need them. At least, he *thinks* he doesn't. So, you see, *that's* where he is."

"Uh, right." I hate it when bright people think I'm as smart as they are. I had to ask, "And where would that be?"

"Out looking for Gloria's killer, of course."

"But he doesn't know she's dead."

"If we know, and the cops know, Henry knows. And Henry isn't one to let other people do his thinking for him. No screaming for help and running to the police for a man like Henry. Take my word for it – he's out there right now, solving this puzzle for himself. My guess is he will headquarter at the music store." She stirred our drinks and licked the knife. "You say you haven't been out to the store yet, right?"

I avoided her direct gaze and said, "Why would I? Manwaring's team is keeping a close eye on the place." Okay, this was not technically a lie, just a slight withholding of information.

Cheyenne handed me my drink, saying, "Sorry, I don't know where the martini glasses are." She then opened the freezer door. "Macaroni and cheese, okay?"

"Oh, you really don't need to—"

"Oh, look…" She yanked something out of the freezer and scraped off an inch of frost. "Lasagna!"

She didn't have to twist my arm. For the first time in the past twenty-four hours I actually felt hungry.

She set the oven temperature, without checking the package, of course. Then she placed her ice cold hand on my forearm and said, "Hey, it's nice of you to go to all this trouble for a man you barely know." She smiled at me as if I were Mother Teresa cradling an orphan. She then clicked her lowball glass against mine. "To Henry."

"To Henry," I said. feeling like shit. I hate martinis, and I hate lying to sweet, lovely women.

Without waiting for the oven to come up to temperature, she popped the frozen entree into it. This was not the type of woman to follow package directions.

While the oven did its job, we went back to the living room to do the same. This time, she sat beside me on the sofa, tucking her feet up beside her. I wished I could have relaxed that well, but my mind was on my missing pooch. I guess my concern showed.

"You're worried about him, aren't you."

She was obviously talking about Henry. I let the misunderstanding ride. "Yes. Yes, I am."

"Einstein's violin…" she mused.

"According to Gloria, her father never heard of the thing."

"Well, he never mentioned it to me." Cheyenne mulled this particular thought over for a moment, then said, "You know Henry thinks Albert Einstein is his old man."

"Yes, I heard something to that effect. Is it possible?"

She took a sip of martini, "According to Henry, when he was a kid, his mother confessed that the man who he thought was his father wasn't. She admitted to him that her husband left her because the jerk couldn't live with the idea of bringing up another man's child as his own."

"Nice fellow. Did she say who Henry's real father was?"

"Never. Said it's best for Henry that he never knows."

"And you say Henry was how old at the time?"

"Eight."

"Shit. Eight years old and Mom tells you it's your fault her husband just hopped a train. That's gotta leave a mark."

Cheyenne tucked her legs up tighter. "Henry felt pretty bad. But then as he thought about his mother hanging out with Albert Einstein just shortly before he was born… well, Henry put two and two together and says he grew to kinda like the answer."

By this point I'd had enough time to do some mathematics of my own. So I asked her, "When did Einstein die?"

"April eighteenth, nineteen fifty-five."

"So, assuming he was still firing loaded shells right up until he passed away, which is a bit of a stretch, that would make Henry at least…"

She nodded. "Older than he looks. But it is possible. I know that Henry is quite a bit older than I am. And I turn fifty-one next month…"

"Fifty-one?" I was genuinely surprised by both the number and by her honesty. "You don't look it. Not that fifty-one is old, but…" I toasted her with my glass. "Happy birthday."

"I owe it all to clean and sober living." She downed half of her martini in one gulp.

"Albert Einstein's son…" Finding this story quite intriguing, I pursued an obvious question. "If it were true, and assuming he could prove the lineage, wouldn't Henry be entitled to some part of an estate?"

"*Estate?* You gotta know Henry. Money doesn't mean anything to him. The man is a card-carrying socialist Even if Henry could prove some legitimate claim on the estate, the man would never bother to fight for it."

"Doesn't approve of inherited wealth, huh?"

"You've seen his home, the cabin. Henry barely approves of *herited* wealth. That's why his wife took off."

"I suppose it takes a special kind of woman to understand a man like that." I hoped I wasn't being too obvious, but I was curious as to what this attractive fun-loving lady sitting beside me saw in an oddball older man like Henry Tapin. She didn't let me down.

"Henry has his good points," she said. "Kind to his mother. A good father to Gloria." Cheyenne emptied the last drop from her highball glass, licking the rim like a child licking a cake spoon before saying, "Oh, and he's hung like a horse."

Huh? I wasn't sure I'd heard right, whether she was joking or not. So I did what I do best – I smiled like an idiot. Finally, after leaving me twisting in the wind, she exploded in laughter. She slapped my knee and said, "I wish I had a photo of your face."

"Yeah, you really got me good. That was a funny one, all right." I laughed and toasted her with my martini. Yeah, this is nice. Sitting back, making jokes about a dead guy's pecker. Of course, she didn't know about the *dead* part yet.

After we had gobbled through our lasagna, and I had helped with the dishes, I told her I truly had to skedaddle. I had lots of work to do and precious little time to do it. There was a place I wanted to visit, and I had to get there this evening, before the building was closed to visitors.

"We'll take mine." She picked up her car keys from the kitchen table.

"No, no, you really don't have to," I said. "I've imposed enough on your generosity already." My heart was not in these words, of course. For several reasons, I would be more than happy to have this woman along with me. She knows Henry. She knows his world. But I'm afraid she'll also soon know I'm just an idiot looking for his dog.

Cheyenne turned and headed for her bedroom. "Give me a minute to throw on a sweater."

"Make it a tight one," I said.

She raised an eyebrow. Maybe two eyebrows – a lovely curl of auburn hair with silver highlights was hiding the other one. "A tight one?" she said.

"I no longer have a badge to flash. So, anything you can flash will be a big help."

She feigned indignation. "Sounds like I'm about to be used as a sex object."

"Do you mind?"

"You kidding?" She said. "How do you think I paid for this place?"

I truly could never tell when this woman was joking. But it was fun guessing.

* * * * *

When Cheyenne suggested we take her car, I didn't give her any argument. If by any chance the police have discovered Henry's body, they would now be on the lookout for my rented Chrysler. But when she got behind the wheel, I did have second thoughts. She had been drinking harder than I had. So I insisted I drive. I got behind the wheel and started off with some small talk. At least, I thought it was small. "So, how'd you get a name like Cheyenne?"

"You mean, is it my stripper name?"

I laughed. "Kinda sounds like one."

"No, Cheyenne is my real name," She adjusted her passenger seat as she spoke. "My stripper name was Marie."

I looked at her but said nothing. *Come on, lady, are you joking or what? Please, give me a clue.* She did.

"You know… as in Madame Marie Curie. Sort of an in-joke among the other dancers." As she spoke, she was pushing her seat back to make room for her long legs. She said, "I was on my way to a degree in quantum physics. I eventually switched my major to math. Specifically, multivariable calculus. But professionally, the Madame Marie moniker stuck." With a bump, her seat clicked into place. My brain, however did not.

I said, "Why do I always feel you're putting me on?"

"Because I don't fit your stereotypical biases. The chick has big tits, takes her clothes off for a living, ergo she must be a bimbo."

"Not all men think like that. I'm just a little taken aback, that's all. It's not every day I meet a mathematical genius stripper."

"Then you should get out more. That's one of the things I like about Henry. When I told him how I earned my way through school, he didn't bat an eyelash. A guy like Henry knows that what a person does to pay tuition or put food on her table has little to do with her innate intelligence. A job's just a job. Besides, I believe intelligence is a highly overrated appurtenance."

"I'd argue with you if I knew what the word appurtenance meant."

"It means smarts have very little monetary value. For every intelligent person who's made a fortune I'll show you a dozen more who don't have a *Berzelius beaker* to piss in. From what I've seen, high intelligence is more often a hindrance to success than an aid. Personal and financial."

"Dysfunctional genius, huh?"

"Look at Einstein. Pretty bright guy, right?"

"That's the rumor."

"Yet his first marriage was a disaster. He had lousy relationships with his two sons. Owned a very modest house, walked to work because he couldn't afford a car, and ended up retiring on a meager teacher's pension of seven thousand, five hundred dollars per annum. All this from arguably the greatest brain in all human history. Seven thousand, five hundred clams a year."

"He'd have done better as a stripper."

"Now you're catching on."

We stopped for gas, picked up a couple of coffees, and continued down highway 186 toward Saranac Lake. While we drove I told her, vaguely, of course, about the green pickup truck I'd spotted at a certain location. I wanted her input on that bumper sticker. Her first suggestion was that the word *Experimental* might refer to the truck's being converted to an alternative fuel like natural gas, propane, or hydrogen. I told her I had already considered that idea but had dismissed it. Those fuels are difficult to find in remote areas like the Adirondacks. Besides, I had the impression that the word was part of a larger phrase, like the title of an organization. I asked her if Henry had anything to do with any such group. She answered that she never heard him mention any such group. She then went on to voice another concern of her own, a concern about my own words, not a bumper sticker's.

"You say you passed this truck when you were on your way into the cabin yesterday, right?"

"Uh, hum," I mumbled. I don't lie well. Not out loud.

"And that's when you spotted the bumper sticker."

"Uh, yeah." I couldn't tell her that I'd actually seen the truck parked outside the music store where I'd found her boyfriend's dead body. Not yet. I will soon. Maybe.

She continued, "On the back bumper, you say… even though the vehicle was coming *toward* you?"

"It was after we passed. I saw it in my rear-view." I thought I'd covered that detail well.

She looked into her passenger side-view mirror so she could conduct a physical test of my theory. "On a narrow, bumpy, dusty road… Where your relative velocity in separation from the target must have been at least, I'd say, a good fifty miles per hour if you were each doing twenty-five."

"I have very good vision."

"You must."

"And don't forget I have training as a cop."

"Right." She was too polite to ask what the hell law enforcement training had to do with achieving superior powers of vision.

I quickly changed the subject. "So, how's your coffee?"

"Hard to swallow. A little bitter." She looked away, out her side window. "You might say it's leaving an unpleasant after-taste."

I'm no genius, but I don't think she was talking about the coffee.

✳ ✳ ✳ ✳ ✳

It's easy to intimidate a witness when you're flashing a badge or ticket pad. But tonight, all I had to work with was charm and good looks. Not mine, Cheyenne's. That's why I had asked her to wear something sexy. But as it turned out, on this first call of the evening, what we needed was masculine allure.

I turned up my smile to full bright as I said, "I understand Amy Tapin was a resident here for several years." I held my head down a smidge and looked up at the female nurse through my dark eyebrows. I'm told this pose makes me look like George Clooney. Granted, the person who told me this owed me money. And several drinks.

The lady nurse sitting behind the reception desk of the Lake Placid Villa Seniors Care facility didn't seem impressed. Probably not a Clooney fan. She was busy typing a hunk of search terms into her desktop computer for me. When the monitor finally coughed up a lungful of results, she read them aloud from the screen: "Patient Amelia Clara Tapin. Released to the care of Henry Tapin, son, January ninth of this year." The nurse then turned her big, round face toward me like she was aiming a satellite dish for better reception. "If you want my opinion, she should never have been released at all. Not in her condition. Totally gaga. But what could we do? We're not running a charity hospital."

"'*Totally gaga?*'" Cheyenne said. "Is that a clinical term?'"

Before the nurse had a chance to take full offence to Cheyenne's swipe, I leapt in and commented, "Owed a few months back rent, did she?"

The nurse looked at her monitor again and said, "More than a few. But between you, me, and the bedpan…" The nurse glanced around to make sure nobody of importance stood within hearing distance before she confided, "Most of us were glad to say goodbye to the old tart."

"*Old tart?*" Cheyenne repeated. But in all fairness, if she hadn't repeated it, I would have.

The nurse looked sideways at Cheyenne, clearly objecting to Cheyenne's… well, everything. And I'm afraid this was mostly my fault. I had suggested that Cheyenne squeeze herself into the snug cotton sweater. The braless absence of mammary support was Cheyenne's idea. I wouldn't have thought she could get away with it. But I was wrong. Quite wrong.

The nurse explained her use of the word *tart*. "I'm sorry, but I don't know what else you'd call a woman who constantly threw herself at every man in the place."

I said, "A bit of a tease, was she?"

The nurse, a rather hefty woman with the skin pallor of expired yogurt, leaned toward me to invite aural intimacy. Her swivel chair squeaked its disapproval to both her posture and her malicious intent. "You promise you won't quote me?"

I put my hand over my heart as if I were facing a judge's bench instead of the counter of a nurse's station and said, "You have my word as a journalist." I had told the nurse that Cheyenne and I were reporters working for a senior citizens' magazine and we were interested in doing a story on this prominent nonagenarian, Amy Tapin. Cheyenne had used the word nonagenarian. I would have said *real old gal.*

The nurse thought for a moment, then decided it was safe to continue sharing more nasty gossip, "Old Mr. Reucassel used to say how Amy Tapin had visited more beds than the tooth fairy."

"You don't say." I glanced down the hallway toward the patients' doors, some of which were open. "Any chance we could talk with Mr. Reucassel?"

"Not unless you're clairvoyant or *she's* a spiritual medium." Great, now the nurse was referring to Cheyenne in the third person.

Somebody had to ask, so I did, "Passed away, did he?"

The nurse nodded. "And thanks to Amy Tapin, he went with a smile on his face and denture adhesive on his willy." With this, the nurse pulled away and went back to her typing.

"Is there anyone else we might talk to?" Cheyenne said. "Other residents, perhaps?"

"Not at this hour," said the nurse.

Cheyenne glanced at a wall clock. "But it's barely past eight."

"Dinner's at five. Most of them conk out right after they eat. Sometimes *while* they eat. You'll have to come back in the morning."

"Conk out?"

I jumped in. "How about staff? Amy lived here for quite some time. There must be some members of your staff who were close to her."

"I seriously doubt it. The woman was not easy to deal with. Half the time she didn't know where she was. And talk… my God, she never stopped. We have work to do. We're short staffed. Do you know how many beds we have here?"

"Far too many, I'm sure." I tried my best to show sympathy and understanding for this poor overworked caregiver who should be working somewhere else. Like maybe airport security.

Cheyenne stepped in. "What about community volunteers? You know… Candy Stripers. High school interns. My God, surely there must be somebody around here who actually cares about the residents."

Speechless, the nurse looked up at Cheyenne in a slow burn. Before her boiler built to a lethal pressure, I jumped in and tried to open a safety valve. "I'm sure they all care." I said, looking pointedly to Cheyenne then back to the tight-lipped nurse. "How about visitors? Apart from her son and her granddaughter, anyone else ever come see Ms. Tapin? Like maybe some old friends?"

"Nobody that I recall. Well, nobody besides Feces, that is."

Cheyenne and I looked at each other silently on this one. There was nothing else we could do. Had we heard right? For a change, Cheyenne wisely kept her mouth shut. So it was up to me to ask, "Did you say… *feces?*"

The nurse said, "That's not her *real* name."

"Her?"

"Fifi. We called her Feces because of the smell."

I think I understood. "I trust Fifi is a dog?"

"French poodle. You know… French?" She touched the tip of her nose. "Allergic to soap?"

"I'm French," proclaimed Cheyenne, now begging for a fight.

I stepped in before I had another homicide on my hands. "You say this pooch… she was close to Amy?"

The nurse went on to explain how Fifi was part of a therapy dog program in which local dog owners brought their pooches to the rest home to cheer up the old folks. I knew all about the program, of course, through my store. The nurse told us how Amy Tapin had formed a strong bond with Fifi, the smelly pooch, a connection the home's resident physician found encouraging considering Amy's deteriorating mental condition. Sadly, that bond was broken when Fifi was pulled out of the program. I asked the nurse why the dog was yanked away. Was it Fifi's poor hygiene?

"No," said the nurse. "It was the dog's owner. The man was a thief. He was using Fifi to gain access to the patients' rooms."

"He was stealing from the residents?"

"While the residents were fussing over his dog, the man would go through their stuff – purses, wallets, drawers, pockets, what have you. The man was a crook. Heck, we found out Fifi wasn't even his dog. He'd snatched her from somebody's back yard."

A dog napper? Images of Stanley flashed across my mind.

Cheyenne said, "I hope you reported him."

The nurse chuckled Cheyenne's ridiculous suggestion away. "Yeah, right… Like we need that kind of publicity."

"So, this man is still on the loose?" I said.

The nurse started typing again as she mumbled, "He's not here, that's all I know. All I *want* to know."

I may have lost the nurse's interest, but she certainly hadn't lost mine. "You have this man's name, I assume? In your computer maybe?"

"I guess so, but…" The nurse stopped typing. She didn't like the direction my questioning was taking. Her eyes narrowed as if she'd just detected a whiff of Fifi. "I thought your article was about Amy Tapin."

"Oh, sure, it's about Amy, all right. But you never know. If this man was as close to Amy as you say, he might have some interesting insights to offer. If we ignore the stealing part, that is." I carefully slipped my hand onto the nurse's hand as I said, "I'd consider it a personal favor." And I gently pulled my hand away.

She looked at the two twenty dollar bills that now lay in her cold, mushy mitt and said, "Russian accent. As I remember, he lived near Saranac." She slipped the cash under her shirt somewhere and resumed typing while mumbling, "Let's see… therapy dogs…"

While she searched her data base for the thief's name, I asked, as off-handedly as possible, "I don't suppose Mrs. Tapin ever talked about having a relationship with Albert Einstein?"

"Einstein? You kidding? When *didn't* she talk about it. My God." The nurse stopped typing again. "You get so sick of it. The same stories. Over and over. But what are you going to do? I guess they can't help it." She went back to her keyboard.

In my peripheral vision I could see the sinews of Cheyenne's neck tighten like the muscles of an angry pit bull straining at the leash. But I kept my attention on the nurse. "How about a violin? Did she ever mention anything about a violin that belonged to Einstein?"

"Violin?" This time, the nurse didn't even bother to stop typing. She waved my question away like Fifi had just farted. "Who knows? We're paid to clean up after them, not take notes."

Cheyenne was ready to explode. Through clenched teeth she announced that she would wait for me outside. Smart girl. I'd never seen ears clench before.

A few minutes later, I left the building and found Cheyenne sitting behind the wheel of her car, still steaming. As I opened the passenger door, she said, "My God. I can see why you left the police department. Having to deal people like that and somehow remain civil…"

"What did you want me to do? Get into a thing with her? Where would that have gotten us?"

Cheyenne said, "Ends justifies the means, huh?"

"It did this time." I held up a slip of paper. I read the note aloud, "Greg Peters, alleged dog thief who knows all about Amy Tapin, her relationship with Albert Einstein, and probably… a very valuable violin."

But Cheyenne was not impressed. "I just wouldn't have the stomach for that sort of thing."

Okay, somebody had to say it. I'm just sorry it was me. "Do you have to like somebody before you pluck their nether regions?"

"I don't pluck, I wax. And if I don't like them, I peel off the wax very, very slowly."

"Well, cops don't always have the luxury of showing such high-minded integrity."

"But… you're not a cop."

I didn't want to get into this with her. I was too tired. Seated now in the passenger side, I fastened my seat belt and said, "I think we'd better get you back to your place."

"Don't you want to see this dog guy? Fifi's owner?"

"Yes, I do. *Alone.*"

"Alone? Why? You afraid he might be dangerous?"

"No, I'm afraid *you* might be dangerous."

She grabbed the note paper from my hand and read it aloud. "South Crescent Road. That's about forty minutes from here. Near Cranberry

Lake." Cheyenne handed the note back to me and guided the car out onto Highway 86.

I suddenly thought of something. "Pull over."

"Why?"

"You shouldn't be driving. I'll take the wheel."

"You were drinking too."

"Not as much as you."

"It's been over an hour."

"We're not swimming, we're driving. Pull over."

"Women metabolize alcohol faster than men."

"Bullshit."

"That too."

"Pull over."

She tried another tact. "I have a touchy stomach. Riding shotgun nauseates me. I have to be behind the wheel."

She did seem quite sober. And I was so damn tired I probably wouldn't have been any safer at the wheel than she was. So I sat back and watched the passing forest. The trees made me think of Stanley. I wondered if he's being kept indoors. He's a good boy. He'd just about burst before he'd soil a carpet. Of course, it's possible he's outside. This would be better for his kidneys but worse for his psyche. He'd be lonely. He likes to curl up with a pal for the night. Okay, I'll admit it – Stanley sleeps in my bedroom with me. At the foot of my bed. More often, on my bed. And while I'm admitting things, the real reason I didn't want to go to Branson with Nina wasn't because of her annoying daughter or the equally annoying country singer. Truth is, I didn't want to go because it would mean putting Stanley in a kennel. I can't do that. All he'd have for company is other dogs. Hell, he'd be better off with a country singer.

Cheyenne turned and looked at me. Misinterpreting my pensive mood, she said, "You blame yourself, don't you."

"Huh?"

"Don't beat yourself up over it. From what you told me, you tried your best to get her to along go with you. It was Gloria's idea to stay there alone."

"Oh, yeah, I guess so."

"Don't worry." She reached over and gently squeezed my forearm. "I have a feeling Henry is doing just fine."

Henry? Oh, right. Shit. Now, I really felt like an asshole. I wanted to tell her about him, but I just couldn't. What if, in order to protect me, she agrees not go running to the police with the news? She'd be an accomplice to obstruction of justice. That's a class A misdemeanor. No, it's better that she remains in the dark about Henry for a little while longer. Better for her, better for me, better for Stanley.

"Henry can take care of himself," she said with a pat to my knee. "The person I'm worried about is his mother."

"Yeah, right. Poor Amy." I rolled my window up tight and zippered my jacket. The night air was making me shiver.

At least, I think it was the night air.

CHAPTER TWELVE

As we turned into the driveway, our old halogen headlights ripped a deep yellow gash out of the night. From out of that wound spilled, first, a lawn mower, then a child's inflatable wading pool, a large willow tree, a front porch, a small garden, and a detached garage. But no pickup truck, green or otherwise. And no dogs. Stanley or otherwise.

I stepped out of the car but then stood still as a grave stone. I listened, my ears tuned for a dog's bark. A familiar bark would be nice, but any bark would do. Even a smelly French poodle's.

Unfortunately, the only sound offered on tonight's playlist was the steady hum of spring peepers chirping their horny little throats raw in some nearby bog. The spooky din sounded like something out of a black and white sci-fi film. I cast my gaze skyward, half expecting to see a flying saucer hovering overhead, but I had to settle for an old rusted satellite dish that was mounted to the peak of a gingerbread eaves. The darkness hid the details, but I'm sure the trim was broken and flaking. It usually is.

I've seen plenty of homes like this up here, and they always make me feel sad. Like abandoned mine shafts in the desert, these old farm houses are remnants of failed dreams and bad advice. As testaments to positive thinking, the original owners often built these sturdy homes of bricks so they would be strong enough to be passed along to children's children. But when faced with the hard realities of thin soil and thick winters, the buildings were lucky if they ever embraced more than one generation, and now the houses survive mainly as income properties, mostly low-cost rentals that rarely feel the tickle of a renovator's paint brush as they wait for the merciful euthanasia offered by a bulldozer's blade. The places tend to live out their final years as the rural equivalent of urban tenements, with mice, bears, and raccoons standing in for the inner city cast of rats, roaches, and drug dealers.

Cheyenne stepped out of the car and silently pointed to an upstairs window where a flickering light indicated a television's glow. The other windows were dark. Upon our arrival, no new lights had flashed on and no curtains had parted, which meant that either the TV was blaring too loudly for the occupants to notice our approach or that somebody has fallen asleep with their wide-screen nightlight on.

"What's our story?" Cheyenne whispered.

"How about, We're looking for the asshole who kidnaps dogs and robs old ladies."

"I guess that's one way of going."

"Wait here," I said as I slipped my little LED flashlight out of my pocket. "Whistle if you see anyone."

"How do you know I can whistle?"

"Because you look like the kind of chick who can."

She smiled.

I started round the side of the house. Turns out I didn't have to use my flashlight – the quarter moon winked just enough light through the passing clouds to keep me from bouncing off any bikes, barbecues, or swing sets.

The double doors of the wooden garage were already raised open. I clicked on my flashlight for a look inside. Just one vehicle - a sedan, the usual road-weary, rusty chariot that such modest digs tend to shelter. I left the garage and continued out to the other building, a small barn.

As I neared, I noticed a tractor looking back at me. Some attachments sat waiting for a session of plowing or seeding or something equally pointless in this lousy soil. Nothing else of interest here, so I switched off my flashlight and retraced my steps through the shadows, back across the yard. When I rounded the corner of the house, I found Cheyenne talking to a woman on the front porch. Cheyenne saw me pop out of the darkness and quickly explained, "I was just telling Shayna, here, about our stupid car."

The woman on the porch took one look at me and immediately tightened up the terrycloth belt of her bathrobe. Cinching the garment like this gave definition to a very round and pregnant tummy. I wanted to ask her if she was Mrs. Peters, but I couldn't – it would give away our cover. Ostensibly, we were not interested in who lived here. We supposedly had other problems.

I waved my arm toward the yard and tried to explain my stroll. "Just nosing around for a tap or pump or something. Didn't want to bother you. Just need some water for the rad."

Cheyenne turned to the pregnant lady and indicated our Oldsmobile. "I've been after him to get something newer, but you know men. They always think they can squeeze one more year out of the old thing. I only hope someday I will get the same consideration." Cheyenne chuckled, hoping to connect girl-to-girl with this Shayna woman. She didn't.

The young woman looked at me and asked, "What were you going to use?"

"Pardon me?"

"For the water. How were you going to carry it?"

I smiled. "Well, I was kinda looking for that, too." The woman probably wasn't buying this shit, but frankly, I didn't care. I wasn't here to sell her anything. I was here because the numbers on her fencepost matched the address that nurse at the seniors home had given me for Greg Peters, the crooked owner of the therapy dog.

Shayna looked across at our Olds Cutlass sitting in the driveway, moonlight glinting its chrome bumper. "Shouldn't add cold water to a hot engine," she said. "You'll blow the gasket. Heck, in a car that old you might even crack the block."

Cheyenne was duly impressed. "Sounds like you know your cars."

"I know enough not to pour cold water into a hot one. Gotta let her cool." Shayna turned back to the door, "You can wait inside if you wish."

Nice lady. I was tempted to ask her if her husband was home, but of course a query like that would scare hell out of her. I also wanted to ask if her hubby or boyfriend had an Eastern European accent like the one that nurse had described. But that was impossible too. So for now Cheyenne and I just accepted her kind hospitality and followed her into her house.

I'd been wrong about the state of the place. The interior has been renovated. Somebody has replaced the original hot water radiators with forced air ductwork. They've refinished the hardwood floors and torn out some of the interior walls. Somebody has also spent a few bucks on spiffy new furnishings – leather sofa, stag horn chandelier, new area rugs, and some fine art pieces on the walls. Originals, not prints.

And talking about original art work, now that I was seeing our hostess in full light, I could see I'd been wrong about her, too. Shayna wasn't the eternally knocked-up, backwoods type my urban prejudices had forecast her to be. Her short bobbed hair bounced clean and well-coiffed. Her skin glowed healthy pink, and her white teeth shouted all present and accounted for.

As we stepped farther into the home I suggested aloud to Cheyenne, "Better take our shoes off."

"No need," Shayna said.

Cheyenne turned to me, but spoke for Shayna's benefit, "Keep your voice down, honey. We don't want to wake anyone upstairs."

Nicely done, I thought. A little less obvious than, *So, you live alone?*

But alas, the clever ploy didn't help much. Shayna just said, "Don't worry." And she motioned us toward the living room. "Make yourself comfortable. I'll put on some tea."

Cheyenne said, "Oh, you don't need to go to any—"

But I jumped in, "Thanks. That's very kind."

Cheyenne caught on. "Yes, thanks," she said. "I'll give you a hand." She then followed Shayna to the kitchen while I stayed in the living room, pretending I had no interest in doing anything but planting my tired butt on the big comfy couch. But I didn't plant it anywhere. I walked it around the room, closely followed by my nose. The place smelled of doggy, alright, but not of my doggy. Had to be Fifi, the farty Frenchie.

The furnishings included a shelving unit that framed either side of a medium screen TV. The shelves held a mix of hardcovers and paperbacks whose spines bragged a wide range of non-fiction, from medieval pottery to computer science. The collection also held several biographies, including a at least a couple about Albert Einstein. But hey, that could be a coincidence. After all, Einstein is one of the most written-about persons of our times after Elvis and The Beatles. I saw no traces of Elvis or The Beatles.

I turned my attention to a small computer desk that was tucked into a dark corner. I leaned in for some serious squinting at the jumble of memos and loose notes that littered the work surface like autumn leaves. I was tempted to switch on the gooseneck lamp for a better look, but I couldn't take the chance. On first glance, none of the notes, names, or phone numbers shouted anything of special meaning to me. The ballpoint jottings included a few Internet addresses, but the dot com jumbles mumbled mostly silly codes that I couldn't decipher. I did, however, notice a couple of the addresses ended in *.ua* and *.by*. I knew the first one was Ukraine. The other could also be an Eastern European domain, but I had no idea whose. One IP address included the name *Einstein*. It was becoming clearer to me that somebody around here has more than a passing interest in Amy Tapin's smarty pants boyfriend.

I eased open the single small drawer for a look under the hood. Here, I found the usual clutter of pens, pencils, and paperclips. But as I eased the drawer out farther I saw, hidden in back, a stack of credit cards. Some were old and worn, some new and shiny.

Before I did any further snooping, I checked behind me to make sure I was still alone. From the kitchen, I could hear Cheyenne's husky voice punctuated by dashes of her bawdy laughter. Figuring she'd probably signal me if our hostess started heading back this way to the living room, I took a chance and switched on that gooseneck lamp.

Fanning out the pile of cards revealed a full house of stolen delights that included debit cards, bank cards, gas cards, and assorted retail loyalty cards. Each piece of plastic was embossed with the name of a different owner – elderly retirees, no doubt, who are now lying lonely and helpless in crib-sided beds in hospitals and rest homes, all innocent victims who made the mistake of welcoming a few moments' warmth from a friendly but smelly French therapy doggie.

I returned most of the cards to the drawer but pocketed a few for later. Even if it turns out this low-life has had nothing to do with kidnapping Amy Tapin or with stealing my dog, at least we can nail him for larceny.

I thought I was done, but as I slid the cards back into to their hiding place, I discovered one more scam this guy was pulling. Tucked away at the back of the drawer, lay two small, clear plastic envelopes, each about the size of a credit card. At first glance, the things looked innocuous. But then I noticed tiny strips of electrician's tape stuck onto them. I recognized these items as tools for more thievery. Back when I was with the Buffalo police, I'd seen these gadgets demonstrated at a computer crime seminar. Called Lebanese Loops, they are used to scam bank cash machines.

I pocketed one of the devices and was just slipping the other one back into the drawer when I heard voices coming down the hall. Cheyenne was speaking loudly in order to give me some warning. I closed the drawer and reached to turn off the gooseneck desk lamp, but then thought better of it. Like movement, a change of lighting is more noticeable than a steady light. Maybe this Shayna woman will think she'd simply left the lamp on.

Cheyenne entered the room carrying a plate of cookies. Shayna followed, holding a silver tray with a pot of tea and three china cups. Geez, I hope this nice woman is clueless about the jerk she is married to.

I hurried over to help with her tray. "Shayna, you're being far too nice to us." And I meant that. I took the tray from her sweet innocent hands.

Shayna said, "I must apologize if the house smells doggy."

"I hadn't noticed," I said. Then I asked a seemingly irrelevant question, "Uh… what kind of dog?"

Cheyenne answered first, "A poodle. Shayna and her husband recently lost her."

"I'm sorry to hear that."

"Thank you," Shayna said. "Fifi was only a few years old. Must have been something she ate."

"Could have been chocolate," Cheyenne said, biting into a cookie.

"She was a therapy dog. My husband thinks she might have gotten into somebody's medication."

Between chews, Cheyenne said to me, "Shayna says you probably know her husband."

"I do?" I helped myself to a chocolate chip cookie.

Shayna said, "You used to work for the Glen Echo Police Department, correct?"

"Actually I kinda *was* the Glen Echo Police Department. It wasn't much of a force."

She said, "You know the Glen Echo Court Motor Inn?"

"Uh, hum." Couldn't talk. Had a delicious cookie in my mouth.

"Gregory is night manager. Gregory Petrescu."

Petrescu? Shit. That was not the name the nurse had given me. Don't tell me I've been nosing around the wrong house. No, that was impossible. Those stolen credit cards… and Fifi.

Shayna added, "You would know him as Peters. Greg changed his name when he came to America."

Man, that was a relief. I'd hate to think I was jerking around the lovely wife of the wrong asshole. "Doesn't ring a bell," I said. "How long has your husband worked at the motel?"

"Five, maybe six months."

"That would be after my time. I left a year ago."

We made some small talk, enjoyed some tea. Ate more cookies. Homemade. Oatmeal. But with chocolate chips instead of raisins. Not milk chocolate, but the good, bittersweet chips. Geez, I hoped this woman has nothing to do with her hubby's hobbies.

Now that she knew I used to be a cop, Shayna relaxed more. She explained that her husband was a Belarusian immigrant, an electrical engineer. But as so often happens with foreign professionals, when the guy came to America, he had trouble getting proper certification to work in his chosen field, so he's been forced to take whatever menial gigs he can scrape up. So far, he's driven a cab in Boston, delivered pizza in Rochester, and telemarketed from a boiler room in Schenectady.

And now he's working as a motel night manager here in the Adirondacks. According to Shayna, her husband likes the mountains because they remind him of the old country. I suspected he also liked these mountains because they offer plenty of cover for hiding yourself away while lying to your wife about being an electrical engineer.

As a cop, I've met quite a few foreign *professionals* with Gregory's story. Most of them, of course, are legit. But some are not. My favorite was a Polish madam who ran a whore house in Tonawanda, New York. She insisted that back in the old country she had been a licensed medical doctor. I never found out if her claim was legitimate, but considering that she had advised her ladies to avoid pregnancy by douching with Snapple, I had my doubts.

While Cheyenne and Shayna finished off their tea, I excused myself to, supposedly, refill our car's radiator. I went through the motions of carrying a large pitcher of water outside and banging away under the hood. A few minutes later, I returned to announce that we were good to skedaddle. We thanked our sweet hostess profusely for her hospitality, and I added that I hoped, if I run into her husband, Gregory, I will tell him what a wonderful American gal he has hitched himself up to. Shayna had no idea how sincere my hope was nor how very soon I intended to run into this slimy toad.

With thanks said, we left. When we were alone in the car – me in the passenger seat again, Cheyenne behind the wheel – I showed Cheyenne the Lebanese Loops. When I was through explaining what they were, she asked, "And did you find anything connecting him to Amy's disappearance?"

"Not directly, but…" I pulled two of the stolen credit cards out of my pocket. "I think I've got enough leverage for a nice little chat."

"Good." She put the car into gear. "So we're heading to the motel? Glen Echo?"

"Yes, I am. Right after you take me back to pick up my car."

She didn't like this idea one bit. "Haven't I been of help so far?"

"You've been a huge help. But this next visit could get a little dangerous."

"I see." But she didn't sound convinced. "If it's dangerous, then don't you think it's time we called in the police?" She gave me a sideways glance to let me know that her comment was not a mere suggestion – it was a threat, a reminder that I was presently just a passenger in her car, and she was behind the wheel.

As she turned the car onto the highway, aiming us toward the motel in Glen Echo, I said, "You must hate flying."

"What do you mean?"

"You know… having to hand all that control over to some idiot professional."

She smiled. And stepped on the gas.

* * * * *

The Adirondacks boast plenty of fancy, five-star accommodations – ritzy resorts with chilled champagne buckets and heated toilet seats. On the other extreme, hunters and hikers have no trouble finding more modest digs – pine-scented lodgings that offer little more than a dry bed and a rusty shower. Positioned somewhere between these two extremes lies the Glen Echo Motor Court. Here, chocolate truffles on the pillows means the last guest owned a dog.

The motel was small, a couple dozen rooms and a half-filled, leaf-littered swimming pool. In all fairness, this spring weather was still rather cool for a dip. As Cheyenne pulled our car up to the office's buzzing neon vacancy sign, my heart rate picked up a bit. Stopping at a cheap motel with a sexy woman does that to me. Kind of like Pavlov's dog but with more salivating.

I placed my hand on the car's door handle and was just about to ask my attractive companion to stay put, but I was too late. Cheyenne was already out of the vehicle and walking to the office door.

I never got to ring that little bell at the front desk either. Before the screen door had slammed shut behind me, the desk clerk was slithering out of the back office. He took one look at Cheyenne, gave her a slimy smile and said in a slippery accent, "Goot iffning." He then sort of glanced at me. "Just two, or have you the childrens vis you?"

In a small way, I was sorry to hear that thick accent. Same for the deep voice. It meant this guy was not the character I'd talked to on the phone two days ago, the confused kidnapper with the ransom demands. That man had spoken perfect unaccented English in a high tenor. And there was something else about this desk clerk that didn't match up. He was tall and fairly muscular. Gloria Tapin had told me the man who contacted her father about the violin was medium height and pudgy. She also said he was balding. This man facing me had a head full of thick curls plush enough to be a motel bath mat, but from a much better motel.

Cheyenne had agreed to let me do the talking, and for a few precious moments she actually honored that covenant. She stood by, obedient as a good puppy, while I said, "Mr. Petrescu?"

At the sound of the full name, the desk clerk's oily smile slid to the floor. How did I know his real moniker? Few people up here would know him as anything but *Peters*.

I continued, "My name's Tanager. I'm not here for a room."

He looked at Cheyenne. Then back at me. *What kind of idiot would bring a hottie like this to a motel and not want a bed?*

I didn't introduce Cheyenne – that would only encourage her to join the conversation. I just said, "I'm looking for information."

Gregory Petrescu hesitated before asking, "You… you are police?" He was not at all happy with this possibility. I'm sure his East European culture looks upon law enforcement differently than ours does. Not more respectfully, just differently.

"No, I'm not with the police. This is a private enquiry." Unsure how to approach my next question, I absent-mindedly lifted a travel brochure from off his counter. I opened it. Had a look. And said, "I understand you used to participate in a therapy dog program. You used to take your dog to visit elderly residents at Lake Placid Villa."

On hearing this, Petrescu's attitude changed from mildly defensive to full *Go fuck yourself*. He was now a maître d' telling me I needed a jacket and tie. "If you not police I don't need talk vis you."

But I pressed on. "Mr. Petrescu, while at The Villa you met an elderly woman. Her name was Amy. Amy Tapin. She liked Fifi very much."

"You must go now."

"We have a problem here." I stepped closer to the counter, as if this man was the school cafeteria lady and I was about to ask for more meatloaf. "You see, this Amy Tapin woman, she has gone missing. And I believe you may be able to help us find her."

"I don't know what you are talking."

Cheyenne, who had held back longer than I had expected her to, brought her plate up to the buffet. "Miss Tapin told you about some items in her possession. Some very valuable items."

"You crazy. You must go. I phone police. Real police." He moved toward the phone, put his hand on the receiver, but he didn't pick it up.

"No, Gregory," I said. "I don't think you will be phoning anybody. I think you are going to tell me everything I want to know. You are going to do this because if you do not talk to me, I will show something to the police." I held out the credit cards I had taken from his home desk.

He looked. He extended his hand to take one. But I pulled the cards away. "You recognize them?"

"I don't know," he said, "Just credit cards, looks like."

"They're more than just credit cards. They're *stolen* credit cards. Do you know where I got them?" I gave him a moment to sweat, then I continued, "I got them from the same place I found the loops."

"Loops?"

"You know… the devices you've been using to rip off cash machines down state." I had read that automated teller machines in Albany and Syracuse were getting hit frequently last fall – about the same time when

Petrescu's wife said she and he were living down there. "For an electrical engineer like yourself, Mr. Petrescu, those machines must have been a cinch to rip off."

He said nothing. I noticed that while I was speaking, Gregory Petrescu had been edging his flat stomach up closer to his side of the counter. And now his large, strong right hand was starting to reach under that counter.

"Uh, uh…" I said. "Hands where I can see them."

I expected he was just reaching for a baseball bat. I was wrong. His right hand pulled a rifle out from a shelf under the desk. He didn't move fast. He didn't have to – I was unarmed.

With the high counter between us, I had no choice but to grab the only parts of Gregory I could reach – his ears. Luckily, they were big ears.

With both my hands full of waxy East European cartilage, I pulled his face forward, slamming it down onto the imitation Italian marble countertop, jamming his nose into a mess of travel brochures. From behind the counter, I heard his rifle hit the floor.

His hands, now empty of weaponry, reached up to grab at me, but there wasn't much he could do. I had all my weight pressing down on the back of his head. I may have pressed a little too hard, though. A thin stream of blood trickled from his nose and onto a brochure that advertised a tour of the home of Robert Louis Stevenson, the famed author who, like so many others at the turn of the century, came up to these unspoiled mountains for the healthy air to cure his tuberculosis and, ironically, clear his respiratory passageways.

While Gregory struggled to get his breath, Cheyenne circled round behind the counter and lifted his sawed-off shotgun from the floor. I eased my grip on Gregory's ears. I then grabbed a wad of paper napkins that were stacked beside a nearby coffee maker and handed them over with an invitation, "We talk now. Okay, Mr. Petrescu?"

I took his silence to mean, *Sure, let's chat.*

CHAPTER THIRTEEN

It took me a while to get the whole story. After all, a Belarusian with a heavy accent, a busted tooth, and his head held back to stop the stream of blood from staining his cotton golf shirt, can be surprisingly difficult to understand. I think he'd bitten his tongue, too.

I would have felt sorry for the guy if I hadn't had the image burned into my mind of those confused senior citizens wandering the halls of their rest homes, leaning on their walkers while getting flak from their nurse for misplacing their wallets, jewelry, and credit cards.

According to Gregory Petrescu, alias Greg Peters, the crazy old lady named Amy had indeed told him about the relationship she'd enjoyed with Albert Einstein back when she was young and gorgeous. And yes, she had also mentioned having a piece of memorabilia from the friendship, namely a violin.

"And you believed her?" I asked Gregory.

"No, of course not. What I look like – stupid in the head? She sick old lady. Say all sorts crazy shit. But then one day her son, uh…"

"Henry," Cheyenne prompted, getting carried away with the moment, feeling the power of holding a loaded shotgun in her hands.

"Ya, Henry. He visit her one time when I am there with Fifi. Old lady starts talking again about violin. She is asking son if he has hid it away in closet for her. Son, he laughs. Laughs hard. Maybe too hard. He tells me pay no attention to what mother say. Says old woman not right in head."

"And this started you to thinking otherwise."

"When a son tries tell you his very own mother is crazy, something is maybe not so crazy."

Gregory Petrescu went on to admit that, while he thought that such a rare item might indeed be worth stealing, no smart thief would go to any trouble until he had done some homework.

I said, "So, you searched the Internet. Looked for someone who might know about such an item." I, of course, had seen Gregory's research notes for myself, web addresses jotted on those memo notes on his home computer desk.

By this time, my interviewee was starting to feel that maybe he'd said enough. Maybe he shouldn't dig his hole any deeper. So, I switched to my good cop mode, put my arm on his shoulder. "Listen, Gregory, I know you're just a poor immigrant trying to make a buck. You wouldn't hurt anyone. I know that. But if the police find the old lady dead, and it turns out you could have helped save her life, yet you didn't, that will make you an accomplice. An accomplice to murder. Just as guilty as if you'd shot the lady yourself. That's the way it works in this country."

Of course, the legalities of my claim were highly suspect, but luckily Gregory was a bogus engineer, not a bogus lawyer. He decided it was in his interest to chat a little further. "There is man. Comes here to motel. Regular customer."

"Regular?" I knew what this meant. "With a girl?"

"Every Thursday I give him room. Cash. No questions."

"He doesn't sign the register. Stays for just an hour."

Gregory nodded. "Used to stay two, maybe three hours. Now, one hour. Soon, half-hour I am thinking." Gregory pulled his crumpled paper napkin away from his nose to see if it had stemmed the bleeding yet. It hadn't.

"Hold your head forward, not backward," Cheyenne said.

As he changed positions, I got back to business, "And you thought this motel guest might be interested in what you had to sell?"

"He is teacher from high school. Science. Mathematics. Physics."

Cheyenne looked askance at this news. She didn't buy it. She said, "Just because he taught science you thought he might be interested in Albert Einstein memorabilia?"

"No, no. Because of license plate."

Cheyenne said nothing. I said nothing. Gregory checked his napkin again for new blood. I had the patience to wait. Cheyenne did not. "And what was on his license plate?" she asked.

"E=MC2."

A vision of two alpaca heads on spikes flashed across my mind, along with their grim message written in blood.

Gregory continued, "When I see license plate, I know this man was liking Albert Einstein very much. So I tell him I know someone has personal item once belonged to Albert Einstein."

"But you didn't have the item," I said, making sure I had this clear.

"I tell him maybe I can get item. He is very excited. Says he is big lover of Einstein. He say he have picture Albert Einstein in his classroom, another one at home. Even computer screensaver is picture of Einstein. I think probably this man have picture Einstein tattooed on his, uh… how you say…?"

"Ass?" Cheyenne prompted.

Gregory gave Cheyenne a big *thumbs up*.

I asked, "Did you tell him specifically what the item was? A violin?"

"I don't have to. Soon as I say it was personal item, teacher say, 'You mean the violin?' Now, I start to think, if he knows about violin maybe this item famous. Maybe it really is worth something. So, I tell him maybe we can work out deal."

"Did you tell him *how* you were going to get the violin?"

"Teacher not ask questions. He knew this wasn't *e-bay*."

Cheyenne said, "So, all that was left was the dickering."

Gregory didn't understand. I rephrased the question. "Money. Did you discuss price with this teacher?"

"I'm not worry. This man drives expensive car. Wears nice clothes. Always tips good for room. Before we talk about money he says he wants know more about item. Wants proof violin really belonged to Einstein."

"He's looking for a provenance," suggested Cheyenne.

Gregory had no idea what she was talking about. Neither would I if I hadn't watched so much public television. "What did you tell him?" I asked our informant.

"I tell him I know item belonged Einstein because it come from Einstein's very own girlfriend. But I think I say wrong thing."

"Why?"

"Because as soon as I mention Einstein girlfriend, teacher say deal is off. He is no longer interest."

Cheyenne turned to me and said, "I don't get it."

I asked Gregory a loaded question, "By any chance does this teacher know about your scam with your therapy dog?"

"He knows I help old people at nursing home, yes."

Cheyenne understood what I was getting at. She said, "So he knows where you met the person with the violin. All he has to do is ask around."

Gregory agreed, "I think I maybe told teacher too much."

I handed Gregory a clean napkin for his nose. "This teacher… what does he look like?"

"Short. No muscles. No hairs on head. Maybe fifty year old. That's how I knew he had plenty money. How else such a man get such a girl?"

I said, "Pretty, huh?"

Gregory sucked in his breath, giving me the international sign for hotsy-totsy. "Long red hair. White skin. Smooth like Bulgarian yogurt. Small. But not small here." He cupped up his palms to his chest and gave me the sign for arthritic hands.

"Nice rack, huh?" Cheyenne said.

Gregory nodded, "Oh, yes. She have rack, too. Across teeth."

For a moment, his cryptic comment left me somewhat confused. But Cheyenne got it, "You mean, she wore braces?"

"For to straighten teeth."

At this point, I heard the creak of a screen door springing open. We all turned to see an elderly couple enter the office, the man holding the door for his wife. The woman stepped into the room smiling, but as her eyes assessed the odd tableau facing her, the gravity of the scene pulled that smile into an open-mouthed gape. She found herself facing a man sitting on a stool behind a counter clutching a bloody napkin to his face, blood still dripping onto the floor. And over on the sofa, a woman was sitting with a sawed-off shotgun held across her lap.

I jumped in, "It's okay, folks. Just a little accident. Nothing to be alarmed about."

Cheyenne tried to back me up on this tale, but what could she do? These people were tourists, not idiots. Sometimes there's a difference.

Backing out of the room as quickly as they had entered, the couple mumbled something about how this might not be the best place in town to spend their honeymoon night.

As I stood watching their car speed out of the parking lot, I noticed that the woman in the passenger seat was dialing her cell phone. I turned to Cheyenne. "I think we'd better get moving. The police will be here any minute."

Gregory was fine with our leaving, but he added, "Please to take shotgun wis you."

He was smart. Police don't look favorably on sawed-off weaponry, especially in the hands of a bleeding recent immigrant. So I decided to do the guy a favor. Not really for his sake but for his wife's benefit. She was a nice lady, and she probably didn't know what her slimy husband has been up to. More important, she has a new cookie in the oven. She doesn't need the father in jail.

"Sure, I'll get rid of the gun for you," I said to Gregory Petrescu. "All you have to do is give me the address of this teacher."

"I told you – he not sign register. No address, no name."

"You never heard his girlfriend call him by name?" I asked.

Gregory thought this one over, "Coach. I think maybe she call him coach. But coach is not name, is it?"

I looked to Cheyenne. "What kind of coach would be short and pudgy?"

"Any of them," she said. "You don't have to be an athlete to coach."

As I left the motel office, my hand still on the screen door, I thought of one more question for our Belarusian friend. It was not a very important question. Just something I thought might be useful to me further down the road.

"So tell me, Gregory, just how old would you say this science teacher's girlfriend was?"

"Young," he said. "Too young. Very much too young."

* * * * *

Cheyenne set out a tray of cheese and crackers and poured us a couple eighteen-year-old single malts. She then invited me to sit next to her on the sofa, but I told her I'd rather go straight to her bedroom. Was I moving too fast? No. That's where her desktop computer was.

While I hopped onto the internet, Cheyenne hopped into the shower and said she was going to change into something comfortable. As an indication of how distracted I was, I let this go by without a lurid thought. Well, without a lurid comment, at least. I took the plate of crackers with me and nibbled, careful not to drop any crumbs into her keyboard.

The website for Glen Echo High School listed teachers by their department. Under *Math and Sciences* I found four names. Three of them were male. Two taught physics, but only one of these coached athletics. His sport was synchronized swimming. I guess that fits. A guy might get ideas sitting around watching young girls sticking their naked legs up in the air. The name of this physics teacher/swim coach was Mr. T. Appleyard. No photo, so I couldn't see if he matched the description given to me by the Belarusian motel clerk. The list of teachers, of course, didn't include home addresses — no point in inviting failing students to drop by and screw with your brake lines — so my next digital visit was to an internet phone directory, Adirondack edition.

You gotta love small towns. If I were searching a landline phone directory for Buffalo or Syracuse, I'd have been presented with dozens of Appleyards. But here in the north woods, where a phone book, if still printed, would be as thin as a directory of Icelandic golf pros, only one Appleyard popped up. His first initial was T, and he lived on Morrison

Lake Road, a location which happened to be an easy commute to Glen Echo High.

I shut down Cheyenne's computer, grabbed what was left of the tray of crackers, and went back to the living room to say thank you and goodbye to my freshly scrubbed hostess. My plan was to spend the rest of the night snoozing in my car. Honest. Or maybe check into a local motel. Honest. But when I entered the living room I found Cheyenne spreading a cotton bed sheet out on the sofa. I protested. Honest.

"Don't be silly." She said as she tucked the fresh sheet around the big plush cushions. "No trouble at all."

"No, no. You've been far too kind already."

"You're tall, but I think this will do if we use a smaller pillow." She added a plush blanket to the temptation.

"I'll just go back home."

"They'll be watching your place."

"Then I'll find a room somewhere. Hey, I'll bet our friend from Belarus will give me a deal."

"After that honeymoon couple report what they saw, that motel will be swarming with cops." She fluffed up a pillow. "So did you find the science teach?"

"I think so."

"You paying him a visit?" She used the singular second person, *you*, not the plural first, *we*. This boded well.

"First thing in the morning."

"Before school?"

"Sun up. Teachers start work pretty early. Especially if they coach a team."

"Any idea what sport?"

"Looks like synchronized swimming."

"Synchronized swimming?" Cheyenne seemed to find this quite odd.

"You know – where a guy stands there blowing his whistle while nubile young women waggle their naked legs in the air."

"Why the whistle? Their heads are under water."

"Without the whistle he'd be just another pervert."

She glanced at a decorative wall clock that was lying on an old typewriter. "Sun up – that's two hours and fifty-seven minutes away. You'd better hit the sack."

"You know what time the sun rises?" I shouldn't have been surprised, but I was.

"Amazes me, too." She pulled back a corner of the blanket as if she were dog-earing a page in a book for future reference. "I'll wake you."

"Thanks." I knew what she was really up to, of course. I was under no delusions. On a first date, my charms might be fetching enough for a kiss at the door. But to insist that I stay the night? Sorry, I'm just not that gorgeous. No, this was her ploy to stay in the game. Keep close. She wants us to continue working together. But why? What was her motive for all this cozy team work?

It sounds awful, but I couldn't help thinking how, if she were somehow involved in Amy Tapin's kidnapping, or even in Henry Tapin's murder, she would be smart to stick by my side, keep a close eye on what I was doing, see what rocks I was looking under.

Cheyenne turned away from me, walked towards her bedroom. The ice cubes clinked in her lowball glass like warning bells as she said, "I'll set my alarm for four-thirty. Time for a quick breakfast before you head out."

I had to say it, "You do realize I'm going out alone."

She seemed unconcerned with my edict. She just shrugged. "Whatever. Just keep in touch, okay? Phone me. I know you're suspicious of my motives, but I want a blow-by-blow."

"Suspicious?" I tried my best to sound like this was a new thought to me.

She turned around to face me eye-to-eye. "You gotta be asking, Why is this chick dropping everything to help me? Investing all this time, trouble, and energy?"

"Well, now that you mention it…"

"Look, Henry's an odd duck, but he's a well-meaning odd duck. Smart. Probably too smart for his own good. I worry about him. Life's not easy for guys like Henry." She added, "And frankly, I'm a little but worried about you, too."

"Hell, you don't have to worry about me. I'm dumber than a bag of lawn trimmings. Not enough intellect to get into any serious trouble."

"I don't believe that for one minute, and neither do you. But it's a cute line. I'm sure lots of women fall for it." And with that, she flicked off the light. "Sleep tight." It wasn't a wish – it was a direct order.

But I couldn't sleep tight, of course. To sleep tight I'd have needed at least two more shots of scotch.

And a big dumb dog lying across my feet.

CHAPTER FOURTEEN

The sun was just rising when I got to Thomas Appleyard's lakefront property. The first rays of dawn stretched their stiff, waking arms out to point out a large, four-bedroom house that lay slumbering upon rumpled green linens of rolling lawn. Down by the lake, a two-story boathouse snuggled up close to the water's edge. This structure's second story appeared to be a guest bunkie. If so, the place violates the Adirondack Park's environmental building codes. You'd think a science teacher would know better.

Just ahead of me, farther along the gravel driveway, a detached garage snoozed with its doors partially open thereby allowing two sets of headlights to peep out at the rising sun. As I drove past the door, one of the vehicles' license plates winked at me.

It read, E=MC2.

Yippee, I've found the correct pervert. On closer examination, the *equals* sign turned out to be painted in. Another law broken. This guy should be careful. When he's not committing statutory rape, he's racking up some serious misdemeanors.

His vanity plate was slapped onto the fancy ass of a late model Infinity. Beside it, sat a Mercedes SUV whose sturdy German booty sported a vanity plate that read, EST8 4U. Sounds like this science teacher's partner sells real estate. Or practices family law.

I parked my car and tip-toed around behind the garage to check out a third car. This older domestic vehicle was cowering in shame under a domestic pine tree where it was collecting domestic tree sap and domestic bird shit. Judging by the junk littering the car's seats – glitzy sunglasses, a couple of fashion magazines, and a pair of pink neon sneakers – I'd say this vehicle belongs to one of the teacher's kids. A daughter, I presume, although I guess I shouldn't presume like that anymore. Not out loud, at least. When I and my sexist biases were finished checking out all the vehicles, I proceeded down the hill to have a look at the boathouse.

I walked quietly. No lights were on. If anyone was currently occupying that upstairs bunkie, they were probably still in bed. As I strode down the gentle slope toward the lake, I zipped up my jacket. Didn't help much. The cold, sharp fingernails of morning breeze tore at my thin nylon windbreaker like a spoiled kid ripping through Christmas wrap. And I soon noticed my feet were getting wet. Not from the sky above but from the ground below. The heavy dew on the long grass was soaking through the suede tops of my Wallabies.

As I neared the lake, a loon laughed. Probably mocking my poor choice of footwear. Above us, the sky was trying its best to lighten, but it had a tough job. The rising sun had decided to hit the snooze button and hide under the covers a little while longer. Coward. It had probably heard about the bugs. I had noticed yesterday that the blackflies were starting to swarm. They haven't reached the voracious, biting stage yet, but they soon will. I just hope the little devils can suppress their crazed appetites for a few days yet, at least until I find Stanley. If the pooch is being kept outside the flies will drive him crazy. Of course, when I had first stepped out of my car, I had kept my ears tuned for a familiar dog's bark. Or *any* dog's bark. But so far, I haven't heard a thing.

When I reached the shoreline, I stepped up onto the wooden decking that ran alongside the boathouse. I quietly edged my way to the building's side window. Inside, I saw two slips but just one boat. It was a mahogany runabout. Probably an antique. Or maybe a replica. I didn't know. And didn't care. What interested me was the name affixed onto the stern in shiny chrome letters.

The Tinef.

Until yesterday I wouldn't have understood the significance. But last night, while my lovely hostess was soaping herself silly in the shower and I was trying to stay focused at her computer, I had pulled up several trivialities about Albert Einstein. One of those trifles was that he had named his sailboat *The Tinef* – a Yiddish word meaning *worthless*. This was probably a big yuk to old Albert, but to me it just reinforced that, along with young female students and personalized license plates, this horndog science teacher has a major hard on for all things Einstein. The rest of the boathouse was empty – empty, that is, of medium-sized dogs and kidnapped elderly ladies. So I turned my attention to the second floor.

I climbed the wooden stairway up the outside of the boathouse, careful to keep my weight as close to the wall as possible so as not to risk any giveaway groans or creaks from either the steps or my knees. If anyone is inside I didn't want to wake them. When I reached the top deck I hunkered low, kept my head below the little window in the door, and crossed to the far side of the frame. With my shoulder blades hunched tight against the wall, I was now in a good position to sneak a quick sidelong glimpse into that window. Never quite got that far, though.

The door flew open. The crazy thing swung outwards, a hundred and eighty degrees – sandwiching me hard against the exterior wall. My first thought was, *What kind of idiot builds an exterior door that opens outwards?* More proof, I guess, that the builder didn't worry about building codes. My second thought was, I can't breathe. Somebody is pressing this against me hard on purpose. This is not good. Maybe I'd better push back.

Frankly, it was no contest. I clearly had the advantage. My back was against the wall – his wasn't. Plus, I was wearing rubber-soled shoes that gripped the decking – he was in stocking feet. And finally, I was a full-grown adult. My attacker was a skinny teenager.

When I pushed, the kid stumbled backwards, his back hit the railing and he went tumbling over the side. But there was no splash. He didn't hit the water. Somehow, he managed to grab hold of the top rail and was now dangling by his slim, pale hands. He kicked out with his stocking feet, trying desperately to swing his heels up onto the deck flooring so he could get a leg up. But he couldn't quite manage the maneuver. This kid was no athlete.

"Just let go," I suggested. After all, he was only a few feet above the water, and except for a pair of socks and underpants he was dressed just fine for a morning dip. But he didn't follow my suggestion. He just kept wriggling like a worm on a hook. So I grabbed the kid's skinny arms. "Can't you swim?" I said.

"It's fuckin' ice cold."

"Hold still. I'll pull you up." As I hefted him, I asked, "Your name Appleyard?"

But the kid had other things on his mind. Two of them, actually. "Shit, dude, I'm freezing my balls off."

I had him safely over the balustrade now, so I let him climb the rest of the way by himself. I backed away, saying. "Sorry if I scared you."

"What the fuck you doing here?" Still catching his breath, the kid collapsed in a heap on the deck floor.

"Long story. Tell me, son," I said. "Has your dad brought home any dogs lately?"

"What?"

"I'm looking for my dog. You seen one around?"

When he'd caught enough breath to speak he said, "Saw you coming down the hill. Thought you were, like, casing us out."

"Nope. Just looking for my pooch."

"And you think my old man took it?"

"Here, let me help." I extended my hand and helped him get up on his feet.

"Lost your dog…" Now standing face to face with me, he looked at my hands. "So where is it?"

"What? The dog?"

"The leash. Where's your leash?" This kid was smarter than he looked.

"Left it in my car."

"What about the bag?" The kid smiled. He thought he had me. "Everybody who walks a dog carries a fuckin' shit bag. It's like the law or something."

"I'm not what you'd call a responsible dog owner."

"Bull shit." The kid turned away from me and went back into his room. I watched as he headed straight for the warmth of his bed, jumped into it, and pulled the covers up under his chattering chin.

Still hanging in the doorway, I checked out the place. The room didn't show any particular personality. Like most guest quarters, it was furnished primarily with discards and spillovers from other, more important rooms. The only sign this bedroom showed of ever having served family duty was a couple of plastic model airplanes mounted on a shelf. A hobby that this teenager had probably outgrown.

I stepped farther inside and asked, "What time does your father get up?"

"Shit, we probably already woke him. And you're lying. You're not looking for any fucking dog."

"I'm not?"

The kid reached over to a bedside table and grabbed a pack of cigarettes. "You're looking for your fucking daughter."

"I am?" This was a new angle.

The kid took out a cigarette and called out, "You might as well come out, Kay. Your old man's already seen your car."

The bathroom door opened. A young girl stepped out. She was dressed in only a t-shirt and panties. She took one look at me and immediately turned to the boy, "You asshole. He's not my fucking father."

"No?" The boy turned back to me. "Then who the fuck—"

But he didn't get to finish his inquiry. We were interrupted by the sound of footsteps coming up the outside stairs and a man's voice calling out, "David, you okay in there?"

"Fuck, my old man." The boy turned to his girlfriend. "Quick, back in the can."

But she didn't have time. The man outside had already reached the top of the stairs and was now looking into the room. His eyes were fixed on the half-naked girl. "Kayla!"

She looked away. Not really from shame. More like boredom.

The middle-aged man at the door stared at the young woman for a period of time far longer than her unresponsive face deserved. Finally, he turned his eyes to me.

The ball was in my court. But I didn't bat it back. The boy did. "Says he's looking for his dog."

That put an end to Thomas Appleyard's interest in me. Like a compass needle that was compelled by the laws of electromagnetic physics to swing north, the science teacher's head returned to the young half-naked girl who was leaning casually against the bathroom door frame. She didn't look back at him. But I did.

This man matched the photo I'd seen of him in the high school yearbook. Of medium height, balding, and with piecing grey eyes, he also matched the description Gloria Tapin had given me of the man who was trying to purchase the violin from her father. Obviously fresh from his bed, wearing leather slippers and a silk robe over silk pajamas, Appleyard, continued to stare at the half-naked school girl. Finally, he said something. "I… I don't understand."

Neither of the kids answered him, so I did. "We should talk, Mr. Appleyard." I gestured to the open front door. "Outside." I then took his elbow and whispered a sweet nothing in his ear, "It's about a certain Einstein item."

Now, I was no sexy young thing in red panties and a pop band's t-shirt, but the name *Einstein* sparked enough magnetic attraction to pull the guy's attention to me, away from the sex kitten who was presently busy biting at her chipped fingernails. He followed me out the door.

I led him along the narrow walkway to the small rooftop patio that extended out over the water. I'd have invited him to take a seat on the cedar picnic table, but the morning dew would have ruined that silk robe, so we just stood by the railing.

"I'm here about the violin," I said. "The Einstein violin."

"Violin? I don't know what you're—"

"Listen, Tom. I know about you and young Kayla in there. I know you've been *tutoring* her at the Glen Echo Motel every Thursday afternoon. I know, and I have a witness. I also have photos." Okay, the photos was a bluff. But the rest was true. How did I know? I knew from the look on this guy's face when he saw that young girl in there. When Appleyard walked in on those two kids, he looked surprised, sure, but that surprise immediately morphed into something else – not anger with his son, as one might expect, but disappointment with the girl. The dark cloud that passed across Thomas Appleyard's face in that instant was not a father's hostility. It was a lover's heartbreak. A spurned lover. *A cuckold*, if you're into medieval literature or porn classifications.

I guess I'm pretty good at reading faces. Hell, I've seen enough of them fall when I've handed them traffic tickets or told them that, sorry, the band doesn't play *Brown Eyed Girl*. But on this particular occasion, I didn't need those special skills of psychoanalytical assessment. You see, young Kayla matched perfectly the description the motel clerk Gregory Petrescu had given me of the freckled, red-headed spinner that the horny Einstein enthusiast has been boinking. She matched right down to the silver braces on her teeth and the silver ring through her eyebrow.

Seeing as I now had this science teacher's balls over a Bunsen burner, I turned up the flame. I placed my hand on his shoulder and said, "Tom, I know you're the fella who's been calling Henry Tapin with offers for the fiddle."

Appleyard was not happy. Teachers don't like losing control. Mine were never thrilled with it. And yet here I was with my big mitt on this man's soft shoulder, holding him literally under my thumb.

Appleyard turned his attention to his house up on the hill. From this distance, I couldn't tell whether his wife was watching us from her bedroom window or not, but that didn't matter. I'm sure Tom Appleyard could. He turned back to me. "What is it you want from me?"

By now, I knew this man wasn't the perp I'd wrestled with at Crazy Henry's store. That man was strong and at least six inches taller than this guy. But that doesn't mean this teacher hadn't hired that muscle. I eased my grip on Appleyard's shoulder. "Tom, I want you to tell me all about this Einstein thing. This violin."

Thomas Appleyard turned his face toward the open doorway of the boathouse bunkie. "I… I can't. Not here."

I needed this man to be able to speak freely. In earlier days, this would have meant inviting him down to the station for a private chat in a dark room with a table and a gooseneck lamp. But those days are long gone. Nowadays, all I have is a pet store with a chair, a stool, and a desk that is currently covered in squeaky toys.

"Throw some clothes on," I said. "I'll buy you breakfast."

A cool gust of breeze whipped up from the lake. Appleyard cinched his robe tighter. But I'm sure it didn't help. The silk could offer no more protection against the chill air swirling up his horny ass than it could against the cold truth slapping his sorry face. The man knew he was caught. Still, he tried to wriggle off the hook.

"I can't. I have a class at nine."

"You know the Golden Dragon?"

He nodded.

"Meet me there. It's just around the corner from your school. We'll be quick." I turned and started down the stairs. But before I got my foot off the top step, I had one more thing to say, one final offer to make. I didn't expect much from it. But I had to try. I said, "Of course, we could call all this off right now. I won't tell anyone about the private tutoring you've been offering that sweet young student in there. It'll be our little secret. All you have to do is tell me where my dog is. Who took him."

Appleyard furrowed his brows so tight his ears almost touched. "Your… your dog? How should I know where your dog is?"

As he spoke, I listened to his voice carefully. Thomas Appleyard had a commanding tone. A voice that has all the answers and can pitch them hard from the front of a classroom. His voice did not match the voice I'd heard on the phone two days ago. That caller had sung in a whole different key. But of course Appleyard could have disguised his voice. Hell, he's a physics teacher – maybe he had altered his phone call digitally.

I turned and continued down the steps. When I reached the bottom I called up once more to my prospective breakfast companion, "You've got one hour. You don't show, I take the photos to the schoolboard."

I waited for his reaction, but the man was no longer taking any notice of me. His attention had reverted to the open doorway of the bunkie where, inside, his son was yelling at the young girl. The boy's razor sharp words spun out over the lake and shredded the morning mist. "My old man? You been fucking my old man?"

"How else do you expect me to pass physics?"

"You could try opening a fucking book."

"I did. It doesn't help."

She had a point. To truly get physics you really do need hands-on help.

CHAPTER FIFTEEN

What the teacher's home lacked in father-son communication it made up for with fine cell phone reception. I sat in my car and checked for messages.

A voicemail from my friend Nina asked how I was doing and how much longer I might need her rental car. She also mentioned, while she "had me on the blower," that she needed an answer soon on Branson so she'd know how many tickets to reserve for the many tribute shows that she and her daughter want to be sure and catch. Oh, and by the way, don't forget that the car is on her resort's corporate card, so it would be nice if I didn't wrap it around any trees or otherwise do something stupid in, on, or under it. "Kiss, kiss, love ya, ciao and toodle-oo."

To be honest, I don't think there's a real future for Nina and me.

The next voice message was from my business partner Marlene. She had left this message yesterday, which was Sunday, and she was calling to make sure that I was coming in tomorrow, which is today. I texted her back and suggested we leave the store closed for a day or two because it looks like I am going to be otherwise engaged. Marlene works hard, I couldn't keep asking her to cover for me.

The third voice in my mail box belonged to Trooper Steve Scott, the young cop whose patrol car I had crumpled and whose mother I had dated once or twice. Trooper Scott didn't say what he was calling about — only that he wanted me to call him back. From the cold tone of his voice it sounded like he was still holding a grudge about my banging up his… well, stuff. I wish there was a way of convincing him that his mother and I were nothing more than casual friends who work in the same bar.

The fourth and final call was from Lieutenant Manny Manwaring. I was hoping this message would say, *Good news, sweetcheeks. We found the perp who shot Gloria Tapin, so you're off the hook. Go have yourself some fun in Branson, and bring me back a souvenir sideburn.* But no such luck. Manwaring just wanted me to please call him back. I found this message rather disturbing – it was the first time I'd ever heard Manwaring use the word *please*.

I didn't call either Manny or Scott back. Whatever they might want to tell me, it didn't sound like good news. I need my freedom a little while longer. At least until I find Stanley. And Amy Tapin, of course.

I had a bit of time to kill before my breakfast meeting with Appleyard, so I decided to take a cruise through the town of Tupper Lake. If I am right, this quick detour will tell me why Inspector Manwaring and Trooper Scott are so anxious to get hold of me.

* * * * *

Unlike some of the more flashy, tarted-up tourist spots up here, the village of Tupper Lake is not afraid to square its shoulders and don the overalls of a real working town, the kind of place where people actually live. The Adirondacks have a colorful history that is certainly worth exploiting, but I'd hate to see the park become just a collection of glitzy attractions selling the Adirondack myth rather than the Adirondack reality. Although frankly, when you consider the winters and blackfly season, the myth is a lot easier to sell than the reality.

It's kind of the same deal with Albert Einstein. According to what Cheyenne has told me, the man never did make any real money. When Albert Einstein passed away he left behind a very modest estate – not much more than any other hard-working university prof would have amassed. And yet today, despite being dead for quite some time, Albert Einstein is making a fortune. Represented by the same Hollywood agency that handles Steve McQueen, Mae West, and Tarzan, Einstein's annual earnings are bettered only by those of Elvis and Marilyn Monroe. And what exactly is it about Einstein that is generating all this wealth? Do the big bucks come from royalties earned on his famous mathematical formula, $E=MC^2$? Do the riches come from copyrights on his dazzling potboilers on General and Special Relativity? Do his assigned heirs – primarily the Hebrew University in Jerusalem – get a piece of the action every time someone splits an atom or when a NASA physicist allows for the slowing of celestial radio transmissions due to a satellite's velocity bending its envelope of time and space?

Nope. Sorry. Think again, this time with more irony.

What generates all this income for Albert Einstein is his handsome puss. That's right. The millions of dollars that this genius of geniuses rakes in each year come solely from selling his image and his myth. So it's not hard to imagine a violin or something connected to that myth being worth a lot of money. But would the item be worth killing for? How about if there's something hidden inside that violin? Like, say, the secret to the origin of the universe. Or a logical explanation as to why disc jockeys are considered musicians. Whatever the thing is, two people have died for it so far. And maybe an elderly lady. My point is, there may be more to all this than an old, out-of-tune fiddle. And that's why I'm so anxious to have a talk with this teacher, Thomas Appleyard. But first I have one small detour to make.

The day was still pretty new as I coasted down the main street of Tucker Lake. From what I could see, most of the retail shops along Park Street were still closed. But things seemed to have livened up as I neared one particular corner. And I wasn't a bit surprised.

The side street that led up to Crazy Henry's Music Emporium had been turned into a circus. The stucco walls of the store and the adjoining coin laundry were shimmering with festive red and blue splashes of dancing lights. But there was nothing festive about the reason these cop cars and emergency vehicles had gathered here.

I slowed. But I didn't stop. I hunkered down, threw on my baseball cap, and lowered the bill. Twinkling roof lights and flashing headlights rimmed the curb like Christmas bulbs clipped along an eaves trough. One dull civilian car sat wedged ass-backwards into Henry's narrow driveway. I recognized this vehicle as the medical examiner's SUV. I also spotted Heather's van. She's a wedding photographer who helps out whenever local law enforcement needs a crime scene imaged. Especially a homicide.

I saw no sign of anyone from the local newspapers, but it was early — their staff reporters were probably still on their bicycles delivering the morning editions. Radio and television crews from Watertown and Plattsburgh should be here soon to confirm what all the amateurs will have already posted on social media: *Henry Tapin, local music teacher and all-round oddball found murdered.* And then the comments will roll in.

Tapin? Hey, isn't that the name of the woman who was killed yesterday at her ski chalet?

It wasn't yesterday. It was two days ago. Get your facts straight, idiot.

Go fuck yourself.

And it wasn't her ski chalet. It was her old man's cabin.

Heard she got eaten by a Yeti.

Yeti's are the Himalayas, turd face. We got Big Foot.

What would Big Foot be doing in a music store?

You can always count on social media to get to the truth.

Now I knew why Lieutenant Manwaring and Trooper Scott were trying to get ahold of me. Somebody's found the body. The labs couldn't have processed fingerprints yet, but as a Person Of Interest in Gloria Tapin's homicide I'm sure Manny's people are itching to question me about this latest dead Tapin. I'll bet if I now cruise past my house, I will find a squad car waiting for me. Well, I'm afraid they'll have to wait a bit longer. I have a breakfast date.

I snaked my way back to the highway and headed for Glen Echo. Figuring as how all the local police units were probably busy at the scene of Henry's homicide, I relaxed, took my hat off, showed my handsome face, and opened my window for some fresh air. I still have lots of time to get to the Golden Dragon, so I might as well slow down and turn on some music. Funny how, when you think you're coasting along safe and sound with nothing to worry about – that's when you tend to step in the poop.

I was coming round a large curve and was entering one of the highway's rare straightaways when I saw it. A quarter mile ahead. A single squad car. It was parked smack dab in the middle of the right lane, my lane, its roof rack flashing a ragged funk rhythm of blue and red. Shit, a road block.

The uniformed officer, a male I believe, had two vehicles stopped and a third pulling up to join the line. I eased my foot off the gas but didn't hit the brake. I just coasted. The squad car up there belonged to the New York State Police. Had to be a rookie – no experienced cop would pick a dumb location like this to set up camp. The long straightaway had too many exits – driveways and side roads that offered easy opportunity to take evasive action. Which is exactly what I did.

Just ahead and to my right, I saw a break in the bushes, a hidden entrance that appeared to be a logging road.

The officer who was stopping cars appeared to be working alone, so when he stuck his head into the next car's window, I seized the opportunity and spun my wheel hard to the right and coaxed the mighty eight cylinders to plow me through the grass, up the road, and into the heavy under bush.

Woops. Small mistake. This wasn't a logging road at all. In fact, not a road at all. A couple of good hard bounces and sharp prangs told me I was on a snowmobile trail. This was not good – I was not driving a snowmobile. Chryslers are considerably larger than snowmobiles.

I should have hit the brake. But I didn't. I kept my foot firmly on the gas. This is exactly why I will never buy a used rental.

I shook, rattled, and rolled the Chrysler along the rutted path a few hundred yards until I was safely out of sight of the highway. Then I took my foot off the gas. I didn't bother braking – the ruts, rocks, and deep weeds had pretty much already made that decision for me. I did, however, turn off the engine just in case I was leaking gasoline.

I sat. Listened. Wondered. Had the officer at the roadblock seen me scoot away? If so, I would know pretty darn soon.

I stepped out of my car, waded through mud and tall weeds until I was back to a point where I could catch a glimpse of the highway. I saw another car drive past, headed in the same direction I had been headed. It soon braked. Moments later, another drifted to a crawl. Meanwhile, one going full speed came by from the opposite direction. Throughout this, I'd heard no siren. It looked like I'd dodged the bullet – the cop hadn't seen my evasive action.

But then all hell broke loose. And most of this hell was about six inches from my face.

Blackflies. Damn things were out in full force. And by *out* I mean out for blood. They have been swarming for days but not biting. That's the way it is with these sneaky devils. For a week or so, every spring, they lull us into a false sense of security, just hanging around, chilling, goofing, loitering without intent, all the while working up their voracious appetites, sharpening their teeth, and tying bibs under their tiny little chins. Then one quiet morning some celestial dinner bell rings announcing that the buffet is open. From that moment on, every man, woman, and child unfortunate enough to be caught outdoors without a medieval suit of armor becomes the chef's Special Of The Day.

I scrambled for my car. Eyes shut. Blind. Flailing, My arms windmilling as I swatted myself silly. Eyes are the first things these devils go for. I don't know if this is an offensive battle tactic or a culinary choice for the tenderest cut of flesh, but spend any time unprotected outdoors in the Adirondacks in springtime and you'll soon look like a Peeping Tom who has the hots for wasp nests.

I jumped into my crippled Chrysler and pulled the door shut behind me. A few flies had managed to hitch a ride in with me, but that was okay. Believe it or not, blackflies aren't troublesome when they're inside a vehicle. That's another crazy thing about these crackpot carnivores. They rarely bite when they're trapped in a confined space. They prefer patio dining. Theory is, they're more focused on getting out and free than in finishing dinner. I can relate to that. I feel the same way about wedding receptions.

Okay, now what do I do. The digital clock on my dashboard with the tiny blackfly walking across it told me it was ten minutes after seven. That means I had twenty minutes to make my breakfast meeting. I picked up my cell phone.

My first call was to The Golden Dragon restaurant in Glen Echo where the owner, Ken Tamori, knows me from when I used to be the town cop. I told Ken that I was coming to meet someone for breakfast but I'd be a wee bit late, so would Ken please ask the guy to wait. Tell him I won't be long. I finished by giving him a description of Thomas Appleyard.

My second call was not so easy. This time I had a bigger favor to ask.

"You said you'd call me." Cheyenne didn't sound happy.

"I *am* calling you."

"You know what I mean – right after you finished your meeting. I've been worried. Are you okay?"

"Fine."

"And you had a chance to talk with him?"

"Uh, the interview process is still kind of ongoing. We're not quite finished yet." I then went on to explain my present predicament. As usual, the brilliant mathematician and spa aesthetician was ahead of me. Before I had time to ask her, she had offered to come pick me up.

"Give me ten, fifteen minutes," she said.

"Fifteen?" This made no sense. I knew I was a good half-hour's drive from her apartment in Lake Placid. "You're at home, right?"

"Uh, no…" She sounded guilty, like she'd been caught. "Glen Echo."

"What the hell are you doing in Glen Echo?"

"When you didn't call, I got worried. So I searched your home address."

"My house? But… have you gone to the door?"

"No, I don't think I should. Because--"

I understood, "Because of the cop car."

"Cop *cars*. Plural." She paused before quietly asking, "You want to tell me what's going on?"

"I do. And I shall. I promise you'll get the whole story. Every detail. I promise."

"When?"

"The minute you drag my tasty ass away from these hungry blackflies."

CHAPTER SIXTEEN

"I'd be happier if you were inside the trunk."

"You're not the first woman to tell me that."

Cheyenne had suggested I hide in her trunk in order to sneak me through the roadblock, but I felt I'd used up my quota of stupid stunts for one weekend. Better to ride boldly in the passenger seat and hope the trooper was looking for a single male driving a new Chrysler, not a married couple cruising along in a beat up Oldsmobile.

The cop bent down to take a look inside the car. I had been right about him – he was young, fresh on the job, and most important, heterosexual.

"Morning, folks," he said, his eager eyes immediately settling on Cheyenne. Seated behind the wheel, she flashed him a big juicy smile.

"Trouble, officer?" she purred. Cheyenne wasn't playing dumb – she really didn't know what the state police officer was looking for. When she had asked me earlier if I knew why the roadblock had been set up, I told her I would explain later, once we got through it. This way, no matter what happens, she can legitimately plead ignorance.

The cop coaxed his eyes to abandon the pretty driver long enough to check out her passenger. "Morning, sir," he said.

"Morning, officer." I spoke up loud and clear. The surest way to draw attention to yourself in a situation like this is to try *not* to draw attention to yourself. "Looking for someone?" I said.

"You folks from around here?"

Cheyenne answered for both of us, "Lake Placid."

I tried again. "Someone in particular?"

The cop seemed fine with my stupid question. "A man. Driving a large sedan. Late model. Caddy or Chrysler. Maybe a Lincoln. Light color. Beige. Maybe gold. You folks know anyone who drives something like that?"

Cheyenne looked toward me to take the lead. She knew darn well that this cop's description matches the rental car we'd just abandoned back in the bushes.

"Doesn't ring any bells," I said.

The officer bent down for a better peek inside. I naturally assumed he was just trying to look down Cheyenne's top. But I guess that's the romantic in me.

"You, uh… you injure yourself there, sir?"

It took me a beat, but I figured it out. "Oh, you mean my head?" I touched the wound at my hairline, the injury I'd suffered at the hands of the perp in Henry's basement.

"Your shirt." The officer pointed to my chest. "You seem to be bleeding on it, there."

I looked. Sure enough, there was a dab of fresh blood on my cream-colored denim shirt. It must have dripped form my head wound.

Cheyenne came to my rescue. "Looks like they've nailed you, honey." She pulled out a tissue from a box that was on the floor behind her seat, and she dabbed at my cheek. "Blackflies got you good."

On this cue, the cop whisked his own hand in front of his own face, performing what the locals call *the Adirondack Wave*. "Tell me about it. Little bastards have no respect for a badge." The officer stood back. Obviously pissed off about having to stand outside like this and be eaten alive, he looked back at the lineup of vehicles piling up behind us. "Waste of time anyway. If you ask me, we're locking the door after the horse has bolted." And with that said, he slapped the roof of our Oldsmobile and said, "Have a good day."

"You too, officer," Cheyenne said with a friendly wave.

Once we were safely under way, she turned to me, "Light-colored Chrysler… Sounds familiar."

"It's a long story."

"Your girlfriend call the cops looking for her car?"

"No," I said. "I suspect this has more to do with a nice gentleman who gets upset if you call his elderly Yorkshire terrier a *puppy*." I remembered how, after I'd questioned him about Stanley, the little man outside Henry's music store had watched me drive away. He was the sort who'd take particular note of details like make and model, especially if the driver of the suspect automobile was sporting a fresh, bloody gash on his big dumb forehead.

Cheyenne, who had no idea what I was talking about, waited for further explanation. She was a patient lady. Understanding. A man could get away with a lot if he were dating a woman like this.

"Cheyenne," I muttered. "I'm afraid I haven't been totally honest with you about Henry."

"No kidding."

As I say, she was a smart woman.

* * * * *

Our drive from the police roadblock to my breakfast date in Glen Echo started off with too much talk and ended with too much silence. Ice cold silence. I leaned forward and turned the car's heater control to high. "This thing work?"

She didn't answer. I understood. I sat back. Said I was sorry again. But it didn't help. Outside, the morning sun was trying its best to warm everybody up, but the chill inside the car was too much for mere solar fusion to handle.

Cheyenne was rightly pissed with me, but in my defense, I tried to explain that I had kept her in the dark about Henry's death for her own good – I didn't want to make her an accomplice after the fact. This was the only time during our drive that she actually laughed. This woman knew bullshit when she heard it. So I admitted I was also trying to protect my own ass and thereby keep it free to find my stolen dog. She didn't laugh at that one. She just said I should have trusted her more. She felt deceived. Insulted. Used. She summed up my behavior by telling me I'd acted just like a typical cop. I thought that was hitting a bit below the belt.

As far as Henry's actual death was concerned, Cheyenne felt sad about losing her friend, but she shed no tears. Turns out, while she admired and respected the man, she said she hadn't known him long enough to really get close to him. I didn't want to speak ill of the departed, but I couldn't imagine anyone knowing Henry Tapin long enough to get close to him.

As we approached our destination – the Golden Dragon Restaurant in Glen Echo – I thanked Cheyenne for the lift but told her not to bother parking.

"You can just drop me off here," I said, my hand on the door handle.

She didn't like this idea one bit. "How you going to get home?"

"Not going home." I pointed down the street toward an old stone building that housed both Glen Echo's town hall and its police station. "After I'm finished with Appleyard I'm making a new Chief of Police very happy."

"You're going to the local cops?"

"Seems as good a place as any. This new guy seems like a nice fella. Capturing me should be quite a feather in his cap. That is, if he has a cap yet. My pooch did quite a number on the old one. Chewed the peak right off. Could you believe the town made me pay for that thing?"

She didn't like my plans at all. "You think that's smart? I mean, you say this dog walker saw you leaving Henry's store."

"Covered in blood," I said with an ironic smile.

"Your fingerprints will be all over the scene."

"And the murder weapon."

Cheyenne's eyes widened. "You handled the gun?"

"Wasn't my idea."

"So you left it there?"

"Had to. It had the perp's prints on it."

"And yours!"

"True."

By this time, Cheyenne's eyes were actually larger than her breasts, which were pretty darn impressive on their own. "And now you're going to turn yourself in? You'll be lucky they don't string you up before dinner time."

"I doubt that. Folks round here eat pretty early."

"You won't be free to look for… for what's his name."

"Stanley."

She turned in her seat to address her idiot passenger head-on. "Look… Before you do anything we'll be sorry for, why don't we see what this teacher has to say."

"*We?*"

"Then we can decide if we should take your story to the police or not." Cheyenne shifted the car into reverse and started backing it into a very tight space, maneuvering her Oldsmobile's rear end almost as expertly as she was finessing her own butt back into my plans.

"*We?*" I said.

"You owe me."

Not wanting to distract her from her difficult parking task, I shut up and took the opportunity to look into her eyes. They were dark eyes. Intelligent eyes. Very little makeup. Crow's feet maybe, but only if the crow was wearing socks. When she finished parking and I had her full attention, I said, "You've been a doll. But I don't intend to repay your kindness by getting you involved any further. You've already done too much. I can't thank you enough for all—"

She shut me up by placing her hand on my arm. Gently, as if she were dealing with a frightened client who had never had a full body waxing before. She said, "Let's just see what this science teacher has to say for himself. Okay? He's obviously the brains. Let's see who's been helping him."

I didn't know whether it was those big eyes, the big brains, or the whole sexy package, but I knew when I was beat. All I could do now was hold on to what little control I still had. "*I* do all the talking," I said.

She smiled and squeezed my forearm. She had a pretty good grip. Must've been all that pole work when she danced her way to a math degree. "There's nothing we can do for Henry now." She said. "Let's go in there and see if we can find his mother."

"And my dog," I added.

"And your dog."

I wasn't being insensitive, just honest.

* * * * *

One quick glance around the room told me I'd been stood up. No sign of any middle-aged genius pedophiles in the joint. But then Ken Tamori, the owner of the Golden Dragon, pointed me toward a seemingly empty booth with a balding head barely visible over the high back. As we neared, we found a science teacher with a passion for all things Einstein slumped forward, his big, calculus-laden cranium now resting on his folded arms.

Thomas Appleyard didn't look up as I slid into the bench opposite him. Nor did he stir when Cheyenne slid in beside me. So I picked up the plastic leatherette menu that lay between us, flipped it open, and proclaimed, "They say breakfast is the most important meal of the day."

He raised his head. His pale eyes brushed lightly over my sweatshirt and skidded to a halt on Cheyenne's cotton sweater. He then raised his eyes to assess the rest of my lovely breakfast companion's charms. Curiously, no embers of lust brightened in the man's dull stare, just cool grey ashes of suspicion.

I introduced my dining guests to each other and apologized for my being late. I asked Appleyard if he had ordered anything to eat yet. Without waiting for an answer, I recommended the Western omelet, but only if my guests' stomachs could handle shallots and green pepper this early in the day. All in all, I tried to sound as cheery as a morning radio show. I couldn't help feeling a bit sorry for this poor sap – he's had a rough morning, what with finding his teenage girlfriend in bed with his teenage son.

Ken Tamori, the Japanese owner of the Golden Dragon, who's been passing for Chinese ever since he sold his Thai restaurant, came by to pour coffee and take our orders. Tom Appleyard said he wasn't in the mood to eat, but Cheyenne said she was. I suspect she always is. Once Ken left for the kitchen, I asked Appleyard a couple of questions about his dealings with Henry Tapin. I didn't push too hard – when interviewing a suspect, I generally like to start off playing Good Cop, reserving my Bad Cop for later, if and when I need him. Turns out, I never got to play that second role this morning. Cheyenne beat me to it.

"I think you're full of shit," Cheyenne said as soon as I paused long enough to take a slurp of coffee. She leaned in close to Appleyard. "You insist you have nothing to do with Amy's abduction. Yet you freely admit you'd do anything to get hold of the violin."

"I said I'd *pay* anything. Not *do* anything."

"He's right," I said, still playing the good guy. "I distinctly heard him say *pay*." I turned back to Appleyard and asked, "So how much was your last offer?"

"Forty-five."

"Forty-five *thousand?*" I was impressed.

Appleyard straightened his posture. "It's impossible to put a price on such an item, but I thought that offer was more than fair."

"Do you even play violin?" I said.

Appleyard, who had donned a sports jacket and tie for his upcoming work day, straightened his cuffs as well as his backbone as he said, "Violin, viola, cello, bass viol, and of course, piano."

"A scientist and a multi-instrumentalist," I said. "You and Henry have a lot in common."

Appleyard had nothing more to say. Cheyenne picked up her cup of coffee. Blew on it. Gazed into it. Then she spoke into it. "I don't think it's the violin that Mr. Appleyard is interested in."

Appleyard's eyes turned toward the smart person at the table. It wasn't me. Cheyenne decided her coffee was still too hot. So she put the cup down and said to nobody in particular, "Don't most violins come with cases?"

"Good point," I said, as if I hadn't thought of it yet. Which I indeed had. I said to Appleyard, "So what is it? What's really in this violin case?

A formula for cold fusion? A more relative theory of relativity? An explanation of how break dancing got into the Olympics?"

Appleyard ignored my nonsense. He had nonsense of his own to deal with. "These photos you profess to have… how do I know you haven't already posted them on the internet?"

"I'm afraid you'll have to trust me on that."

Hearing this exchange, Cheyenne looked at me. *Photos?* What the hell was I talking about? Happily for me, she played along. She held her tongue as well as her curiosity.

Appleyard sat back and said, "I don't believe any such photos exist. I believe you're bluffing."

"Ever the scientist. Faith isn't good enough for you. Smart man. You want scientific proof. I'll be happy to show them to you if you wish." I paused before adding, "As soon as you answer a few more questions."

"Now," said Appleyard. "I presume they're on your phone."

"My laptop. In my car. Just let Cheyenne and me have our breakfast. And while we eat, you can tell us where Amy is. Then we'll go out, pull up the photos. You can watch me delete them. Or keep them as a souvenir — your choice. There are some nice ones of you and young Kayla leaving the room together. Gregory what's-his-name, the desk clerk, he has a real talent for photography. I think before he was a fake engineer he was a fake photographer."

"I said *now.*" Appleyard started to slide out of the booth.

But I grabbed his wrist and held him back. "Look, Tom, I'm not saying you shot Gloria or kidnapped her grandmother. Hell, I'm not even saying you stole my dog. I've already met the jerk who snatched my pooch, and his wrists are a lot bigger than yours." I released his wrist and continued, "The violin… forty-five thousand. That's a lot of money. You started out much lower. So tell me, who were you bidding against?"

At this point Ken arrived at our table with our food. I had ordered my usual omelet with sides of sausages, fruit, and whole wheat toast. Cheyenne decided to go with the same thing except with fries and a muffin. As I surveyed my plate, I couldn't help but think, if Lieutenant Manwaring catches up with me, this could be my last decent meal for quite a while. So I dug into it heartily. Meanwhile, Tom Appleyard just sat and watched. And thought. And listened.

After a few moments of silence, punctuated by the smacking of lips and clicking of cutlery, the science teacher finally decided to say something helpful. And curiously, his first word was not a word at all.

"DNA."

"Pardon me?" I wasn't sure if I'd heard right, what with all the chewing. chomping, and clinking.

"I need the DNA to prove my lineage."

Cheyenne understood. "You think you're related to Einstein."

"Professor Einstein is my grandfather." Appleyard made this statement as a simple matter of fact. No boast. No embarrassment. Like he was telling us his shoe size.

I tried to make sense of his wild claim. "You mean… Amy Tapin is your grandmother?" I looked to Cheyenne. "That would make Henry his… uncle?"

"No, no, no." Thomas Appleyard clearly had no patience with idiots. "Amy Tapin is no relation of mine. My grandmother lived in Rochester. She was a musician. Studied at the Eastman School of Music. Majored in viola performance. Summers she worked here in the mountains. A hotel near Saranac."

"And that's where she met Einstein," Cheyenne said.

"The resort had a staff orchestra. They played for dances, concerts, that sort of thing. Somehow, Grandma met Albert Einstein. Story goes, he was captivated by her playing. He invited her to his cottage. They played duets. Violin and viola. He especially admired her Hoffstein."

Cheyenne turned to me and explained. "German composer, late eighteenth century. Hoffstein made his mark, primarily, as Germany's first commercial music publisher of—"

I held up the palm of my hand like the traffic cop I once was and explained to Appleyard, "She likes to show off." I then used that handy outstretched palm to smack the bottom of my ketchup bottle and dislodge a dollop onto my omelet.

Appleyard said, "Approximately nine months after Grandma's little summer of duets with Opa Einstein, my mother was born."

Cheyenne turned to me again, "*Opa* is German for—"

"*Grandfather*, I get it." I turned back to Appleyard, "This must have been about the same time Albert was getting sailing lessons from Amy Tapin. Makes me wonder where the ol' boy found time to build atom bombs."

Appleyard took exception to my remark. "Opa Einstein would have nothing to do with the development of nuclear weapons. He was a pacifist."

Cheyenne spoke up again, "Einstein wrote that his greatest regret in life was helping Roosevelt to develop the atom bomb. Just five months before he died, Einstein said he—"

"Okay, okay, I get it," I wanted to get these two eggheads back on track. I said to Appleyard. "So now you're after Einstein's DNA to prove your own lineage. What's the violin got to do with it? Are you expecting to lift some DNA off the chin rest? Did old Albert drool?"

Appleyard said, "According to what this Amy Tapin woman told certain people in her nursing home, she used to cut Opa Einstein's hair. He didn't like barbers."

I waved my loaded fork in agreement. "Anyone who's seen his photos can attest to that." A piece of sausage fell off my fork. Cheyenne snatched it like a hungry terrier.

Appleyard said, "Apparently, the Tapin woman saved the hair. Says she hid it away. In a case."

I stopped waving my empty fork. "The violin case."

Cheyenne leaned back from the table and wiped her hands with her napkin so she could massage Appleyard's story with clean fingers. "Hair… could work. Others have tried to obtain samples of Albert Einstein's DNA. One woman in Florida who wanted to prove she was related to him got permission to take a sample from his brain."

"They have Einstein's brain?" I asked.

Appleyard picked it up from here. "Slices of Albert Einstein's cortex have been stored at several universities. But in all cases, the tissue has been improperly handled and has proved useless for DNA analysis. I am hoping the deoxyribonucleic acid molecules in his hair will prove less fugitive."

"Usually is," Cheyenne said with her usual air of authority. "Mitochondrial DNA is very stable. It's not as informative as nuclear DNA, but it should be serviceable enough to prove likely genetic succession."

I asked Appleyard, "Did you tell Henry *why* you wanted the hair?"

"He claims he never saw any evidence of any hair nor of any violin case. He's lying, of course. He just doesn't want to know the truth."

"No? Why not?"

"It might prove he is indeed *not* related to Albert Einstein."

I put my fork down. Suddenly I felt full. Too many nuts served with one meal can do that. My plate was now empty, and the way I saw it, so was this man's hope of ever claiming his innocence in the kidnapping of Amy Tapin. I pushed my plate away and said, "So, what you're admitting is, you have an overwhelming motive to get hold of that violin case, a motive nobody else in the world would have except you."

"I know I am incriminating myself by admitting this. But if you think I am willing to kill for this DNA sample, or to kidnap an elderly lady for it, you are mistaken."

"But you do admit you broke into the Tapin cabin to try and get it."

"I admit no such thing."

"You had someone else break in for you," I said.

At this, Thomas Appleyard clammed up.

Assuming I'd hit the nail on the head, I proceeded to countersink it. "You going to tell me who this man is? Who's helping you? Or shall I just go ahead and post those photographs?"

As regards what happened next, I have nobody to blame but myself. I should have seen the suspicious bulge in Appleyard's pocket when I'd first arrived, but the little twerp had already been seated. And the way he was tucked far inside that booth… well, he could have been carrying a rocket launcher in his Dockers and I wouldn't have noticed. Until now.

From under the table, I felt a cold steel barrel press against my kneecap as Appleyard said, "We're going outside. You are then going to take me to your car. I want to see that laptop."

Cheyenne knew nothing about the gun barrel nuzzling my knee cap, but she understood the bluff I was pulling. She backed up my lie. "Forget it, pal. Talk first, photographs second. Who was your accomplice? Who's been doing the heavy lifting for you?"

I tried to settle her down. "Mr. Appleyard has a good point. I think I should take him outside to see the photos."

If Cheyenne was confused, she hid it well. She stuck to her role of bad cop. She addressed her remarks to me now, as if Appleyard weren't at the table. "No photographs until he tells us who he got to break into Henry's cabin for him. It's a cinch this little doink didn't do it. Not alone. Look at him. He's pathetic. An over-the-hill geezer who can't get his little shriveled pecker up without the help of an underage girl. He obviously hired muscle. He certainly doesn't have any himself."

With a weak chuckle, I said, "Now, now, there's no need to say something we might later regret."

Appleyard jammed the gun harder into my kneecap. "Now."

"Fuck you," Cheyenne suggested. "First tell us who owns the green pickup. The one with the bumper sticker on it."

At the mention of the truck, a spark of recognition flashed across the science teacher's eyes. This man knew something about that vehicle. I had to keep him talking. But first I had to stick a cork in Cheyenne. I turned to her, "We're going outside now, Mr. Appleyard and I. You are going to hang back to pay the bill." I indicated her purse that was sitting on the bench beside her. "You got cash in that thing?"

She nodded. She must have known I was bluffing. She knew there were no photographs. Yet here I was inviting this guy to come view them. What was I up to? She had no idea. Neither did I.

The situation was delicate. A crazy little man who thinks he's Einstein's long-lost grandson had his shaky finger on a handgun's trigger. There were four other diners in the restaurant. If there was a scuffle and the weapon should go off, someone might get hurt. And then the crazy gunman might turn the gun on himself. And if that happened we'd never find out who owned that truck. Who has kidnapped Amy. Who has my dog.

I said to Appleyard, "Put the weapon in your pocket and we'll leave. I'll walk ahead of you."

"Weapon?" said a confused Cheyenne proving that sometimes smart people can miss the point.

As Appleyard got up from the table, he slipped the gun into his pants pocket but kept his finger on the trigger. I followed.

Before I left the table I said to Cheyenne, "Leave a nice tip. Ken always slips me an extra sausage."

* * * * *

The door of The Golden Dragon restaurant closed behind me. Slowly. Quietly. Like it expected never to see me again.

Out here on the main drag of Glen Echo, the weather had brightened up considerably. While we had been indoors discussing nonexistent photos and a dead guy's DNA, the sun had been busy with more positive pursuits – burning off the high haze and cueing the robins that it was time to change key. Yes, it was going to be a glorious morning, the kind of morning that makes a man glad to be alive. Especially when he has a gun pointed at his back.

I stepped onto the sidewalk and, instinctively, turned toward Cheyenne's Oldsmobile. But then I caught myself. I spun a smooth pirouette that would have been the envy of any Lake Placid figure skater and proceeded in the opposite direction. I hoped Appleyard hadn't noticed my little slip-up.

As we walked along Main Street, Appleyard was careful to lag just a few steps behind me, just out of reach, with his hand in his pocket, firmly clutching the gun. Cheyenne, for once following my orders, was still in the restaurant, paying the bill.

I filled Appleyard in on our destination, "Just up that alley. The municipal lot." I had a plan, sort of. I was going to wait for just the right moment and precisely the right location to overpower my assailant. It shouldn't be difficult — the guy was a bit older and a lot smaller than I was. All I have to do is draw him close enough. This job, of course, will be safer to do away from this busy street.

We proceeded up a narrow pedestrian walkway that squeezed between a couple of storefronts. This alley soon emptied us into a metered parking lot behind the Main Street stores. Here, as soon as I confirmed that we were alone, I stopped walking and started performing. "Oh, shit," I said, surveying the dozen or so cars parked around me.

At this point, Appleyard, noting that nobody was around to see us, boldly withdrew his pistol from his pocket. Meanwhile, I went on acting up a storm, pretending that I'd lost something.

"My car," I whined, extending my arms toward the sidelines. "I thought I'd parked over there by the wall. But I don't see—" Then, "Oh, right. There it is. I forgot." I turned and walked straight toward Appleyard, pointing over his shoulder. "I parked it by those garbage bins back over there."

Appleyard glanced over his shoulder to see what the hell I was pointing to, and when he did I started to pounce. But I didn't finish. I stopped dead, frozen solid by the sound of a gunshot. And surprisingly, the shot hadn't come from Appleyard's gun.

The bullet chalked the asphalt halfway between Appleyard and me, and for an instant, neither of us moved. Appleyard seemed slightly surprised by the shot, but curiously, not frightened by it. It was almost as if he'd been expecting it.

I glanced upwards and searched the horseshoe of surrounding rooflines. We were corralled by the strip of stores that lined Glen Echo's main street plus a row of townhouses that ran behind us, none of which was over three stories tall. The gun shot seemed to have come from one of the stores' flat rooftops, but I couldn't tell which one.

Appleyard spoke, but not to me. He called out to the sky, "It's all right. He's showing them to me."

Damn! If I wasn't so afraid to move, I'd have kicked myself in the ass for being an idiot. I should have known he'd keep his accomplice close by. As Cheyenne had so undiplomatically pointed out in the restaurant,

Thomas Appleyard did not look the type to pursue any criminal action alone.

Appleyard ignored what had just happened and waved his handgun at me. "Please proceed."

What else could I do but proceed? But to where should I proceed? I had no vehicle parked in this lot. It was all a bluff. So I picked out a car and walked towards it, my footsteps slow, my mind racing. *Maybe I'll try the door handle and when it doesn't open I'll say I must have locked the keys inside. Then I'll suggest he shoot the lock free, and while he's distracted I can make my move and grab his gun. Yeah, that might work. Might not, too. But it's all I have.*

As it turned out, I never needed any more, because after about ten steps another shot rang out. It came from behind me. This time I didn't freeze. I spun around, fully expecting to see Appleyard standing there, clutching a smoking gun in his soft white hand. But I was wrong on both counts. Appleyard was not standing. He was falling. Backwards.

Dead. He was out before he hit the ground. A bullet to the head will do that.

He landed face up, the red bullet hole smack dab in the middle of his brainy forehead like he'd just joined a Far Eastern faith. A faith with remarkably good aim.

Now I moved. Better late than never. I dove for cover behind the nearest vehicle. But I needn't have worried. No shots followed.

After a moment or two of silence – I have no idea how long – I stuck my head up over the vehicle's hood. My eyes searched those rooftops again. Checked all the windows for movement. Nothing. No sign of anyone up there, so I took a chance, left the shelter of the car and went to have a look at the victim.

I felt his neck for a pulse. Found nothing. There was no more I could do. No bleeding to stop. No pain to ease.

All Thomas Appleyard's problems were clearly over. So, I turned my attention to my own. First, I took out my cell phone and dialed 911. I spoke as quickly and precisely as possible: "A man has been shot. Seems dead. Glen Echo. The municipal parking lot behind the Dollar City store. Name of the victim is Thomas Appleyard. Shot sounded like a rifle. Or a large caliber handgun. Two shots fired. Probably from a rooftop of one of the stores. I am in pursuit of the shooter."

She asked me to identify myself, of course. I turned off my phone, of course. They'll have to work for that information. Won't take long, of course.

I took a good, long look at Appleyard's handgun that was now lying at his feet. I was sorely tempted. I could really use that weapon right now. But I resisted. Who knows where Appleyard got the thing and what crimes the weapon could be traced to. So, I left it lying on the asphalt and hurried back to the street.

When I emerged from the alley, I found the street relatively quiet, just a few pedestrians roaming aimlessly, which is exactly the way it should be at this time of the morning. Stores in tourist towns don't need to open early – most of their customers are sleeping late. Apart from the Golden Dragon, many of the retail shops wouldn't be starting their business day for at least an hour yet. So nobody saw me emerge from the alley. Except for one. As soon as she saw me, Cheyenne came running.

"Stay there," I yelled. But she obeyed my order as well as Stanley would have. As she sprinted toward me, my eyes scanned the sidewalk, the road, the storefronts, the rooflines for signs of that shooter.

"I couldn't find you," she said as she neared. "Where the hell were you? What happened?"

I grabbed her by the shoulders and spun her a one-eighty, back toward her car. She never missed a beat, "How'd it go? Where's Appleyard? Did he tell you who was helping him? Did he say if—?"

"Shut up." I hated to be rude, but I was trying to listen.

From the other side of town, I heard a siren's wail. Faint. But growing louder. I couldn't tell specifically who it was – ambulance, fire, or police.

But I saw no reason to stick around and find out.

CHAPTER SEVENTEEN

This time, I offered no choices. I took the wheel. Cheyenne, stunned by the news that the science teacher was dead, quietly eased herself into the passenger seat. As she got in, I happened to notice her place her purse on the floor, between her feet. It was a big purse. Or small feet.

Her purse. I hadn't given it any thought before. But I did now.

The thing was large. A shoulder bag. She usually stowed it in the trunk rather than tote the heavy thing around with her. But this morning she had carried it with her into the restaurant. That was curious.

I pointed to the handbag on the floor. "Don't you usually leave that thing in the trunk?"

"Yes. Well, sometimes. Not always." She could tell something was up, but she didn't know what.

"And this morning you decided to carry it with you."

She answered hesitantly. "I... I had something in it. Something I thought I might need."

"Uh, huh..."

The bag was certainly large enough to hold a handgun. And not just a dinky lady-sized one, either, but the sort of weapon that might have some serious range to it. That sniper on the rooftop had been an excellent shot. Could Cheyenne have shot that well? Hell, what am I saying – everything Cheyenne does, she does well.

She said, "What are you getting at?"

I considered answering truthfully, but decided to just let it go. "Nothing."

I shifted the car into gear. Shifted my brain, too. I was being silly. The bullet that had just drilled through Appleyard's forehead had originated from at least fifty yards away. No handgun has that kind of accuracy. It had to be from a rifle. This purse of Cheyenne's is big, but it isn't big enough to hold a sniper's rifle. Not even a folding carbine. Certainly not one with a scope attached.

Cheyenne said, "Did you notice the truck?"

"Pardon me?" My mind was still on the possible contents of that stupid purse. I was thinking about how comfortable Cheyenne had been last night, holding that shotgun on the motel clerk. Yeah, she'd held guns before.

Cheyenne said, "When I was coming up the street some guy took off in a truck. He was in a hurry."

"Green?"

"Dark green. Could be a Chev."

"Was this before or after the shooting?"

"I told you – I never heard any shooting. I was paying our bill. You owe me. Plus twenty-five percent tip."

"Damn!"

"Too much?"

"Where? What direction was the thing going? This way?" I pointed to the road ahead of us. "North?"

"Actually, this street runs more northwest."

"But he was headed in this direction?"

"Yes."

"Did you notice a bumper sticker?"

She didn't answer me. She was clearly more interested in my suspicious attitude. "What do you think I have in my purse? A Howitzer?"

"I just never saw you carry that purse around before, that's all."

"Pull over," she said.

"Why?"

"I want you to search my bag. Better yet, why don't you go through the whole car. You haven't checked my trunk. Who knows? I could have a bazooka tucked away under the spare."

"That's not what I meant."

"And when you're done with the car you can go over my person. You haven't given me a good frisking yet. Don't skip anything. I know we haven't known each other for long, but we did have had breakfast together."

"I'm sorry. I'm tired. I'm not thinking straight. Old habits are hard to break – I tend to suspect everyone."

"Especially ex-strippers."

"Don't be silly. That has nothing to do with it."

"And while we're talking about suspecting people," Cheyenne said. "Why shouldn't I suspect you? I mean, you're the one leaving the trail of fresh corpses in his wake. Gloria. Henry. Now this teacher. But you don't see me asking you to empty your pockets. And why? Because from the start I've been willing to give you the benefit of the doubt. Although I'm starting to wonder why."

"I'm sorry. It's been a tough morning."

"And judging by current trends I'd say it's going to be a tough afternoon. So be careful how you treat me, buster, because frankly, right now I may be the only friend you've got."

"*Buster?*" I said. "Who uses the word *buster?*"

"I thought it was more polite than *asshole.*"

By now we had argued ourselves all the way out of Glen Echo's town core and were silently cruising on Highway Thirty. After a moment's peaceful contemplation, I asked her, "That green truck… you didn't happen to see a dog in it, did you?"

"Dog? I don't know. Could have been. There might have been a bumper sticker too. Not sure. He was moving pretty fast."

We spent the next hour searching for that green truck. First, north on the highway. Then up and down a few side roads, all the while carefully keeping clear of any sound of sirens that were responding to that parking lot shooting. I was tempted to drive past my house in Glen Echo, see how much heat I was attracting, but I couldn't take the chance on being spotted. Back in that parking lot, when I'd called in the homicide report on my cell, I knew I was identifying myself with the call, but I had no choice. I had to make that call. Appleyard looked fairly dead, sure, but I'm no doctor. What if there was a chance of reviving the guy? Besides, if that phone call didn't identify me, several witnesses at the restaurant certainly could. They had seen me leave with the murder victim, and at least one of them, Ken Tamori, knew me by name.

Of course, the smart thing for me to do now would be to head straight to the cops and turn myself in, just as I had originally intended to do. But I couldn't. Not now. Not at this point in the game. Not when the late Thomas Appleyard has so kindly introduced me to his partner – that sniper. This guy has to be the muscle who kidnapped grandma Amy Tapin and now has my dog. I'm far too close to this perp now to leave the game and sit on the bench.

Should I do the smart thing? No. Better to do what I do best – stumble along and follow my hunch. The way I look at it, any idiot can do the smart thing.

* * * * *

It took about fifteen minutes to drive to Lake Placid. As we coasted along town's main street, I tried my best not to attract any attention. This was not easy. Not with this woman. Cheyenne has lots of friends in this town, and whenever one of them recognized her or her vintage Oldsmobile they turned and waved. And not only would Cheyenne wave back, the crazy chick would lean across me, hit the horn ring, and honk a friendly *howdy*.

When we got to her bookstore, I pulled into the alleyway that runs to her parking spot round back. Cheyenne then hopped out and opened the rear entrance door to her building for me. I then climbed the stairs to her flat. Alone. Cheyenne didn't join me. She had some shopping to do, so she circled back to the street. I needed a hat – something to shade my locally familiar face, but a little less distinctive than the one I had with me. Any moment now, the description of a baseball cap with a large bass clef embroidered on it would be circulating to every cop, park ranger, and Boy Scout in the mountains, so I needed something new.

I didn't have to wait long. When Cheyenne came back to her apartment, she proudly opened her shopping bag to show me her purchase. I had requested, if possible, a cap with an NHL logo. Preferably the Buffalo Sabres. Failing that, the Toronto Maple Leafs. But I didn't get either. Not even close.

"What the hell's this?" I said lifting a limp piece of felt out of the bag. "Isn't a cap supposed to have a bill on it? You know, like a duck?"

She smiled, still proud of her purchase. "I just don't see you in a baseball cap."

"But you *do* see me in this?" I held the thing up between two fingers like I was holding the tail of a dead rat. A *French* rat.

"It'll give you an intellectual air." She slapped the beret on my head and pulled me into the bathroom to shame me with the vanity mirror.

I said, "I look like somebody stole my brushes and easel."

"You're wearing it wrong." She adjusted the silly chapeau to a jaunty tilt.

I said, "Now it looks like I'm keeping the New York subways safe."

She completed the picture by hanging a brand new pair of dark glasses on me. "There," she announced. "Now your own mother wouldn't recognize you."

"If she did, she wouldn't admit it." The plastic sun glasses were not the aviator style I'd requested. Not unless that aviator was Amelia Earhart.

I thanked her for her trouble and stuffed the offending accoutrements back in the bag. I then sat down at her desktop and got back to more productive pursuits. From the Internet I learned that Thomas Appleyard had indeed been a noted citizen. He belonged to several local service clubs including the Masons and Rotarians. He was a member of the local astronomy society and president of a local chess club. His name also featured prominently in Glen Echo's weekly duplicate bridge results. All fascinating pursuits, I'm sure, but not exactly the ideal places to connect with the subgenre of citizens I was looking for – suspected or convicted felons.

Somehow, Appleyard has managed to hook up with an associate who is handy with a rifle and, likely, with burglar's tools. The usual place for this sort of meet-and-greet used to be a local bar, whorehouse, or drug den. But nowadays, the internet has taken over these social functions.

There was nothing more I could do right now, so I logged off. Before shutting down, I printed up a photo of Thomas Appleyard I had found on a Glen Echo High School yearbook web site. It wasn't a great reproduction, but it was good enough for my purposes.

Having exhausted my high-tech resources I went out to have a low-tech chat with Cheyenne about our next move. She was sitting in the living room, and she seemed rather quiet. I guess the loss of her friend Henry was finally sinking in. I told her about what I'd found, or not found, on the internet. We discussed what local bars might be the best places for someone like Appleyard to find criminal assistance. On this subject, she and I were both experts.

"There's nothing in Lake Placid," Cheyenne said. "It's all swishy tourist spots. Same for Saranac."

"There's a joint outside Tupper where the occasional bad actor is known to hang." I checked the wall clock. "But it doesn't open till five or six." It wasn't even noon yet.

"What about Malone?" said Cheyenne. "There's a club up there might fit the bill. Called Doc's."

"How do you know about Doc's?"

"I get around."

"Yeah, but it's a—" I was going to say *strip joint*. Then I remembered how Cheyenne earned her way through university. "Madame Marie Currie?" I said.

She nodded.

I stood up to stretch my legs. If I didn't, I was afraid they, and I, were going to fall asleep. I was beat. I said, "Malone is a long way from here. At least an hour. Same for Watertown and Plattsburgh. If we're going to travel that far this search could take days. We don't have days. *I* certainly don't, anyway. And neither does Amy Tapin."

"Or Stanley," Cheyenne added.

I smiled a *thank you*. That was kind of her.

At this rather tender moment, a noise caught my attention. Nothing unusual, just somebody slamming a car door. Somebody out front. But for some reason, this particular car door sounded familiar. And not a good kind of *familiar*. I went to the window for a look.

Yes, it was a car door all right. And yes, my ears had successfully identified the make and model. It was a Ford Interceptor, standard issue SUV for state law enforcement. The car was parked across the street. One uniformed trooper was standing on the sidewalk waiting for the other trooper to exit the vehicle. That partner, still behind the wheel, was using his rear view mirror to adjust his hat. I never liked those hats. They make a cop look like he's waiting to stomp out a forest fire. Now that I think about it, those dumb hats are probably the main reason why I've always stayed with municipal departments.

When the trooper finally deemed himself fit to be viewed by the fine taxpayers who had paid for his silly headgear, the guy stepped out of his car. I wasn't surprised to see it was Trooper Steve Scott, the young cop who had nabbed me in the forest after we crunched fenders. Nice to see Manwaring gave him a new vehicle.

Okay, so what does this mean? Have these two uniforms come to get me? Has Manwaring somehow linked my name with Cheyenne? Or is Trooper Scott in town on some other errand? Of course, it was always possible he and his partner are just stopping here for an early lunch. There are plenty of fine eating establishments in Lake Placid. Trouble is, most law officers can't afford them.

I turned to Cheyenne and said, as calmly as possible, "I think we have to go, now."

Cheyenne looked out the window to see what had suddenly alarmed me. "Think they'll have the back door covered?" she asked.

"I doubt they have the manpower available." I picked up the bag containing the silly French hat and dark glasses plus the photo of Appleyard.

"How would they know you're here?" Cheyenne said. "Could they have linked you with me?"

"Tell you what…" I moved toward the door. "Why don't we discuss this in your car." From downstairs, we heard the troopers knock on Cheyenne's front entrance, the door beside the book store. "Your front door locked?" I asked.

"I think so. But if Brad sees them, he'll tell them to go round to the back." I assumed Brad was the clerk in her bookstore.

We scurried down her back stairs and out the rear exit. I had guessed right – no police officers were posted back here.

Cheyenne quickly opened a rear door of her car. I got the idea and crawled in. She went around to the trunk and came back with a blanket. I scrunched down on the floor, and she tucked me in for the night.

From the scratchy wool darkness, I said, "This thing smells like garden fertilizer."

"That's Crusader," she said from the driver's seat. "I keep him at Sunnybrook."

"You got a horse?"

"Half owner. Not sure which half."

"Race horse?"

"Dressage. You ride?"

"Not enough to know what *dressage* means."

From under my smelly cocoon, I could feel the vehicle bounce over the curb, take a sharp left turn, and hit the main drag.

"There they are," she announced. "Looks like they've seen us."

"Don't talk. They'll see your lips moving and know you're not alone."

"Von of zem's standing outside, keefing a lookout."

Great, now she was attempting ventriloquy.

"Go slow and don't stare," I whispered aloud, with no logical reason for whispering.

"He's vaving at me. '*Hi zer, handsome.*'"

Great, this bad lounge act was flirting, probably waving back to the trooper.

The engine picked up speed and we continued smoothly away from both her place and, I hope, Scott's parked squad car. If there is any traffic it must be moving well. I was dying to sneak a peek out the back window, but I didn't dare. All I could do was peer up at the back of Cheyenne's head, her thick auburn curls cascading over the seat back. She probably dyes out whatever grey she's got.

We slowed. She glanced into her rearview mirror to give me a play-by-play. "Looks like he's calling the other guy back from the front of the store and… Yup, there he is. He's pointing this way." He voice rose. "Shit, I think they're going to come after us." And with that, she stepped on the accelerator. We then pulled around something.

"Watch your speed. You don't want to give them a reason to chase us."

"Looks like they already have a reason." She stomped on the accelerator like she was killing a bug.

"What are you doing?" I called to her. "They're law officers. You can't outrun them."

"I got eight cylinders that says you're wrong."

"Shit, why do all the women I meet drive too fast."

"Probably because you drive too slow. When I have a minute I'd teach you the Theory of Relativity."

Enough of this crap. I threw the stinky blanket off and sat up. Out the back window I could see Trooper Scott and his buddy about three blocks behind us pulling their SUV away from the curb. Meanwhile, the street ahead of us was bustling with mid-morning tourist traffic. "Don't try it," I said. "You might hurt someone."

"Don't worry. This is the mountains. People come up here for adventure."

"I'm not kidding, slow down. They've got us. Game over. Time to pull over."

But my pleas only encouraged her to step harder on the gas. She said, "I'm beginning to think you're a bit of a wuss."

We were now passing the Olympic sports arena where, thanks to the long gentle curve in the road combined with the town's unusually narrow main street, we were temporarily out of sight of the two troopers. I grabbed Cheyenne's shoulder. "Take the next right. Go up the side street."

"And then where? Half these streets are dead ends. We'll be boxed in."

She was right. The downtown retail section of Lake Placid was strung out along one narrow street that runs along the shore of Mirror Lake. Off that street, the town had little going for itself 'round back. Still, I had to do something to make this crazy lady slow down before we hurt somebody.

I leaned forward and stretched my arm between the split front seats until I could reach the dash. "Pull off now or I'll take those keys out of the ignition."

She looked at my hand and probably thought about slapping it away, but instead, she made a right turn onto what looked like a small street. But it wasn't a street. It turned out to be an entranceway to a parking lot of a motel.

"Park anywhere," I said.

"They'll see us."

"Just park the fucking car." We were in full view of Main Street. But I didn't care.

She slowed down, picked a spot, and wedged us in between a small minivan and a giant SUV. She then shifted into park.

We were now facing the main drag that we had just departed. She slumped down in her seat, her eyes peering over the dashboard like a frog. But instead of watching for passing iridescent dragon flies, she watched for a dark blue SUV with yellow trim.

The siren's scream grew louder, and the glowing lights flashed brighter until the vehicle popped into view directly in front of us. The two troopers inside would have spotted us easily if they had turned their heads. But they didn't. They looked straight ahead trying to avoid pedestrians on the busy, narrow street. They passed us by. And we waited. And we listened. And we heard the siren's cry dissolve slowly into the crisp mountain air, eventually to be replaced by a songbirds' sweet trills.

Cheyenne looked up at the nearby maple tree. "*Turdus migratorius,*" she said.

"Looks like a robin."

"It is."

"So why didn't you say *robin*?"

"Because I'm a pretentious prat." She smiled and asked, "Any idea why your friends came to my place? How they connected me with you?"

"They're not my friends." Actually, I did have an idea how they found me. But before telling her about it, I asked her to show me her cell phone. Meanwhile, I fished mine out of my pocket.

Sure enough, the two devices were the same makes and models. So I turned mine on and called up the contacts list. All the names on it were strangers to me.

I showed her the phone. "Must have grabbed the wrong one this morning when I got off your couch."

"That's mine! But how…?"

I finished the story, "When Appleyard got shot, I called 911."

Cheyenne said, "They think I phoned in the homicide report." Then she asked, "Why the hell did you call 911?"

"What was I supposed to do? Leave him lying there?"

"But you said he was dead."

"I still had to call it in, didn't I?"

She teased me, "There you go, Norris, acting like a cop again."

"Could you do me a favor?"

"What?"

"Could you stop calling me Norris?"

"It's your name, isn't it?"

"Friends call me Tanager."

"But I like Norris."

I held my ground. "Tanager, like the bird."

"Tanager…" she mused. "*Piranga olivacea.* Originally thought to be in the family *Thraupidae* but now classified as *Cardinalidae.*"

"Just Tanager will do." I climbed out of the car, went around, opened her door. "Mind if I take the wheel?"

She slid herself out. "Where we going?" she asked.

"See an old friend. You'll like him. He rarely obeys speed limits. Or any other laws."

* * * * *

Garth Rundle was not glad to see me. But he hid it well.

"Tanager, you tone-deaf cocksucker, what are you doing roaming these mountains without supervision? Last thing I heard, you and the chubby chick were running a gift shop in Saranac."

"It's a *pet* shop. In Lake Placid. And Marlene is not chubby. She is zaftig. How you doing, old buddy?" Garth was neither old nor a buddy, but I was about to ask him for a favor.

Of course, by now it didn't matter much what I said – Garth was no longer listening. His slimy attention had slid off me and was now oozing its way up the legs of the hot babe who was gliding into the room behind me.

Cheyenne emerged from the tavern's beer-soaked shadows and stepped into the dusty spotlight of the service bar. I noticed, as soon as she had entered the empty nightclub she was walking differently. Like she was wearing high-heels instead of sneakers. I guess old habits are hard to break.

Before I had a chance to make the proper introductions Garth jumped the gun with, "I know you." It was an accusation not a greeting. Like he was picking Cheyenne out of a lineup.

"Probably from the country club." Cheyenne said taking a stool at the bar. "The spring cotillion?"

Standing behind the bar, Garth went back to doing what he had been doing when I had first come in, loading beer bottles into an under-counter fridge. "Nope," he said. "That can't be it. Had to miss the spring cotillion this year. Clashed with my Toastmasters Club quarterfinals."

Cheyenne probably thought he was joking. He wasn't.

Garth popped open a bottle of beer and slapped it down in front Cheyenne, announcing, "On the house." Then he opened one for me. "Shall I start a tab, officer?"

"How come I have to pay and she doesn't?"

"It's Ladies' Night."

"At two in the afternoon?"

"We get a lot of Canadians in here, so I've switched to metric time." He turned back to Cheyenne. "The curling club?"

She shook her head. "Sorry, I prefer my ice under my nose, not under my toes."

"She's a poet. Hey, that's it." Garth snapped his fingers in celebration. "The book club. Poetry night. We met at the library."

"'Fraid not." Cheyenne raised her beer and downed half the bottle in one long swallow.

I left my bottle sitting where it was. Too early in the day for me, especially considering I hadn't had any sleep for seventy-two hours. "Garth," I said, "if I wanted to hire someone to do a little job – say, bust into a place, lift an item or two – is there anyone you might recommend for such a venture? Off the record, of course."

Before possibly incriminating himself, Garth asked, "You're not carryin' a badge anymore, right?"

"Right."

"Let me think… That's a tough one…" Garth pondered the problem. Meanwhile, he went back to loading his fridge.

I waited, gave him a few moments, then goosed him along with, "No one springs to mind, huh?"

"You kidding? Plenty spring to mind. That's the problem. You gotta narrow your search, officer. This item you wish purloined – is it readily negotiable? Does it come in small plastic bags? Does it have wheels? And if so, how many? I know a guy who can make an eighteen-wheeler disappear faster than Doug Henning." Garth turned to Cheyenne, "You're probably too young to know who Doug Henning was."

Cheyenne said, "Canadian magician. Impressive moustache. Big smile. Now deceased."

Garth was impressed. "You must be older than you look."

I said, "No, just smarter." I unfolded the photo of Thomas Appleyard that I'd pulled from Cheyenne's printer. "This gentleman ever come in here making the same inquiry I just posed?"

Garth took the photo and held it under the pin spots that shone down on the pyramid display of premium liquor bottles that have remained untouched since the place opened. "This guy? Uh, huh. Yeah, sure. It's Tom. Tom, uh…"

"Appleyard?" Cheyenne prompted.

"That's it," said Garth. "Tom Appleyard. High school teacher. Short. Losing his hair. Bit of a know-it-all. Answers your questions long before you bother asking them."

I said, "So he's a regular here?"

"Here? You kidding? No way. That guy wouldn't be caught dead in a joint like this. Don't think he even drinks." Garth handed the photo back to me. "No, I met Tom at the gourmet club."

Cheyenne couldn't hide her surprise. "You belong to a gourmet club?"

Garth ignored her insult and pointed at the photo. "Weird fucker. Quiet. But smart as hell. Hangs with that bunch of brainy hermits. The, uh…"

"Cold River Council?" Cheyenne said. I wish she hadn't.

"That's the bunch." Garth turned his attention back to Cheyenne again. "Tell me, honey, how long you been up here?"

"Present abode? One year, two months, and eight days."

"You mind some advice?"

"From you? Anytime." She was putting him on.

Garth leaned on the bar with both elbows so he'd be nice and close to his audience. He spoke softly. "Don't hide from the weather. You can't let Old Man Winter win. You gotta fight him toe-to-toe. You gotta get out of the house. Be a participant. A player. You gotta join, join, join." He banged his fist on the bar demanding that all beer bottles jump in agreement. "You gotta join till it hurts."

I explained to Cheyenne, "I don't think there's a club or social organization north of Albany that Garth does not belong to. I'll bet the only one he's missed is the Girl Guides."

"You'd lose," said Garth. "Wanna buy a cookie?" Garth turned his attention back to Cheyenne, "All's I'm sayin', babe, is don't become a mushroom like so many newbies to the Park do. Sitting inside with their devices. Scrolling through social media. Surfin' porn. Shit, nowadays men would rather look at pictures of tits than step out the door and see the real thing." Garth turned back to me. "Remember couple of years ago when I tried putting dancers in here? Brought some girls from Albany. A few from Montreal. Shit. Didn't work any better than the trivia nights. Or the karaoke."

"You could try bands again," I suggested.

"You still playin' rock?"

"Blues, R&B, funk…"

"Shit, I'd do better with the strippers." On the word *strippers*, Garth turned back to Cheyenne and squinted. "Geez, I know that face… Model Railroading club?"

Somebody had to steer this conversation back on track, so I grabbed the wheel. "This Tom Appleyard guy… far as you know, he ever ask around looking for some help? You know… No questions. No names."

"Muscle? No, not that dude. Not the sort. Far as I know, that guy's as straight as a Sunday preacher." This thought inspired Garth to turn to Cheyenne once more. "That's it. Church. Glen Echo First Evangelical. The choir. You sing."

"Ah, ya got me," Cheyenne admitted.

"Aha! I thought so." Garth was happy now. "Didn't recognize you out of your choir robe."

"Nobody ever does." Cheyenne toasted this thought with the last swallow of her beer.

* * * * *

When we returned to the sunshine, Cheyenne asked which bar we were headed for next. I think she liked this aspect of detective work. I hated to poop in her pilsner, but I told her I didn't think we should waste time visiting any more beer joints. From the way Garth had described him, it's hard to imagine Appleyard would ever be comfortable recruiting help in such a place.

On this subject, Cheyenne had a suggestion of her own. "Appleyard is a teacher, correct?"

"Correct."

"So maybe he asked one of his students to lend a hand."

"Don't you think that's asking a lot of a kid? Breaking and entering? Murder?"

"If the money's good enough…"

I wasn't buying this idea. "That stunt in that parking lot… Right between the eyes. From at least a hundred yards. No kid's that good a shot."

"And the sniper never fired at you?"

"Don't think so. Could have. Easy. I was out in the open. But no. Once Appleyard was taken care of, the shooter took off. Left me alone."

Cheyenne understood, "To take the heat."

"Looks that way." We had reached her car. "Mind if I keep driving?"

"You're the boss."

I wish I could have believed that. I opened the driver's side door. But before I had my butt in the seat I heard someone from behind us call out.

"Tanager, hold on." It was Garth. He was walking towards us. Not hurrying, of course. Garth doesn't hurry for anyone. He could if he wanted to. He's built for it. Small and wiry. But that's not his style. He's too cool.

"Home-builts," Garth said when he finally reached reasonable speaking distance. "Kit planes."

"What about them?"

"That's where I know your boy. I just remembered. It wasn't the train club. It was the kit airplane club. Appleyard was a member."

"Kits? Like models?" My mind flashed back to the plastic airplanes I'd seen in Appleyard's son's bunk room.

"Not models," Garth said. "Real planes. One's you build in your garage." Garth pointed towards a shed behind his restaurant. "I've been working on mine for about eight years. I figure if I live for another eight, I should have it finished."

Cheyenne, from the far side of the car, said, "Tom Appleyard was building a kit plane?" From the intense expression on her face it was evident she thought this information was a lot more important than I did.

Garth said, "A few years ago, I went to a couple of meetings. That was enough. Dull bunch. Not exactly the best place for social networking."

"No women, huh?"

"None I'd like to get off the ground with." Garth swatted a black fly. Then another. "Probably not important. Just thought you might want to know." Garth turned to retreat inside before he got eaten alive. Unlike us, he was standing in the shade, which the bugs like.

I asked the back of his head, "What was the name of this club?"

"EAC. Adirondack chapter." With arms flailing, Garth picked up his speed. I'd never seen him move this fast. The little buggers almost had him jogging.

"EAC?" I asked. But I was too late. Garth had disappeared inside. So Cheyenne answered for him.

"Experimental Aircraft Club," she said, flashing one of her juiciest smiles yet. She understood the importance of that one particular word to me.

A picture flashed across my mind, an image of a green pickup truck with the word *Experimental* on it.

Cheyenne continued, "It's an FAA designation. Their official name for a home-built aircraft is *Experimental*."

I turned and we followed Garth back into the bar. Cheyenne ordered a second beer, and this time, I had one as well. Garth told me that the EAC Adirondack chapter was small, so we shouldn't have much trouble tracking down a member who drove a green pickup. Garth even furnished me with the name and phone number of the president of the local chapter.

Before leaving his bar I had one last favor to ask of Garth. I decided to make it a tit-for-tat sort of deal.

"Garth, how'd you like to have the best band in the mountains play for you any Saturday night you wish, no charge."

I watched the wheels turn as Garth tried to figure out what the catch was. It was like watching a kid examine a wrapped package received from his spinster aunt. Was it going to be a computer game or socks? Finally, he asked, "Whose band?"

"My band."

"Aw, shit." Poor Garth. It was socks.

I said, "You gotta admit nothing else has worked in here. Why not give blues and funk a try?"

He knew there was a slim chance I might be right. But he also knew there was a catch. "You said for free. Nothing's for free."

"Tell me, Garth… what are you driving these days?"

CHAPTER EIGHTEEN

Back in Lake Placid, Trooper Scott had seen us leave town in Cheyenne's Oldsmobile, and by now he would have posted a bulletin on it. So I asked Garth to lend us one of his spares. Like many people out here in the sticks, Garth keeps several vehicles in service. With almost no public transport, very few taxi cabs or car rentals, it's always smart to keep a spare vehicle ready to roll. Besides, as every man knows, it's hard to throw out a working car just because it has a few holes in the floor.

This one barely had a floor.

I shifted her into second, and the old girl rasped her disapproval as if I'd asked her to play a fifth game of pickle ball. The transmission sounded like we were grinding keys at the hardware store.

"I thought you said you could drive a standard," Cheyenne said.

"This clutch is shot. We should have taken the van."

"No way." Cheyenne patted the dashboard of Garth's vintage Datsun 240Z as if it were a puppy's forehead. "A hundred and forty-six cubic inches, one hundred and fifty horses, Chapman struts on back, MacPhersons on front, a single over-head cam, and disc brakes. For its time, this baby had everything."

"Except a decent stereo system." I pulled the cartridge tape out of the dash and handed it to her to put away. "See what else you can find."

Cheyenne lifted a box of tapes out from the hatch area behind us. While she clattered her way through them, I wrestled the stick shift into a quieter gear. Garth had given us a choice of two vehicles. One was a two-year-old minivan, and the other was this fifty-year-old 240Z. I didn't need to guess which one Cheyenne would fall in love with. When she insisted we take this sporty Datsun, Garth didn't argue. That should have been my first clue that this old girl was not all that she seemed. I'm talking about the car, that is.

I struggled to shift into third, but the sleek bit of flash, with her new coat of makeup, wasn't thrilled with my choice. I'm not talking about the car now.

"Pull over. Let me try." Cheyenne said.

I brushed her meddling hand away from the stick shift. "You just see if you can find something we can listen to that doesn't sound like a moose clearing his sinuses." The tapes in the box were part of Garth's extensive eight-track Country Classics collection. Apparently, Garth had tried to purchase the car's eight-track player alone, but the owner wouldn't sell the vintage tape player without the vintage car attached.

I reached down to crank up the window. Surprisingly, the handle turned just fine, free and easy. But no glass ever appeared for my efforts. This, combined with yesterday's rain, put me hip to why the floor mats were damp.

By this time, I felt I may have made a mistake trading this sick wreck for Cheyenne's healthy Olds. But my attitude changed when, near Saranac Lake, I spotted an unmarked radar unit sitting on the shoulder of Highway Thirty. As we passed by the state trooper, he barely gave us a second look. All he did was chuckle at the middle-aged goofball seated behind the wheel of the snazzy sports car wearing the dark glasses and the French beret with the hot babe seated beside him.

We were headed to the Adirondack Regional Airport, It's located eight miles northwest of Saranac Lake. Earlier, back at Garth's bar, I had tried phoning the president of the Experimental Aircraft Club, but he didn't answer, so I figured my next best bet was the airport. Garth had told me this is where many of the members of the local EAC rented hangar space.

As we drove through the town of Saranac Lake I kept my eyes peeled for any more police. Happily, I didn't see any, but I did run across one person in uniform who, despite my clever disguise, almost gave the game away.

We were stopped at a pedestrian crossing near the elementary school when I recognized the lady crossing guard. Back in Glen Echo, when I was police chief, I had once detained this woman for shoplifting a pair of reading glasses from a drug store. I had let her off the hook, though, because she explained that, due to cataracts, her eyesight had been so lousy she hadn't realized she'd walked past the cashier. It seemed like a reasonable excuse, given her age. But now, as I watched her guiding a group of school children across the busiest street in town, I hoped she had been lying about that poor eyesight.

As she led her young charges to safety she looked my way and waved. "Hi, Chief Tanager. Love the hat."

Well, at least her eyesight was okay.

* * * * *

Adirondack Regional Airport is certainly not O'Hare, Kennedy, or even Buffalo International, but it's big enough if all you want to do is fly to Plattsburg or Boston. The terminal building is a one-story brick affair with no control tower but a darn fine lunch counter. Trouble is, that lunch counter serves only breakfast and lunch. I don't know what the local pilots do for dinner. I guess that's why they fly to Plattsburg and Boston.

When we walked into the terminal, Cheyenne headed straight to the ladies' room – a facility she had wisely avoided at Garth's bar. Meanwhile, I rattled around the empty lobby. Eventually, a man stuck his head out an office door to see what all the damned rattling was about.

If a Hollywood director were casting the role of a brick-jawed, sixty-year-old airline captain with a dimple on his chin so deep it echoed, this was the guy to go with.

"Can I help you?" His voice was as deep as his dimple.

"Yes. Maybe. I hope so. I'm looking for a pilot."

"You've come to the right place." He smiled. I turned away to avoid the glare. He said, "You looking to charter?"

"No, I don't want to fly anywhere. You see, it's kind of a long story, but my, uh… my sister was in this car accident…"

His jaw suddenly tightened from stone to, I guess, harder stone, and he started heading for the front door. "Is she all right? Are you looking for a medevac flight? Where is she?"

"No, no. The accident happened three months ago."

The granite jaw turned to sandstone. "Three months?"

I found my groove and went with a peppy rhythm. "It was quite serious. Car went over a bridge. Caught fire. She almost died." I was in the pocket now. "In fact, we would have lost her if it weren't for this wonderful man who came along and pulled her out of the burning wreckage. I gotta tell ya, this man was quite a hero."

"Sounds like he was quite a hero."

Was there an echo in here? Maybe it was that dimple. I continued, "Yes. And like so many heroes he didn't stick around to bask in his glory."

"They never do."

"No, I think it's a union thing." I smiled. He nodded, in stern agreement. I continued with my tale, "After the ambulance showed up, the man split. Disappeared. Never to be heard from again. We never got to thank the guy. My sister never got to express her immense gratitude to this brave man. And that's what brings me here today."

"I understand."

He did? That was strange considering I barely understood what I was getting at. I said, "You see, I've found out that this man was a pilot."

My audience nodded knowingly, as if to say, *Of course he was a pilot. All great heroes are pilots. What else did you expect him to be —a cop? A bass player? A pet shop owner?*

I continued, "I found out that this man flies out of this area. Maybe this airport. But unfortunately that's all I know about him – that, plus the fact that my sister remembers he was driving a green pickup truck."

"A green pickup…"

"Late model. And I believe he was a member of the Experimental Aircraft Club. Geez, I sure would like to find him. Thank him. Maybe give him a reward if he'll accept it."

At this point, Cheyenne emerged from the ladies washroom. The airport guy saw her and flashed a smile so bright it could blind a polar bear. As she neared us, he said to her, "Nice to see you're feeling better."

"Uh, yes…" Cheyenne didn't understand. She looked questioningly at me. We hadn't discussed this story. I was ad-libbing my melody line to go along with the changes.

The guy said to Cheyenne, "Sounds like you're one lucky lady to have made it out alive."

Cheyenne looked back at the restroom wondering what calamity she had just dodged inside that stall.

The pilot decided it was time to formally introduce himself. He was Jim Whiteside, Director of Operations of Adirondack Regional. Cheyenne told him her name. I joined in but gave him a phony name just in case the guy had heard about me from when I worked as Chief of Police. Turned out I needn't have worried. Jim Whiteside was new to the area and to the job, all of which he made crystal clear when he told Cheyenne about his recent divorce that had precipitated his move from California where he had been in charge of a much larger, and sexier, operation with longer, thicker runways, a tall, sturdy upright control tower, a hard-wired electronic landing system, and a tasty lunch counter that served hot, steamy sausage rolls.

I think this guy liked Cheyenne.

Anyway, I grabbed hold of the control yoke and banked the conversation back to the reason I was here. Did this man know of any pilots who drove green trucks? He said he didn't, but he was new here, so he called in an employee from one of the hangers, a denim over-alled mechanic who had been working on planes since Orville and Wilbur were still twisting rubber bands. This old guy was a great help, and by four o'clock Cheyenne and I were walking out of the airport with a couple of good leads plus an open invitation from Jim Whiteside to go flying any time, although I think the invite was meant more for my *sister* than for me.

The elderly airplane mechanic had mentioned two pilots who, as far as he could recall, drove green pickups. One was a physician named Dr. Johannasen. When I asked if this man might belong to the Experimental

Aircraft Club, the mechanic said he doubted that any practicing surgeon would have enough spare time to mess around building a plane in his garage. Besides, the good doctor already owned a nice Beech Sundowner.

The other owner of a green pickup had indeed built a plane of his own. The mechanic knew this because, while this pilot was constructing his kit plane, he had made a pest of himself at the airport, hanging around, borrowing tools, and asking for free advice. That was a few of years ago, though, and since then this man hasn't been seen around here. Apparently, the plane the fellow had built was a floatplane and therefore doesn't use a conventional landing strip. Unfortunately, the mechanic couldn't remember this float plane pilot's name, but that was okay – he knew the guy had a waterfront home near the community of Gull Lake. So all I had to do was drive to the lake and ask around. I should have no trouble finding someone who flies a float plane in and out. Simple and easy, the mechanic said.

So I grabbed hold of Cheyenne's hand, and together we skipped off to her car, happy in the realization that soon we would be saying hello to one confused, kidnapped elderly lady and one blissfully trusting pooch.

Simple and easy.

CHAPTER NINETEEN

Gull Lake is one of those settlements that's so small the *Welcome* sign and the *Please Come Back Again* sign are painted on the same moose. Unfortunately, I couldn't find that moose. After driving through the village once without actually realizing it, I turned the car around and took a second shot. The GPS on my phone insisted I was at the correct junction of two roads and one lake with a government boat launch, but I saw no signs of an actual settlement. No general store. No post office. No gas station. Just a thin fringe of modest homes rimming the rocky shore of a fairly large lake.

On this second pass, I noticed an elderly woman dressed in sandals and a bathrobe pushing her aluminum walker up her driveway away from her mailbox. She had a handful of mail and flyers stuffed into the wire basket of her walker. When she saw that my car was slowing down, she waited patiently to find out what I might want. That's the difference between city folk and North Country folk – when people up here suspect that you might need assistance they don't turn and run the other way – not unless you're wearing a suit and carrying a Bible. And even then, many of them will still hang back to politely tell you their mortal souls were already saved last month, thank you.

I climbed out of Garth's vintage car but was careful to keep the vehicle placed between myself and the elderly lady so I wouldn't intimidate her. "Good afternoon," I said. And it really was a good afternoon. Warm and sunny. "I wonder if you might be able to—"

"Nice wheels."

"Thank you." I imagine her hearing wasn't too good, so I spoke up. "I'm looking for a particular house. Don't know the address or the name, but I know it's on this lake and that the owner flies his own plane. A seaplane. So I thought maybe—"

"What is it? A sixty-nine? Seventy?"

It took me a beat to catch on. "My car? A seventy-two, I believe. The house I'm looking for would have an airplane and maybe a green—"

"Not the original paint, though."

"No, I believe she's been repainted."

"Thought so. That robin's egg blue didn't come out until seventy-four."

Through her open passenger window, Cheyenne joined the party, "Sounds like you know your cars."

"My late husband had a Z. Second hand. It was a present. Me and the kids chipped in. Give it to him when he retired."

"I'll bet he was thrilled," Cheyenne said. "Is it still on the road?"

""Fraid not. Car's gone. And so is my husband."

"Oh, I'm sorry," I said.

"Joe dearly loved that car. In fact, near as we can figure, he's still in it."

I didn't understand. "Still in it?"

"We warned him. Told him not to take it out on the ice. Especially that late in the season. But you couldn't tell Joe nothin'. Never found him nor the car. So, what's she do? Zero to sixty in under seven, I bet."

"That's about right," said Cheyenne.

By this time I figured I was wasting my time here, so I finished up with, "You have a nice day, now. Okay?"

"And you stay off the ice," she said.

"You bet." And I got back into the car.

But the elderly lady wasn't through. "And drive slow. Else you'll bust your oil pan on that dirt road."

"What dirt road?" I said. The highway we were presently parked beside was paved smooth.

"The road that leads to that house with the plane." She pointed down the highway. "Next right. Far end of the lake. Mile and a quarter. Last property. Road's a bitch. That's why he flies in."

I pushed my luck and asked, "You wouldn't happen to know what sort of vehicle this pilot drives would you?"

"Got two. A Subaru and a F-150 pickup. Both four by fours. In winter couldn't get nothing else in there. Your snazzy Datsun, forget it. Not over snow."

"The F-150… is it green?"

"As a leprechaun's pecker." The lady turned away from us and started walking up her driveway. As she left I heard her say, "Yup, the Z's a fine car, all right. Lousy boat. But a fine car."

We took off and found the side road easy enough. But after fifteen minutes or so of bouncing and banging over roots and rocks without seeing a residence with a floatplane, I grumbled to Cheyenne that we might be putting too much reliance in the NASCAR granny's memory. But Cheyenne kept the faith, and sure enough, after a few more minutes of pan-scraping and tooth-rattling, we rounded a curve atop a cliff, and below us, across a small bay, we saw it – a small yellow floatplane sitting moored to a dock.

We followed the road down the hill and around a bend to the subject property, but we didn't stop. Not yet, we didn't. I wanted to know what might be waiting for us. So we continued a ways past the hidden, unadorned driveway and along what was left of this rumor of a road. A hundred yards later, the rumor finally died, dissolving into an open field of sand and sparse grass. I turned a one-eighty and parked behind the cover of a grove of sumac. From here, looking along the lake front, we could see the plane, a house, a garage, and a small barn. If this place had originally been a working farm, my guess is it must have raised sheep. I couldn't imagine anything else possibly thriving on this craggy landscape. Nowadays, of course, the property was most likely just a residence.

When we had passed it by, I hadn't seen any name posted on a mailbox, so we still didn't know exactly whom we were dropping in on. But that didn't matter. Not anymore. We were now well beyond the point of no return. Our car was in trouble. I hadn't told Cheyenne, but for the last ten minutes, the needle on our engine's temperature gauge had been sitting in the red. My guess is, we had done some lethal damage to our car's undercarriage, probably around the rusty radiator.

I parked in the weeds, shut down the overheated engine, and gave Cheyenne the bad news about our mortally injured vehicle. As always, she saw the glass, or in this case the radiator, as half full. "Good," she said. "Then this time we won't have to lie about our car troubles." And with that, she opened her door to get out of the car.

"Hold on a minute," I said, grabbing her arm. "The last time we pulled this off we had anonymity on our side."

She realized the problem. "Oh, yeah, right. This person or persons unknown may have already seen you."

"Seen me and taken a shot at me."

She shut the door to keep the flies out. We sat, staring at the house. "Looks like nobody's home," she said. "Don't see any cars around."

"No green trucks either."

"Could be parked in that garage."

I sat back to ponder our next move. "I need to do a little reconnaissance. But in broad daylight like this I'll be asking to get my ass shot off."

"We could wait till dark."

"Could be a long wait," I said.

She brushed fresh dust off the clock face on the dashboard. "Sun sets in three hours and twenty-seven minutes."

My eyes were still on the house. "If that were your confused grandmother tied up in there, would you want to leave her for a further three hours and twenty-seven minutes?"

Cheyenne looked at me thoughtfully before saying, "You must have been an awfully nice cop."

"A pussycat," was all I could say. I was busy mulling our situation over. Finally, I said, "There's no other way to do this. I have to march up to that house and knock."

"Right. Let's go." Cheyenne started to open her door again. But I grabbed her arm again. It really was muscular. I don't know if I could take her in a wrestling match or not, but I'd enjoy trying.

I said, "If I don't come back in fifteen minutes, you crank this baby up and drive as far as she'll take you. Turn the heater on. That should give you an extra mile or two."

She understood, "Bleed heat off the engine."

I stepped out of the 240Z saying, "Until then, leave the vehicle hidden here. That way he won't know that you are all I've got."

"Hey…" she objected.

"I'll bullshit him that I've got backup. My posse's hidden in the trees. We have the place surrounded."

"Too bad you made me toss that shotgun away."

"Too bad about a lot of things." I walked around to her side of the car and leaned into her open window. I kissed her. It wasn't a big, sloppy tongues-trying-to-unstop-the-drain sort of smootch. Just an offhand goodbye-to-the-wifey-at-the-airport kind of kiss. But I followed it with, "Maybe when we're finished with all this, we can do that right."

She smiled.

* * * * *

The walk to the house took just a few of moments, but it gave me an opportunity to check for signs of life. There weren't any. The homeowners appeared to be out, probably still at work, wherever that might be. After all, it was late Monday afternoon.

The house was forty or fifty years old, but in good shape. It sat well back from the lake's shoreline and high enough up the grade not to worry about spring flooding. Wood framed and sided in vinyl, the structure stood a story-and-a-half tall. Three dormer windows peered out of the steep roof. Probably two bedrooms and a bath. Surprisingly, the building appeared to have a full basement, which is not always the case here in the Adirondacks where so many structures are built on rock.

I wasn't trying to sneak up on anybody – quite the opposite, actually – so when I put my big feet on the wooden steps of the front porch I planked them down good and hard so as to announce my approach to anyone inside. It was like whistling on a hike to alert the bears.

My noisy approach worked. Somebody had indeed heard me, and the voice I heard made my heart soar. Sound's crazy, maybe it's my musician's ear, but I immediately recognized his bark. "Hey, pal," I called blindly, through the closed door. "How ya doing, buddy?" I'd hate to admit this to anyone who doesn't own a dog themselves, but yes… my eyes teared up a bit.

I opened the outer screen door and knocked on the closed inner one. The barking grew louder, more frantic, and I soon heard claws scuffling and climbing their way up the other side of the door. This was particularly great news. It meant the thief hadn't tied him up or caged him. I know some dogs don't mind being confined – I even sell travel crates for just such a purpose – but Stanley always hated confinement. He must have suffered a bad experience before he had come to me. I've never been able to place him into a crate without a lot of whining and whimpering. Some of it coming from the dog.

Except for Stanley's eager *Come on in and join the party* bark, my knock remained unanswered. I tried the doorknob. I wasn't surprised when it turned. At the end of a deserted road like this, there would be little point in locking up.

I edged open the door just a few inches – a wet brown nose forced it the rest of the way. I tried to keep him contained – I didn't want him running loose. But turns out I had nothing to worry about. He had no intention of leaving my side.

"You miss me, pal?" The pooch answered by jumping up and trying to lick my face off. I only wished I could have shown this kind of honesty moments ago when I'd kissed Cheyenne.

As I patted his big head, I looked down the hallway. "Are you alone?" I called out to the house, "Anybody home?"

My question, I suspected, was needless. Unless the inhabitants of this place were stone deaf they could hardly have missed the racket Stanley and I had just made. Of course, now that I thought of it, poor old Amy Tapin could be hard of hearing. So I called out again, this time louder, "Amy? You here, honey?" I stepped farther inside the house. "Amy? Amy Tapin?"

No electric lights were turned on, but plenty of daylight filtered through the shear drapes and large windows to tell me that the place was clean and well-kept. Sexist that I am, I could feel and smell a woman's touch. I didn't detect the presence of any kids, though. The place was too tidy. Plus, people with children tend to festoon the walls with family photos. All I saw here was decorative prints and a couple of large aerial photos that were probably shot from that plane parked down at the shoreline. Of course, all this was just my fleeting first impression. I wasn't here to search details. I was here to find an imprisoned elderly woman.

With Stanley sticking close at my heels, I combed through the main floor, anxiously opening every door. Nobody hidden in the living room. Nothing in the dining room, same for the kitchen. I did notice a doggie bowl with some water in it sitting on the kitchen floor. Whoever lived here may have committed some terrible crimes, but I am truly in debt to them for taking good care of Stanley. Hard to hate somebody like that. But hey, the day is young.

I hurried up the stairs.

A narrow hallway led to a large master bedroom with two dormer windows poking out of the slanting ceiling, one on either side of a queen-sized bed. Behind the open door, a large wardrobe stood with its cherrywood back up against an inner wall like it was trying not to be noticed. I swung open the doors of the piece. No hostage inside, just clothes, a man's and a woman's. What this couple actually looked like, I had no idea. No family portraits on either of the nightstands nor on the walls.

Across the hallway, a second bedroom was furnished as a den or an office. A quick glance at the book shelves told me what I already knew — someone here had an interest in carpentry and home-built planes. He or she also seemed to enjoy murder mysteries. I hoped this interest was strictly literary.

Next door to this room, a small bathroom was wedged in between the home's end wall and a linen closet. Neither the linen closet nor the curtained bathtub contained any bound and gagged ladies, so I hurried back to the staircase. As I ran down, I was careful not to trip over the rather bored pooch at my feet. Stanley already knew this place far too well to act interested in my search.

I continued down a second flight of stairs, past the first floor, and down to the basement. Stanley stayed close, his interest peaking. He probably hasn't been down here before. Or maybe he thought I was looking for his leash.

The basement stairway emptied into a finished recreation room that was seemingly built around a big screen TV. Off this room sat a furnace room and a laundry room. No workshop. The homeowner probably has an outbuilding for that. Lastly, a two-piece washroom squatted in a corner, and a small cold storage cupboard hid under the stairs. No elderly ladies were tucked away in either, just toilet rolls, canned goods, and beer. When you live this far out of town, you have to store away plenty of essentials.

Satisfied I had touched all bases, I led Stanley back to the stairs. "Well, fella, looks like you're the only treasure to be found here today." I patted him, then planted my foot on the first step of the stairs. But that's as far as I got. I didn't fall. Something had caught my eye.

A face. No, several faces. They huddled together inside a picture frame, one of several cheap frames that were screwed onto the basement's cement block wall. When I'd first come down here I had walked right past these photos without taking any notice. My mind was on other things. Plus, I couldn't see too well – my eyes hadn't yet become accustomed to the dull light. But now…

This one particular frame held a standard group photo of a standard graduating class. Nothing unusual about the faces – just your usual array of proud but stern students, mostly male, all about the same age and none of them seemingly impressed with this, or any other, fact. But it wasn't the somber head shots that had caught my attention – it was the items sitting on top of those heads that had stopped my further progress up the stairs.

Hats. The graduates were wearing beige Stetson hats. All with purple bands. I was looking at a graduating class of the New York State Police Academy. And they were looking straight back at me. Except, they didn't seem nearly as surprised about this as I was. I have, of course, seen many similar graduation photos. Matter of fact, I have one, myself. I think it's at my mother's house. Or my ex-wife's. Not still on a wall, though.

Stanley, who was now halfway up the stairs, looked back to see what was keeping me. I let him wait. My eyes were busy skimming over this gallery of cadet faces, searching for a particularly eager puss. And it didn't take long before I crashed into it. Head-on. Again.

In this photo, Trooper Steve Scott looked a few years younger and a couple pounds thinner, but it was him, all right. Who else could it be? It all made sense to me now. My mind jumped back to our first meeting, the car crash on that forest road when I was leaving the cabin. At the time, I had assumed the young Trooper was responding to the 911 call placed by that nice kid down the highway. Sure, I should have been suspicious about this officer's quick response. But hey, my mind was on other things – like the mortally wounded woman bleeding to death in my back seat. Could Trooper Scott have been in the area because he had just shot Gloria. Was he now returning to the scene of his own crime in the guise of answering the bulletin I'd phoned in? Didn't cross my mind at the time. Sure as hell did now.

I returned my gaze to the photo gallery to check out the other pictures mounted to the concrete. I skimmed quickly over a collection of familiar standards – the usual stuff a guy hangs in his rec room or den. Shots of baseball and hockey teams. A couple more school class photos. Most of the standard glories a guy gathers before settling down to domestic bliss.

I took a closer look at those school photos. Sure enough, one of them was taken on the front steps of Glen Echo High. This would explain how Trooper Scott might know our local science teacher and Einstein groupie, Thomas Appleyard.

As I poked through Scott's past, Stanley grumbled. *Are we going? Some of us have to pee.* There was nothing more I could do here. I had my dog, but I did not have Amy Tapin. It was time to search the out buildings. First, though, I have to call Manwaring and warn him about Trooper Scott. But before that, I have to go and get Cheyenne before she assumes the worst and tries to drive off for help. I hurried up the stairs, Stanley loping ahead of me.

Outside, I was happy to see our borrowed sports car still waiting patiently in the grove of sumac at the far side of the field. I waved. Cheyenne started the engine and headed this way. But of course she didn't get far. The thirsty thing seized up and quit about fifty yards short of the house. Cheyenne abandoned the sad, old Japanese corpse, and came running the rest of the way on foot. Stanley, who was busy watering a flowering pin cherry, barked at her. It was a happy bark. *Great. Maybe this party will pick up now that the girls have arrived.* He finished up and then galloped down the drive to greet her. While Stanley enjoyed an enthusiastic rub down, I brought his massage therapist up to speed on my discovery of who owned this place.

Not surprisingly, Cheyenne caught on quick. "Scott, huh? That explains a lot."

"Maybe to you it does. To me it opens up a lot more questions than it closes." I started back to the house. "Wait here. I have to call Manwaring."

Cheyenne started walking the other direction, up the driveway. "I'll have a look in the garage."

"No, no, no you won't. Just stay here, hold onto Stanley. I'll be right back." I scurried back inside the house and headed for the land line that I'd seen in the kitchen. But when I picked the thing up I got no dial tone. I went to my second choice, the extension phone in the living room.

Same thing. Dead.

Okay, a disconnected line is nothing to get excited about – not out here. This house is the very last connection on a rural line – both phone and electricity would be hit and miss. We'll simply have to use one of our cell phones. I hurried back outside and asked Cheyenne to go fetch hers or mine from the car. While she ran off, I headed up the drive to have a look at the garage. Meanwhile, poor Stanley stood there trying to decide which of us to follow. I called to him, "Come on, pal. I need your nose." Surprisingly, he came to me.

As I lifted the large garage door, the rising curtain of late afternoon daylight presented me with the star of today's show – a green Chevy truck complete with the suspect bumper sticker. Unfortunately, no human cast member was here to take a bow – no evidence of Amy Tapin. Stanley did manage to find a cat which promptly took off. He didn't chase it. He never does.

The garage was easily large enough for two vehicles, but the green truck was the only one in it today. Back in that community at the top of the lake, the NASCAR granny had mentioned seeing a Subaru coming and going. My guess is, that second vehicle must belong to Scott's wife.

I now walked over to the third building on the property, a small barn which included a workshop. Here, I found two items of interest. One was a large storage tank. It smelled of gasoline. The guy at the airport had told me how pilots who keep their aircraft at home often store their own supply of high octane aviation fuel. The second item was an old classic wooden motorboat. The craft was sitting on a trailer, probably ready to be hooked up to the hitch I'd seen on the green truck. Sadly, this old mahogany watercraft was the only vintage item here – no signs of any elderly ladies.

When I returned to the house, I found Cheyenne sitting on the front porch holding her phone, looking at the item with disgust. I recognized that look.

"No signal, huh?"

"Not a fart. Hills are too high."

"Then we're off for a hike." I glanced down the road. "Keep your ears open. We hear a car, we dive for cover."

Cheyenne stood up and wiped the dust off the bum of her jeans. "You think his wife knows what hubby's been up to?"

"Don't know. I suppose he could explain Stanley as a stray he picked up."

Finished with her own butt, she patted Stanley's. "Any idea why he took Stanley?"

"Who knows? Maybe insurance. In the last couple of days I've been stirring up a lot of shit. If I ever did uncover something incriminating against Trooper Scott, he could use Stanley as a bargaining chip, incentive for me to keep my suspicions to myself. I don't know. Whatever the reason, I'm sure it was an impulse purchase." I turned away and started down the driveway.

I expected Cheyenne to follow along. Silly me. "You thirsty?" she said.

"Guess so, but—"

And before I could stop her, she bounced up the steps and disappeared into the house. She had a point, I suppose. It was going to be a long trek out.

A moment later, she magically reappeared holding two sweating cans of ice cold beer. I had to laugh. "No fruit juice?"

"Plenty." With a satisfied smile, she handed me a can of beer, and the three of us started merrily down the Yellow Brick Road. We didn't get far into the Land of Oz before Cheyenne stopped. "Oh, shit…"

I thought I knew what was bothering her. "Yeah," I said, "There's nothing we can do about it – we're going to get eaten alive." I swatted at a cloud of black flies that were trying to gain entry to my tiny brain by way of my big ears.

Cheyenne gently placed her hand on my forearm. "Listen…"

I did. But I couldn't hear a damn thing. I was too busy swatting myself deaf. When the little buggers get in your ears they tickle like crazy.

"Hear it?" Cheyenne's ears were sharper than mine, probably because she hadn't spent as much time standing in front of weak guitarists with strong amplifiers.

I held my breath. It took me a little longer, but I eventually heard the sound of fat tires crunching over thin gravel. All I could do was repeat Cheyenne's sentiment, "Aw, shit."

As usual, Cheyenne offered an optimistic scenario. "Maybe it's the wife."

I didn't waste any time arguing. I grabbed Stanley's collar and pulled him off the drive and into the woods. Stanley was fine with this idea, but Cheyenne had other plans.

"The house," she cried as she took off up the driveway.

"No," I said. "We'll be trapped."

She called back, "He's a cop. He's got to have a gun in there somewhere."

"Forget it. He'll have his sidearm with him."

"I'm talking rifle." She had to yell now – she was that far away. "I've never met a cop who wasn't a hunter."

"You have now." But I was wasting my breath – she was already leaping up the porch steps and grabbing for the screen door.

I stayed planted right where I was, my fingers hooked into Stanley's collar. I kept my eyes on the road. Soon, through the delicate lacework of spring foliage, I watched quick flashes of reflected sunlight off chrome strobe through the forest glen like the flickering images of an old-time silent movie. Except, this film wasn't so silent. I could hear the hum of the big 3.5 liter V6 engine as the Ford Interceptor rounded the last bend of the road.

No, it wasn't the wife's car. Not unless the wife drives a New York State Trooper's car.

CHAPTER TWENTY

There was a time when I'd have done the smart thing – turned tail and run deeper into the cover of the forest, disappearing far into the trees before Trooper Scott could spot me. That way, I could double back and surprise him when he was inside the house questioning Cheyenne. But Gloria Tapin's death had left me shy about leaving women alone in the woods with homicidal maniacs. So, I decided to race this one back to his house.

With Stanley at my side, I crunched through the forest's carpet of pine needles and leapt up onto the hard dirt roadway. I still had a good hundred-yard lead on the approaching car. As Stanley and I sprinted, I could hear Trooper Scott's cruiser growling round the final turn, nipping on our tails.

Stanley won the race. He scampered up the steps and loped through the open doorway, straight into Cheyenne's welcoming arms.

I never made it that far.

I had my left foot on the top step when the bullet hit. My leg folded under me. I collapsed backward, tumbling down the four steps onto the ground. From here, flat on my back, I looked up at pale blue sky. No sharp pain, not yet, just the vague sense of being hit in the back of my leg with a shovel. There was nothing I could do now but lie flat in the dirt. And wait.

The dust raised by my falling onto the sandy soil was now settling on my face. So I closed my eyes. When I opened them, I turned my head toward the house. I saw Cheyenne standing above and just beyond, framed by the home's open doorway. Her hand had gone to her mouth. Her dark eyes had opened wide with terror. But she quickly blinked those beautiful eyes shut when a bullet splintered a chunk of wood out of the door jamb just inches from her lovely cheek bones.

"Get the fuck inside," I suggested. And for once she followed my advice.

With some difficulty and a bit of pain, I rolled myself over onto my side and cocked my head to see behind me. I was in no hurry, of course. I wasn't trying to avoid the next shot – I couldn't, not with this useless leg. No, I just wanted to face my executioner. If this bastard intends to finish me off, he will have to look into my eyes as he pulls the trigger.

The patrol car was stopped halfway up the driveway. Trooper Scott, in a pose that aped a thousand cop movies, was hunkered behind his open door with his Glock 37 held firmly in both his hands, his forearms resting on the frame of the open window. He didn't move. Didn't speak either. He just stayed frozen in that defensive cop crouch waiting to see if I was truly down and no longer a threat. Eventually, he made his decision. He smiled. Or at least his lips did – I have no idea what was going on behind those mirrored sunglasses. He slowly straightened himself up to his full five-foot-eleven inches which he probably called six feet.

He was still in uniform, except for one item – he'd left his silly hat in his car. For the first time, I noticed he was balding. That must be rough for a young guy. No wonder he resented me. I still have a pretty full head of hair. Well, *full* might not be the best word.

With the caution of a hunter approaching crippled game, Scott stepped towards me. As he did, and despite the rising pain in my leg, a calm washed over me. It was like I'd been immersed in a warm bath. I went with it. I lay back. Stared up at the late afternoon sky.

High above me, a hawk spiraled upwards for a better look at the silliness below, his wing feathers splayed wide to catch the rising thermals. I watched as the magnificent bird soared effortlessly through a line of wispy clouds, their undersides washed in rose from the low sun. If the end was indeed nigh, this was a damn nice backdrop to go out on. A perfect tableau to be etched on a man's eternal screen saver. Beats hell out of dying in an inner city concrete canyon. Or worse, in a hospital room.

I listened to the big clunky cop shoes scuff nearer, across the loose gravel. And I pondered. So why had he shot me? And why was he now about to finish me off? I could only assume he must know I found my pooch locked inside his house which means I can now clearly link him to the homicide of Henry Tapin. But what about Cheyenne? What will he do about her? Stanley should be safe. He can't talk.

I arched my back for a better look. Damn! The pain from my leg was finally introducing itself to my brain. That warm bath was now stinging hot.

I propped myself up onto one elbow so I could assess the damage to my leg. What I discovered was two bloody wounds – one where the .45 caliber slug had drilled into the front of my thigh, and the other on the back, where it had exited. This was good news. It meant the slug probably hadn't hit my femur and I may one day walk again. Of course, such optimism was rather pointless considering Trooper Steve Scott was about to put his next bullet into my brain. My only hope now was to stall him long enough for Cheyenne to find that hunting rifle she suspects exists. Hell, she might be right. She usually is.

Trooper Scott, now about twenty feet away from me, stopped walking. His mirrored sunglasses shifted their focus to something lying behind me. I craned my neck to see what had captured my executioner's attention.

It was Cheyenne's cell phone – the one she had abandoned after failing to get a signal. The useless device was lying on the second step of the porch.

Scott's lips snaked into a reptilian grin. "Didn't work, did it."

"What? The phone? Of course, it did. Called Manwaring. He's on his way."

"Bullshit. No signal here. Hills are too high." He waved his .45 handgun toward an overhead wire. "That's why the land line."

"Which you just cut. How'd you know I was here?"

"Mrs. Boscarino said someone was looking for me."

He must be talking about that nice NASCAR lady at the top of the lake.

The trooper turned and looked back at our Datsun. "Clever boy. You've switched rides since Placid."

Recalling our first meeting, I said, "You going to tie me to another tree?" As I spoke, I started edging myself toward the porch and that useless cell phone.

Scott looked genuinely sad as he pondered my impending doom. "Boys in Ray Brook say you were a real smart cop. Too smart for your own good. Too smart for everyone's good." He looked up to the house where Cheyenne was now hiding.

I was close enough to the porch steps now, so I picked up the phone. Trooper Scott didn't bother to stop me – he knew the device was useless. Still, I held the phone up and continued bullshitting, "When conditions are right, these babies will work anywhere. Has something to do with sunspots or pollen count or something. Seems today's conditions are spot on. I assure you, Manwaring is on his way."

Trooper Scott didn't answer. Was there a glimmer of doubt behind those dumb sunglasses? Maybe.

I kept pushing, "Hey, don't take my word for it." I held out the device to him. "Try it yourself."

The trooper considered my offer. Should he approach me? If he reached for the phone would I grab his arm and yank him out of those big dumb cop shoes? If he guessed I would, he had more faith in my strength than I had. Sure, this kid and I are about the same size, but he's probably visited a gym in the past year for something other than meeting sweaty women.

"Toss it here," he said, holding out a strong, but soft, hand.

"Sorry. My shoulder's fucked. You'll have to come get it.

He was dumb, but not dumb enough. He stayed where he was. So I changed the subject to something else that was on my pained mind. "Thanks for taking care of my pooch."

"No problem. I like dogs."

"Good for you," I said. "How about old ladies? You like old ladies?"

On this subject, Trooper Scott had nothing to add. He just looked down, cast his gaze to the dirt. Which was all the answer I needed.

"Aw, shit. You dumb fuck. You killed her."

"Wasn't me," he said quietly.

"But she's dead."

Scott toed the dirt like he was getting ready to sign his confession on the dotted line. "Happened when we busted into the cabin."

"You and Appleyard."

Scott's tone of voice rose in both volume and pitch. "Shit, everybody knows when Crazy Henry goes into town he takes the old lady with him. Always. So, in we go. And there she is. Locked up. In the bedroom."

"Locked up?"

"Yeah, I couldn't believe it either. I mean, what if there was, like, a fire or something? But nope, there she was. Locked up tight. She starts screaming. Thinks we're doctors come to take her away. Appleyard tries to quiet her down. Tells her we're not going to hurt her, we're just looking for something. The violin. Asks her where it is."

"Poor thing must have been terrified."

"More angry than scared. Appleyard grabs her, tries to shake some sense into her. But she's all ape shit. Tries to run. Trips over her housecoat. Head bounces off a table. A heavy one."

"The one with the jigsaw puzzle."

"Yeah, well… that's one puzzle that'll never be solved. Not by her, anyway."

I put the rest of his story together. "So you and Appleyard decide to make the most of a bad situation – hide her body and hit Henry up for ransom on his supposedly kidnapped mother."

"Nice guess, Chief, but you're wrong. We just took off. I signed up to help my old science teacher search a cabin, and that's all. The ransom idea wasn't ours."

"Then who's idea was it?"

"Who else? Her kid's. Crazy Henry. The piano dude."

"Henry?" My mind went back to that crazy phone call. That high-pitched voice… yeah, I guess that could have been Henry Tapin trying to disguise himself. The formal, educated grammar certainly fit. But why?

I had lots of questions, but Trooper Scott had decided he was through giving the news update. His attention returned to that cell phone. He waved his gun at it. "Give me that phone."

"First, tell me what Henry was up to."

"What do you care?"

"Consider it honoring a dead man's last wish. You *are* going to kill me, right?" I was trying to stretch this out. Cheyenne needed time in there.

With a self-satisfied grin, Scott decided to honor my request, "Figure it for yourself. Henry Tapin comes home to the cabin. Finds Mommy on the floor. Stiff as a carp. He could see the place had been broken into. Somebody had busted down the old woman's locked bedroom door. So what's Henry going to do? Call law enforcement?"

I said, "They'd discover that he had left a frail, confused elderly woman alone, locked up."

"They'd also discover a barn load of weed. The guy hadn't transplanted his seedlings yet. But that's not the worst part. Seems Henry had recently had Mommy's life insurance increased. To the hilt. I checked, myself."

As Scott spoke, I could hear some clattering from inside the house. Cheyenne was up to something in there. I had to stall. I said, "The death clearly looked like a homicide. With Henry as sole beneficiary, he would be suspect *numero uno*."

"So, Henry dumps his mother's corpse somewhere – the lake, I figure – and he makes up a story about her being kidnapped."

I said, more to myself than to Scott, "But why kidnapped? Why not say his mother just wandered off?"

"I wondered about that too," Scott said. "But Appleyard, he's pretty smart. He figured it out. Says, with a kidnapping, when the old lady's body finally does turn up, Henry won't have to explain why he never reported her missing – he just says the kidnapper told him not to go to the police."

"True," I said. "But if Henry wants to collect that insurance money, sooner or later the body has to be discovered. Can't be Henry, though. The beneficiary finding the body… that would look too suspicious."

From behind me, I heard a window slide open. Sounded like an upstairs dormer. I couldn't turn my head to look. Had Scott heard it? He knew Cheyenne was in there – he'd already taken a shot at her.

"Okay," I said to Scott, keeping his attention away from that window. "I understand why he leaked the news about the kidnapping. But why leak it the way he did? Why the crazy wrong-number call? And why to me? I barely knew the guy. Why not just pick a name out of the phone book?"

Scott said, "A call to just any Joe Citizen wouldn't work. No guarantee Joe Citizen would put two and two together and pass the news along to the authorities. But an 'accidental' call to a smart, conscientious ex-cop who Henry once played with in a rock and roll band…"

"Rhythm and blues."

"Crazy Henry knew you'd come through." Scott laughed. "Of course, I doubt even Henry figured you'd come through *this* well – digging into the case all by your lonesome and getting his daughter killed."

"Bullshit," I said. And on cue, from inside the house, Stanley barked his complete agreement.

Scott looked up to the house to see what Cheyenne was up to, so I decided it was time for a stronger distraction. A tantrum might help. I threw the phone down on the ground and yelled, "You over-groomed, under-brained trigger-happy fuck wad! *I* wasn't the one responsible for Gloria's death. An idiot with mirrored sunglasses, polished boots, and a shiny new badge killed her. Geez, man, what the hell were you doing out there, anyway?"

"Killing alpacas," Scott said, his attention still on the upstairs window behind me.

"I know that. But why?"

Seeing nothing interesting happening in the window, Scott turned back to me. "Still trying to squeeze Henry for that violin. I thought a little added incentive might help. So I left a message. If Henry didn't 'turn over the violin, maybe his daughter would be next. I didn't mean it, of course."

"But you did mean it. You shot her."

"Self-defense. She shot first."

I thought back to that day at the cabin. "You must have been on the property when we arrived."

"On my way out, actually. Heard your car coming, so I ducked inside."

"Inside what? One of the outbuildings."

"The backyard shitter."

"You were in the outhouse all the time I was searching the cabin?"

"Hoping you wouldn't need to take a dump." Scott shivered. "Geez, I hate spiders."

"How did you get my gun?"

"Grabbed it from your car while you were checking out the grow op. Thought it might come in handy. It did."

"And when I went out to search for a phone..."

"All I wanted was to get as far away from that cabin as possible. But your lady friend had other ideas. Christ, Tanager, why the hell would you leave a woman alone in a situation like that?"

"She had a gun, knew how to use it."

"Damn straight she knew how to use it. Fuck, man, I had no choice."

In the windshield of Scott's patrol car, I could see the reflection of the house behind me. No sign of Cheyenne yet. "So, what's your next move? Dump our bodies in the water next to Amy's? I imagine that lake is getting crowded."

Scott started thinking aloud to himself. "What I should do is plant the violin case in your car. Next to your body. That might do the trick."

"The violin? You have it?"

Scott laughed. "You know where it was?"

I took a guess, "Henry's music store."

"Bingo. Lying there in plain sight. The basement. A pile of old instruments and junk. Trouble was, Henry was lying there, too. With a bottle. Trying to drink himself to oblivion. Seeing as how I was in uniform, he assumed I'd come to arrest him."

"Arrest him for what?"

"Take your pick – the grow-op, elder abuse, the phony kidnapping. So I went with it. Told him I'd let him off the hook if he'd just tell me where the violin was. But when he handed the fiddle over, he decided to get cute, make a grab for my side arm."

"Your service Glock."

"On special occasions like that I carry an unregistered piece."

"Which now has my prints on it."

"Hey, nobody invited you to stick your nose into this, Tanager. I was on my way out when I saw you looking in that front window. So I booted it back to the basement."

"With the violin," I said.

Scott corrected me, "With an empty *case*. No violin. Never was." Scott laughed. "You know what was in that fucker?"

I quoted a line from a classic film. "The stuff dreams are made of?"

"It is if you're dreaming 'bout hair."

In the windshield reflection of Scott's car, I saw a shadow moving across that upstairs window. "So what's your plan now?" I said to Scott.

"The way I see it, you are already a suspect in three homicides. You and your sexy accomplice in there are neutralized trying to evade arrest. I bet I make detective for this."

Before I had a chance to congratulate him on his upcoming promotion we were once again interrupted by the bark of a dog. This time we both looked up to the house.

Stanley had his big wet nose stuck out the dormer window. Beside him, Cheyenne was clutching the walnut stock of a bolt-action deer rifle.

"Drop your weapon," she called out to Scott, her deep voice ringing out with casual but firm authority, as if she were simply instructing a spa client to *flip and I'll wax the naughty bits.*

But of course Scott didn't drop anything.

This was a standard Mexican standoff – the only difference being Cheyenne's gun was pointed at Trooper Scott, while his gun was aimed at an injured idiot lying helplessly in the dirt.

I couldn't see exactly what was happening behind those dumb mirrored sunglasses, but I imagine Scott's brain was busy trying to figure out how much Cheyenne knew about firearms. After all, the weapon currently pointed at him was his own rifle, and Scott had most likely stored the thing unloaded. Could this woman have known enough to load it? And if she had, had she known enough to flip off the safety? And did she then know how to cock the bolt and deliver a cartridge into the chamber? From down here, it looked like the thing might be cocked, but we were too far away to be sure.

"I said *drop it*," Cheyenne repeated.

Scott looked up at the pretty lady holding the big ol' gun. Hell, she was old enough to be his mother. Could she be a serious threat? Probably not. So he said, "You aren't going to shoot anyone, ma'am."

Ma'am? Wrong thing to say, and the wrong *ma'am* to say it to.

The first bullet hit the dirt just inches from the young trooper's foot. Cheyenne then raised the rifle muzzle by just a hair. "Right or left?" she asked. "Which ball you least attached to, kid?"

Scott decided this woman knew her firearms as well as she knew her male anatomy. So he bent down and carefully placed his .45 handgun on the ground.

"Now down," she said. "Spread eagle."

Under the circumstances, the lady was giving the correct tactical order, and Scott knew that. But he didn't go along with the command. Instead, with his hands held high where she could plainly see them, he proceeded to slowly back away, down the drive toward his waiting squad car.

"I said lie down," Cheyenne shouted.

But he didn't. He continued backing away. "You won't shoot. You don't need to. I'm leaving. Threat neutralized." Scott kept shuffling backwards all the way down the driveway until he reached the open door of his car where he then slid in behind the wheel.

Cheyenne tried firing a couple of warning shots in his direction. With his vehicle facing us, her first bullet drilled through the center of his windshield and took off his inside rear view mirror. Her second shot popped off his outside driver's mirror. Undeterred, Scott started his engine. He slid the gearshift into reverse and, using his one remaining passenger-side mirror, backed the car down the driveway. Once he reached the end, though, he stopped. He didn't turn the vehicle around and leave. He just stopped. He shut off his engine. And he sat. And he waited. And he watched. And he thought. *What should I do next? I can't just leave them here. They're onto me.*

Meanwhile, Cheyenne came running out of the front door, the rifle still clutched in her hand. Stanley was by her side. As she crouched down to have a look at my leg, I congratulated her on her skill with the rifle.

"Mom hunted," she said. "I used to tag along."

"Your *mother?*"

Cheyenne looked closer at the blood stain blossoming through my chinos. "Hold this." She handed me the rifle. "I'll go find something to bandage this up." She stood up to go back to the house.

"Take Stanley with you," I said. "He'll only get into trouble out here."

She turned, patted her thigh, and called him to follow her. He did.

While waiting for my nurse to return, I kept an eye on the idiot in the car. He, in turn, kept his eye on the idiot on the ground. After a moment, one of the idiots got out of his vehicle, walked around, and opened the rear cargo door. I had a hunch what he was going for, and I was right. He casually lifted his tactical shotgun out of the cargo hatch. He then pulled out a box of shells. And with these in hand, he got back into his front seat again.

Meanwhile, Cheyenne came out of the house carrying a first aid kit, a wet cloth, and a pair of scissors. This time, she'd been smart enough to leave Stanley inside. She kneeled down and slit the leg of my pants open with the kitchen scissors.

As she worked, I filled her in about the shotgun Scott had lifted from his hatch. "We can't just sneak out through the woods," I said. "Even if my leg was up to it, he'd pick us off before we got fifty yards."

She put the scissors on the ground to have a good close look at the carnage she had uncovered. "You're bleeding, but not too badly. No arteries seem to have been hit." She changed subject, "How about after dark?"

"I think that's your best bet," I said. "You can take Stanley. But whatever you do, don't let him lead the way. The dumb pooch will just take you on a tour of raccoons' nests."

Cheyenne said, "You're not coming?"

"I'll hang here. Rattle around the house. Make some noise. Talk to the furniture. That way, he'll think we're both still here."

She opened the first aid kit box and fished through it. "You think he's that dumb?"

"Possibly, but I'm only going by looks."

She took a roll of gauze out of the kit. But before unrolling it, she looked down toward the lake. She thought a moment, then said, "Of course, there *is* another way."

I was with her. "By water."

Cheyenne craned her neck to look down the shoreline. "I don't see any boat around, but he must have one."

"It's in the barn."

"Any chance we can put it in the water?"

"Not without getting our asses shot off. The thing's on a trailer. He'd pick us off."

She started winding the gauze around my wound. "No canoe?"

"Haven't seen one."

"Well, that leaves just one choice." Her eyes went back to the waterfront, to the plane that floated so quietly and benignly at the dock.

I said, "Don't suppose you can fly?"

"I bet I can taxi." She continued rolling gauze around my bare upper thigh. She then ripped a split in the gauze and started tying the final knot. "That feel okay?"

"Just fine," I lied.

She yanked it tight. Very tight. One of us swore. I think it was me. Through clenched teeth, I pondered aloud, "I wonder if planes need ignition keys."

"Some do," Cheyenne said with a degree of authority which she promptly explained, "Bar owner I worked for in Syracuse flew a Cessna. Took me up once. Let's see…" Still kneeling beside me, Cheyenne closed her eyes to help her visualize the plane's cockpit. "There was a choke. He closed that. Primer. Mixture. Magnetos. Two of those, I believe. And something called carburetor heat. I'm not sure exactly how that was used. And yes, there was an ignition key." She opened her eyes and looked at me. "You must know how to hot wire a car."

"We'll find out. You know how to steer the thing?"

"Up in the air you use the wheel, or more properly, the yoke. On land, the pedals."

"And on water?"

"I believe the pedals are attached to rudders on the floats. But they're retractable. Gotta make sure they're lowered."

I said, "Whatever we do, I suggest we do it soon." I nodded towards the far horizon. "Sun's getting low. Don't want to do this after dusk." A bark from inside the house punctuated my point. Somebody didn't want to be left behind.

Cheyenne handed me the rifle and got to her feet. "I'll go get Stanley."

To her retreating rear end, I called, "See if you can find me a pair of pliers, a knife, a screwdriver, and some form of alcohol."

"Alcohol? But I already sterilized the wound."

"I'm not a good flier. I saw some vodka over the fridge."

CHAPTER TWENTY-ONE

"Contact!"

"Okay."

I said, "You're supposed to yell *contact* back to me."

"Oh, sorry."

I said, "Keep your eye open for Scott." Then I touched the naked wires together. A spark flew. The propeller spun. The engine coughed. But it didn't catch. I unhooked the wires and said, "A little more fuel."

She was sitting in the pilot's seat. I was crouched low with my head tucked between her legs, and amazingly, all my attention was on the back of the instrument panel.

From above me, I heard Cheyenne pump the primer lever. Then she tickled the mixture knob just a hair towards rich. "Okay. Try again."

There was probably a prescribed method of doing this, but we didn't have time to look for the owner's manual. "Contact," I yelled.

"Contact," she answered.

Once again, I touched the wires. Once again, a spark flew. Once again, the propeller spun. But this time the engine's four cylinders exploded into life.

Task completed, I slid myself out from under the panel. I continued sliding my whole body backwards until I was fully outside the cockpit and standing on the float. Enjoying the idling propeller's gentle breeze, I straightened up as best I could, which wasn't a whole lot. My leg hurt like hell.

The float I was standing on was situated on the pilot's-side of the plane, the float closest to the dock. Cheyenne was now crammed into the far seat — normally, the passenger seat. There wasn't much room in this thing. The plane, a side-by-side two-seater with a small single seat/cargo hatch in back, was a kit-built affair about the size of a Cessna 152. I was surprised it had a key ignition, but I guess that's a smart idea if your aircraft is going to be parked on a lake all day while you are off working a double shift catching bad guys. Or helping them. I was also surprised the aircraft had dual controls — this seemed pretty sophisticated for a homebuilt. But maybe that's some sort of FAA regulation.

From inside the cockpit, Cheyenne said, "I'm going to leave this carburetor heat knob thing in the off position, okay? I suspect it prevents ice in the carburetor during humid weather. Relative humidity is pretty low today. Bleeding hot thin air into the carb would only lessen our performance. Right?"

"Uh, yeah, right, sure. Sounds like a good idea." I had no idea what the hell she was talking about. I did, however, know something about the Remington rifle that she had found in Trooper Scott's house. I had placed it in the back seat, just in case we needed it. So far, we hadn't needed it. A few minutes ago Steve Scott had stuck his head up over the rise above us to see what we were up to, but he hadn't dared try to crawl closer down the hillside. He knew our deer rifle had a longer and more lethal range that his tactical shotgun. I hadn't seen any sign of Scott in the last few minutes, so I suspected he may have gone back to his car and was now driving out, probably planning to head us off at that hamlet at the top of the lake, which is exactly where we were heading. We need to get to that highway. Happily, we will be headed in more-or-less a straight line across the lake, while he will be stuck meandering through the forest, along that cow path of a road.

My final chore before climbing into the plane was to load our third soul on board, the passenger who was currently standing on the loading dock, licking his balls goodbye. Sometimes the pooch has a sixth sense about joining in with idiots, and today he had two of us coaxing him along.

At this point, Cheyenne was messing with the mixture control lever, trying to get the engine running smoothly, and I was standing on the float, listening to the engine's tone and trying to keep my head away from the spinning propeller. When Cheyenne finally thought she had the engine purring, she looked to me for approval. I was about to give her a big, encouraging thumbs up, but I never got the chance. Instead, I watched Cheyenne's eyes suddenly open wide with concern.

She was looking past me. She yelled something that I couldn't hear above the engine. Then she pointed up the hill behind me. I turned around to see what had gotten her so excited.

It was Trooper Scott. He was in his squad car, up top of the rise, driving along the ridge. His car was headed toward a gentle slope that curved and tilted down to the water. Hitched onto his back bumper was the boat and trailer that I'd seen in the barn.

I didn't bother grabbing the gun and firing off a warning shot — it wouldn't have been heard above the roar of the airplane engine. And shooting out a tire wouldn't have hampered his task – he had only a hundred yards to go before reaching the spot where a flat table of rock made for a natural boat launch. Happily, it would take Scott a few minutes to maneuver his trailer around and back it into the water. So I got ready to do some fancy maneuvering of my own.

I bent down to grab Stanley and hoist him from the dock into the plane. Trouble is, the pooch hates being hoisted. I think it has something to do with his once being hoisted into the vet's in my loving arms and then having two of his favorite parts lobbed off. Anyway, that's why, when I stepped off the float and onto the dock and edged my way closer to him, sweet-talking as I bent down to grab him, the pooch said *fuck you, Tanager* and jumped off the dock and into the water.

I looked to Cheyenne to see if she was following the action. She was. She pointed to Scott's boat, then started waving a frantic semaphore that said, roughly, *Get your wounded ass in gear and into this fucking plane.* Believe it or not, I think she actually expected me to leave without Stanley. Fat chance, lady.

I jumped into the lake. Grabbed the dog. But with my injured leg, I couldn't manage to climb back up onto the dock. So I held onto Stanley's collar and dragged him to the rocks.

Lifting the wet pooch up and onto shore wasn't easy. Dry, Stanley weighs a good fifty pounds. Wet, a bad seventy. My leg was killing me, but somehow I struggled up onto the rocks and retraced my steps to the dock. With a helping hand from Cheyenne, I managed to stuff the armload of dripping canine into the plane's cargo area behind the front seats.

By now, Scott had his boat in the water and was untying the ropes that secured it to the trailer. I did the same with the lines that moored our plane to the dock. With one foot still on the float, I grabbed a strut and shoved the plane away from the dock. I then eased my sore butt into the left-hand seat while Cheyenne advanced the throttle and started piloting us out into open water.

Technically, I was now sitting in what is usually the pilot's seat. But thanks to the dual yokes, Cheyenne was able to take control from the passenger side, which was peachy-fine with me. My wounded leg couldn't possibly operate the steering pedals which are probably called the rudder pedals if you know what you're talking about.

Scott had parked the plane conveniently pointed toward the lake, so we had no tight maneuvering to do. And being early evening, there was no wind, which was also good. As Cheyenne gained confidence, she edged the throttle farther in. The engine's rumble rose in pitch, and we picked up speed. She called out to me over the propeller's chugging growl, "You okay?"

I was sopping wet, and my leg hurt like hell, but I gave her a happy thumbs up. I didn't try to talk over the noise. Earlier, we had noticed audio jacks in the dash for the pilot and passenger to use, but Trooper Scott hadn't been considerate enough to leave any headsets in the plane. Not that we had much to discuss.

I twisted around and looked back behind us. I couldn't hear anything above our own engine, but judging by the plume of black smoke belching from his boat, Scott had fired up his. He fiddled around organizing something in the vessel, and then he hit the throttle. His prow rose as he advanced the speed. It soon lowered as he reached full throttle.

"Here he comes," I yelled.

Cheyenne gave our engine more juice, and the prop's circle disappeared in transparency. The race was on. I had no idea how fast this plane could go. Or more correctly, *should* go.

We had a couple of miles of water to plow through before we would reach the small settlement on the highway at the far end. Our original plan was to make this voyage at an easy cruising taxi speed, but that was back when we thought we'd be racing a cop car hobbling its way through thick forest, not trying to outrun a speedboat.

I leaned over and checked our speedometer or whatever you call that instrument in a plane. The needle said we were going about thirty. I don't know if that was miles per hour or knots per hour or furlongs per minute, but it didn't matter much – I could easily see that Scott was gaining on us.

I mentioned this to Cheyenne, our pilot in command. She advanced the throttle.

"Careful," I yelled as the engine's whine rose about four semitones in pitch. "We don't want to take off." I said this with a laugh. Imagine, the very thought of such a ridiculous notion.

Cheyenne pushed in the throttle knob a little further. "Tell me something," she said, obviously wanting to take my worried mind off her aggressive driving. "Back at Henry's cabin, when your car collided with Scott's vehicle, you say he was on his way in, right? Answering the 911 call?"

"That's what I assumed."

"But he had just shot Gloria."

"He must have been on his way back to Ray Brook when he heard the call come in for an NUI."

"NUI?"

"Nearest Unit Investigate. So he told dispatch he was on it, pulled a one-eighty, and retraced his steps back to the cabin."

Cheyenne looked at me. "Why?"

"It gave him a perfect opportunity to be first on the scene, fudge anything that he might have missed. Don't forget, he didn't know I was coming back."

"And that's when you crunched fenders."

"Thereby giving him a handy patsy to pin Gloria's homicide on." Now it was my turn to change subject. I pointed out the windshield at the lake in front of us. And the island rushing toward us. "You see that?"

My bouncing finger was pointed at a rocky dome of granite sticking out of the water, a little island that was too small to be seen until you were almost on it. We were almost on it.

Unperturbed, Cheyenne said, "Is he still gaining?"

I turned around in my seat to look back at Scott's boat. I liked what I saw. I yelled the good news to Cheyenne, "I think we're losing him. You can slow down. Ease up. Maybe even turn. Right or left, your choice."

But the rocky island was still coming straight at us. Or vice versa. Maybe she hadn't heard me. The engine was awful loud. And my voice was probably weak from pain. And blood loss. Point is, she didn't slow down. In fact, she advanced the throttle. A lot.

I yelled again. Right into her ear. This time with more obscenities. But it didn't help. What the fuck was with this chick? I mean, I had studied her when she sat behind the wheel of Garth's sports car. She was a bit enthusiastic, sure, maybe even aggressive. But she didn't go full Mario Andretti like this. Has she flipped out? Is she nuts? Are all geniuses nuts?

Seems this one was.

Enough of this shit. I reached for the throttle knob. She slapped my hand away. Meanwhile, the island kept coming. I could have muscled her hand off that throttle, but this was no time to wrestle for control. Maybe she had a plan she hadn't told me about.

I turned and looked out my side window. Our aluminum floats were scratching over the ripples like fingernails clawing at corduroy. And then suddenly, like magic, the fabric smoothed out to silk. Our floats were no longer splashing. No longer spraying. They were now barely skimming along the surface. I turned around to look back at Scott's boat again.

The good news: He was even farther back, losing ground. No threat at all. The bad news: There was now open air between our floats and the water. In other words...

I turned to Cheyenne and said as calmly as I could, "You, uh... you do know we're flying, right?"

She smiled. And then she pushed the throttle a final quarter of an inch. All the way. To the firewall. Full power.

I didn't say anything. This was not the time for discussion. I just sat back. Braced myself. And watched.

I watched the nose of our plane rise. I watched my pilot gently pull the stick back. I watched more pale blue sky fill the windshield. I watched my pilot gently urge the stick to the right, and at the same time, ease the right pedal forward with her sneakered foot.

The plane banked. And when the wings reached an angle with which they were apparently satisfied, Cheyenne leveled the yoke and held it there.

The wings held their bank, and the lethal dome of granite passed harmlessly beneath us with a few feet to spare. Soon thereafter, Cheyenne eased the stick back the other way until the whole deal had been undone and we had returned to straight and level flight. Except we were now higher. A lot higher. I couldn't help but be impressed. This entire maneuver had been performed very smoothly. Very skillfully. And very dishonestly.

"Why the fuck didn't you tell me you could fly a fucking plane?" I enquired.

"Wasn't sure I could."

"*Wasn't sure?*"

"Like I said, I watched a pilot do it once."

I thought about this for a moment, then I asked a very important question, "Did you happen to watch him land?"

"Yes."

"Good."

Then she said, "But not on floats."

With as much cool understatement as I could muster, I said to her, "I've heard float landings can be rather tricky."

"Yes, I've heard that too."

I left a few moments of silence. I didn't want to be a distraction to her. But I had noticed we were still climbing. So I asked, "We, uh, headed to Saranac Lake?"

"Sure, if you want. Saranac's fine."

I figured Saranac Lake would be the best place to land for several reasons. First, it was large enough for a plane to land on. Second, it had a good-sized municipal police department on hand, many of them friends of mine. And third, it had a hospital.

Bat-shit crazy or not, Cheyenne seemed to be doing a fine job of flying this thing, so I started to relax a bit. We should be over Saranac in ten or fifteen minutes. But Cheyenne had one more surprise up her sleeve.

"Just one stop to make, first."

Huh? What the fuck? Had I heard right? *A stop?*

She continued, "Just have to drop something off at a friend's. It'll only take a minute."

Okay, that's it. Up till now I had been very understanding. Sure, she'd scared the hell out of me with this stunt. But maybe I had it coming for being dishonest and not telling her sooner about her friend Henry's death. But now… a completely needless detour and possible crash landing for no good reason? This gorgeous brainiac needed a leash more than my pooch did.

I screamed my next words, although the dramatic affect was severely diminished by the engine's roar. "You really are fucking nuts. Do you really think you're that bright? Do you really think you're such a fucking smarty pants you can do anything? Shit, you've never landed *any* kind of plane let alone a fucking floatplane. Hell, if we walk away from just *one* landing it will be a miracle. And you want to press your luck and try *two*? No, no, no. No way, lady. We're landing once and only once, and that landing will be in Saranac, right next to the hospital, the one with the nice handy doctors, nurses, trauma unit, and mental health professionals."

She patted my knee. "Don't get your panties in a knot. Just have to drop something off."

Drop something off? What could she possibly be referring to? I looked around the cockpit. Nothing here. Nothing on the floor. Nothing on her person. A few bulges under her clothes maybe, but they seemed to be the same bulges I'd been admiring for days. What could she possibly have to deliver? Me? My dog? The plane itself? Is there something hidden in the cargo hold?

I grabbed the back of my seat and pulled myself around to have a look in the back. The pooch, was there, of course. And the rifle. But nothing else.

Then I noticed that Stanley was busy trying to get at something under the seat. Under Cheyenne's ass.

I watched him scratch away at the plywood floor, jamming his furry muzzle under Cheyenne's butt like she was the new poodle on the block. He worked away at it, biting and snorting, exactly like he does at home when he's trying to pull one of my socks out from under the sofa. Suddenly, with a triumphant tug, the pooch yanked his prize free.

It was a small purse. Or carrying case. No, that's not it. It's a shaving kit. The kind a guy uses to pack his razor, toothbrush, and nail clippers. Except this one probably predated nail clippers. It was old. A tarnished brass zipper ran around three frayed fabric sides. The leather top, cracked and burnished, had been tooled in shallow relief and embossed with flowers and a line drawing of a musical instrument. A violin. And wait, those weren't flowers. They were drawings of atoms, the traditional illustrations of electrons orbiting a nucleus. So this was what was inside the violin case. Einstein's shaving kit. Sure, why not? The thing was probably given to ol' Albert as a novelty gift.

I stretched out my arm behind the seat and tried to grasp the thing. But I couldn't reach it – there was too little space. So I had no choice but to leave the thing where it was. But that was okay. I didn't mind. To tell the truth, I was far beyond caring. This stupid bag of hair had already cost three lives. Four, counting poor old Amy's. And soon to be seven if we three don't get this plane down intact.

I turned back to Cheyenne. "So, that's where Amy kept her boyfriend's shorn locks."

Cheyenne knew what I was referring to. She didn't know, however, that the leather bag was presently clutched between the slobbering jaws of my dog. She said, "It was in the plane all along. I found it when you were fishing Stanley out of the water. Scott must have stashed it here."

"So where we taking it?"

"Long Lake."

I understood. "N.J.'s restaurant."

"I'm sure Henry's friends won't mind keeping it for me until things die down."

"For *you?* What are you going to do with it? Sell it?"

"Sell it?" She looked at me with disappointment. "I would never do a thing like that."

"It *is* just hair, right?"

She laughed. "A *lot* of hair. Sealed tight in a plastic bag. Amy must have given Albert quite a few trims."

"So, what do you want it for?"

She looked at me as if I were the crazy one in this cockpit. "DNA, of course. Proof of bloodline."

I couldn't believe it. This thing was like some sort of sickness. "Don't tell me you think you're related to Einstein too."

"Not me, silly" she said. Then she patted her stomach. "My baby."

I skipped the congratulations. "You're knocked up?"

Cheyenne glowed as she announced to me and to her ever-expanding universe, "There's a very strong possibility I am carrying Albert Einstein's grandchild."

"Oh, for shit's sake," was all I could say. This obsession with genealogy was a disease. A sexually transmitted one.

Cheyenne said, "Henry and I only did it the once. But hey, sometimes once is enough."

"Or too much."

She motioned toward the package in the back seat, still unaware that the precious proof of her baby's genius lineage was presently clamped between the furry lips of a rather non-genius pooch. "If the authorities get their hands on that stuff, I'll never see it again, and my child will never know for sure who his or her famous paternal grandfather is."

"And why Long Lake?"

"Noah J's Cafe. My friends. They'll hold it for me."

"I see." And so I did. I saw that Cheyenne and her whole gang of Einstein groupies were out of their overdeveloped minds.

With nothing more to contribute to this biological discussion, I sat back, looked out the side window, and watched the world pass underneath my genealogically unexplored butt. I've never put a lot of store in pedigree. Certainly never had the urge to dig up my family tree and see what's rotting away at the roots. Apart from possibly discovering a propensity for certain nasty diseases, the whole exercise has always seemed rather pointless to me.

After a few moment's thought, I decided to point out a slight flaw in the plans of this beautiful genius seated next to me: "You do know, once he's prosecuted for those homicides, Scott will likely admit that the shaving kit was stored in this plane. And when he does, the authorities will want to know what happened to this priceless bag of historic DNA."

"And we won't know what he's talking about." She looked at me pointedly, as if we were signing a contract together. "We never saw it. It will be just Scott's word against ours. Right?" Since she knew she was clearly asking me to lie for her, she added a little incentive, "I helped you get your dog back."

Damn. I sat back and asked, "So, how pregnant, are you?"

"To tell the truth, I'm not absolutely sure if I am or not. I was just on my way to purchase a test kit the day you dropped into the spa. But of course, I dropped everything to help you... help you find your little doggy." She was pouring this on pretty thick.

"Sorry I interrupted your plans."

"That's okay. Glad I could be of help. But if I am preggers, it would certainly be nice to know my baby's lineage."

I looked out the window at the giant jigsaw puzzle of roads, valleys, mountains, and lakes that were passing beneath our aircraft's floats. At this late hour, the puzzle was getting hard to fit together – the sun had set, and the frayed edges of the individual pieces were quickly fading into the gray twilight. I could barely make out the highways and hamlets we were flying over.

I had to take control of this insanity, and I had to do it fast. "We have to land now," I said. "We can't wait. Next lake you see, put this thing down. And once we're down, we're staying down. I don't care where we are. This game is over."

Cheyenne pointed to a lake off to our left. "That's it. That's Long Lake." Then she added, "Most likely."

"Just put it down," I said.

She banked the plane to the left, toward the small, narrow ribbon of silver-purple water. She pulled the throttle back. The engine's peppy song dropped to a somber ballad and the plane's nose lowered. Cheyenne responded by pulling back hard and fast on the yoke. Too hard and too fast. The plane shuddered its disapproval. She eased the yoke forward again. The shudder stopped. We were now gliding nose down toward Long Lake.

Most likely.

Long Lake rubs up against a ridge of high hills which border the water's eastern shore. Coming at it from the south like this gave us a clear, fairly unobstructed approach. That was our plan, anyway. As I say, it was hard to make out the exact contours of the landscape in this evening light. I felt we were descending a little too fast, but I kept my thoughts to myself.

She appeared fully at ease. Sure, I wanted to continue harping on how stupid I thought this whole stunt was, but this was not the time to start an argument. Not the time to destroy her confidence. In the past couple of days I'd learned that Cheyenne was an exceptionally bright person who could handle just about any challenge thrown her way. But was she this bright? A police pilot once told me that landing a small plane at an airport is actually quite easy. That same pilot, however, told me that landing on water was a risky task even for an experienced pilot.

My pilot today had never landed anything anywhere anytime.

I tightened my seat belt, twisted around, and checked on Stanley behind me. There was no way to strap him in back there, but he seemed fine, happily chomping away on that leather shaving kit full of hair as if it were a rawhide chew toy. I wonder what dog spit will do to DNA tests. Serves Cheyenne right if she learns her baby is related to a Labrador retriever.

We were now well below the tops of the surrounding hills. I lowered my gaze to watch the glassy water skimming beneath our floats. I didn't know how strong Cheyenne's eyesight was, but I knew I couldn't possibly judge exactly how far we were above that mirrored surface sliding below us. Not with any accuracy, at least.

Turns out, neither could Cheyenne.

"Oh, fuck," she said as she jerked the stick back, jamming it into her cotton-denimed, possibly pregnant stomach.

I cracked opened my door and pushed it into the slipstream. If we ended up at the bottom of the lake I didn't want to be trapped inside this homemade coffin.

The plane's nose tilted up, sending the back end of the right-hand float bouncing off the water. This caused the plane's nose to fall and slam the other float flat onto the smooth water. It hit hard. At this speed, the lake's surface was like granite. I don't know what gage aluminum pipe Trooper Scott had used to brace these floats, but I soon found out it wasn't meant to take this kind of punishment. One more hard bounce and our left float strut folded like a cheap lawn chair, and the next thing I knew my world was spinning. The little plane was cartwheeling like a gymnast with an inner ear disorder. After two or three somersaults, we finally came to rest. Upside down. Floating on what was left of our wings.

The world had suddenly gone quiet. No moans, no groans – not even a dog barking. I struggled to turn and see how Cheyenne was doing, but I could barely budge. I was hanging from the seatbelt, and the tension made it impossible to undo the buckle.

Beside me, Cheyenne, also hanging upside down, had her eyes closed. I called out but got no reaction. Meanwhile, Stanley was no longer on the floor of the cargo hold. Without the benefit of a safety harness, he had taken the worst of this. He now lay motionless behind and below my head on what used to be the ceiling.

Even though my door was open, very little water was coming into the cabin – the thick, hollow wing, which had been perched above us, was now beneath us, keeping us afloat.

With a hard tug, I managed to unsnap my seatbelt. As I fell onto the inverted ceiling, I tucked my neck and shoulders so they would take the hit rather than my head. I then unbuckled Cheyenne's harness and carefully lowered her limp body from her inverted seat. She moaned. Then she swore. Finally, she apologized for the poor landing. With my door already open, it was easy to drag her out my side and onto the upturned wing. Happily, no great urgency hastened our exit – thanks to those big, thick wings, the plane seemed to be in no immediate danger of sinking.

As I lay Cheyenne on the doped fabric that covered the wing, she coughed and snorted. Then she rolled over, raised her head to get her bearings, and actually looked like she was contemplating swimming to shore.

"Lie still," I said. "Don't try to swim. Just hold onto this, okay?" I placed her hand on a busted strut.

I slipped back into the cockpit. With some difficulty, I reached across and gently pulled out Stanley's limp body. I placed him on the wing.

Meanwhile, Cheyenne was getting herself worked up about something. "The kit," she said. "Get the shaving kit."

I didn't tell her to go fuck herself. Not aloud, anyway.

Stanley's eyes were closed, and he didn't seem to be breathing. No sign of life at all. I lowered myself off the wing and into the water until I was face-to-face with the pooch. I then wrapped my hands tight around his muzzle and blew as hard as I could into his nose.

It didn't take long at all. After just one hefty lungful from me, damned if the mutt didn't open his eyes. And as soon as he saw what I was doing to him, damned if the mutt didn't bite off half my nose. The water turned red with my blood and the air turned blue with my words.

From behind me, I heard Cheyenne say, "The shaving kit. We gotta get the hair."

I was fully in the water, but Cheyenne wasn't. Half crawling, half swimming, she pulled herself along the wing, so she could slink herself back into the cockpit. That was her plan, anyway. But with her weight, and now Stanley's bulk lying on it, the wing spar finally gave way. The strut pulled loose, and the whole wing tipped, dropping Cheyenne and Stanley into the drink with me. I grabbed Stanley.

With the buoyancy of that wing compromised, the lake water started pouring into the overturned fuselage. The plane's cabin was going down fast, and there was not a damn thing Cheyenne nor I could do about it but stay clear and clutch onto the broken half of wing that was still staying afloat.

To her credit, Cheyenne offered to give me a hand with Stanley, but I assured her the pooch and I were alright. I could see that a couple of motorboats were speeding this way. Some cottagers had seen our plane come down.

Later, and for ever after, thanks to a very kind promise from Cheyenne, the official medical report would read that my nose had been sliced open by a jagged piece of aluminum airframe.

Hey, what else could I do? Go through life admitting that the scar on my nose was the result of my French kissing a dog?

CHAPTER TWENTY-TWO

The cocker spaniel had a good baritone voice, but when he sang *Hound Dog* he drifted off key. Still, the song elicited a big ovation from the crowd. Elvis tunes always do. Especially when sung with someone's hand up your butt.

We were sitting in the Grandview Theater in beautiful Branson, Missouri, enjoying a born-again Christian ventriloquist whose doggy dummy, Old Shep, was famous for doing public service announcements extolling the virtues of sexual abstinence.

Sure, easy if you're a hand puppet.

Suspicious Minds closed the show, and we were soon outside, squinting into brilliant sunshine. Normally, I prefer attending my stage shows in the evening, but the good folks of Branson seem to think nighttime is for sleeping. Apart from that, the town is nice enough. They don't have as many blackflies as we do up north. Instead, they have Elvis impersonators who don't move their lips.

Before tackling the long flight of steps that led down to the street, I grabbed hold of the cast iron railing. My leg hadn't completely healed yet, and I was still a little shaky.

"Here, let me help." Cheyenne took my elbow. Her touch was strong but gentle — two welcome qualities in an aesthetician. And in a girlfriend. When we reached the sidewalk, we stopped to wait for Nina and her daughter to catch up. "That was fun." Cheyenne said to me. "I'm so glad

Nina asked me along." Turns out Nina knew Cheyenne from the spa where, for years, Cheyenne has been waxing Nina's bikini line. That's right, Cheyenne has seen a whole lot more of Nina than I have. Or ever will. But that's okay.

Nina and I have discovered we are not a match made in heaven. This divine realization came to us when Lieutenant Manwaring offered me a job with his squad and I put him off, saying I wanted time to think about it. Nina thought I was nuts. How could a guy who makes his living selling monogrammed doggie bowls not immediately leap for a prestige gig with The New York State Bureau of Criminal Investigation? Pissed with me, Nina confessed that she could never get serious about a man of such modest ambition. I congratulated her on her good judgement, and we mutually agreed that Nina should find someone else to join her on her upcoming trip to Branson. So Nina invited her *fave* spa attendant, to go along. Turned out, Cheyenne has always wanted to visit Branson. Amazing, huh? I mean, who'd have thought that a babe with a master's degree in multivariable calculus and an I.Q. higher than a lobster's golf score would be hot to watch stars from yesteryear try to remember song lyrics? Anyway, Cheyenne told Nina she'd love to join in on the fun but only if she could bring a pal along to share her room. This was fine with Nina, even when she learned that Cheyenne's pal was yours truly.

So here we are, the four of us enjoying a great lineup of the most talented, family-friendly entertainers to ever stand under a toupee. And talking about family-friendly…

Cheyenne found out she is not pregnant, just perimenopausal. As a result, she no longer has any genetic interest in those DNA-laden barber trimmings from Einstein's noggin. She does, however, believe the hair would be of immense historic importance to the right museum or university. But here's the catch: We've lost the stuff. The shaggy treasure is gone. Seems when the police divers pulled Scott's plane out of the lake, the leather shaving kit had been ripped to shreds, presumably by a vicious animal.

Cheyenne had a pretty good idea who that vicious animal was. So, for the next week, while I was stuck in hospital with my bad leg, Cheyenne kept a close eye on Stanley. Or at least, on one end of him. For days, she sifted through pooch poop, examining each precious turd with tweezers and a nit comb. But in the end, so to speak, she found nothing.

While Cheyenne was busy following Stanley around with a spaghetti strainer, Lieutenant Manwaring was busy sifting through my story about Trooper Steve Scott who has since been charged with first-degree murder in the homicides of Gloria and Henry Tapin. Thomas Appleyard, the horny science teacher, will likely get away with a lesser charge in the somewhat accidental death of Amy Tapin.

It was during his visits to my bedside that Manwaring tried to romance me into carrying a badge again. I must admit, the job tempts me. Trouble is, a police investigator has to be available twenty-four-seven, which would seriously mess with my band work. I can't quit playing. Music is important to me. Nina could never understand this. But Cheyenne does. This woman has her priorities straight. She knows what is truly important in life.

"Beer," Cheyenne said on cue.

"Huh?" I enquired.

Cheyenne checked the clock on her phone. "We have time for a drink before the ABBA show." Cheyenne surveyed the street for a likely watering hole, her head of lush curls rotating like an auburn radar dish.

I took out my phone and turned it on. As I waited for the thing to find a signal, I said to Cheyenne, "Think you could find happiness with a guy who is both a bass player and a working cop?"

"Doubt it. When would he have time for me?"

Smart girl. I tapped a number into my phone.

Cheyenne saw me tapping and said, "Oh, no. Not again. I swear you're worse than a mother separated from her child."

"Gotta make sure she's keeping her kitties away from him." Marlene was boarding Stanley for me at her place. She has a couple of cats. Stanley likes cats, but they don't always like him.

While I waited for Marlene to answer, Nina and Brianna, came out of the theater and hurried down the steps. Brianna was tugging on her mother's sleeve, probably reminding her that, if we don't get our asses in gear we're going to miss the ABBA cover band's tribute to dental whitening strips.

Marlene answered on the fourth ring. I thanked her, once again, for watching Stanley but added, "I, uh… trust he's getting along with your kitties okay?"

"You know your dog thinks he's a cat, right?"

"Yeah, he likes everybody."

"No, I mean the crazy pooch really thinks he's a cat. This morning he coughed up a hair ball."

"Don't you mean, *fur* ball?"

"No, it's hair. Long, coarse, silver-gray. I have no idea where he got it. None of my cats has gray hair."

"Gray *human* hair?" I held my breath in anticipation.

"I guess it could be."

"What did you do with it? You didn't throw it out, did you?"

"A hair ball? What do you think I did with it, knit a cardigan? Of course, I threw it out."

I glanced sideways to make sure Cheyenne wasn't listening. Luckily, she was busy talking with Nina. I covered the phone and whispered to Marlene, "They haven't collected your garbage yet, have they?"

"No…" Marlene was starting to suspect something was up. Namely, my blood alcohol level.

Nina and Brianna were now walking away, going off on their own. Cheyenne turned and started back toward me. I had to talk fast. "Marlene, hon, do me a favor. Search through your garbage. I want you to put that stuff aside for me."

"The hair?"

"Stash it in a safe place."

Marlene was no dummy. "You think it's Einstein's?"

"Please, listen to me. Under no circumstances should you let anyone know that you have that hair. Do you understand? Not a soul. That's very important."

"Why?"

"Because people will kill for it. It's priceless."

"But it's gross. It's been marinating in a dog's colon for two weeks. It smells like rancid kibble."

"Just find it and hide it away. Somewhere safe. Believe me, science and posterity will thank you."

"I don't get it," Marlene said. "Even if it is straight from Einstein's very own personal head, why would anybody in their right mind want the junk now?"

Almost on cue, Cheyenne clapped her hands together and announced, "Change in plans. Nina and Brianna are going to see the ABBA tribute by themselves. That leaves you and me free to go catch the tribute to the man himself, *Mister Las Vegas*." Then she added. "I don't get it. Why would anyone in their right mind prefer a fake *ABBA* show over a fake *Wayne Newton* show?

Meanwhile, Marlene said, "Who in their right mind would want a hunk of hundred-year-old hair?"

I answered both questions at the same time: "Takes all kinds, I guess. Let's just be thankful they have their own room."

Both women seemed satisfied with my answer.

THE END

ABOUT THE AUTHOR

Best-selling author Richard Adamson has worked as a scriptwriter and story editor on several television series, a script doctor for films and Broadway stage, and as a monologue writer for such diverse talents as David Letterman and Yakov Smirnoff. Prior to becoming a professional writer, Adamson earned his living in Toronto as a jazz pianist.

WAKE THE
NEIGHBORS
RICHARD
ADAMSON

NOTE FROM RICHARD ADAMSON

Word-of-mouth is crucial for any author to succeed. If you enjoyed *Einstein's Fiddle*, please leave a review online—anywhere you are able. Even if it's just a sentence or two. It would make all the difference and would be very much appreciated.

Thanks!
Richard Adamson

We hope you enjoyed reading this title from:

BLACK ROSE
writing™

www.blackrosewriting.com

Subscribe to our mailing list – *The Rosevine* – and receive **FREE** books, daily deals, and stay current with news about upcoming releases and our hottest authors.
Scan the QR code below to sign up.

Already a subscriber? Please accept a sincere thank you for being a fan of Black Rose Writing authors.

View other Black Rose Writing titles at www.blackrosewriting.com/books and use promo code **PRINT** to receive a **20% discount** when purchasing.

www.ingramcontent.com/pod-product-compliance
Lightning Source LLC
Chambersburg PA
CBHW060538190726
48283CB00003B/780